THE DARK KNIGHT RISES

THE OFFICIAL MOVIE NOVELIZATION

THE
DARK KNIGHT RISES

THE OFFICIAL MOVIE NOVELIZATION

A NOVEL BY GREG COX

BASED ON THE SCREENPLAY BY
JONATHAN NOLAN AND CHRISTOPHER NOLAN

STORY BY CHRISTOPHER NOLAN
& DAVID S. GOYER

BASED UPON CHARACTERS APPEARING
IN COMIC BOOKS PUBLISHED BY DC COMICS

BATMAN CREATED BY BOB KANE

TITAN BOOKS

The Dark Knight Rises: The Official Movie Novelization
Print edition ISBN: 9781781161067
E-book edition ISBN: 9781781161074

Published by Titan Books
A division of Titan Publishing Group Ltd
144 Southwark Street, London SE1 0UP

First edition: July 2012
1 3 5 7 9 10 8 6 4 2

A CIP catalogue record for this title is available from the British Library.

Printed and bound in the United States.

DID YOU ENJOY THIS BOOK?
We love to hear from our readers. Please email us at
readerfeedback@titanemail.com or write to us at
Reader Feedback at the above address.

www.titanbooks.com

THE DARK KNIGHT RISES

EIGHT YEARS AGO...

"Harvey Dent was needed. He was everything Gotham's been crying out for."

Police Commissioner James Gordon stood before a podium in front of the courthouse where the late district attorney, supposedly martyred in the line of duty, had once fought for justice by prosecuting the city's powerful underworld kingpins. Somber dignitaries, including the mayor and city council, were on hand to honor Dent's memory. A black funeral wreath framed a large color portrait of a handsome man with wavy blond hair, a strong jaw, and a winning smile. Harvey Dent looked every bit a champion of justice, but Gordon had seen his other face. The commissioner hesitated briefly, before continuing.

"He was...a hero. Not the hero we deserved. The hero we needed. Nothing less than a knight, shining brightly even in Gotham's darkest hours. But I knew Harvey Dent. I was...his friend. And it will be a long time before someone inspires us the way he did." Gordon gathered his notes, anxious to get this over with and exit the podium.

"I believed in Harvey Dent."

The words caught in his throat. With any luck, people would think that he was simply overcome with emotion. God forbid they should guess what he was really feeling. That was a secret he shared with only one other man, a man who had sacrificed his own legend to preserve Dent's legacy and reputation. A man whose face Gordon had never seen. Gotham's true dark knight.

Is he watching this? Gordon wondered, his eyes searching the crowd. *Where is he now?*

And will Gotham ever see him again?

CHAPTER ONE

SOMEWHERE IN EASTERN EUROPE

A land cruiser sped over a rugged mountain road, past rocky slopes devoid of human habitation. Scraggly patches of scrub and greenery dotted the barren gray hills. The cruiser had the road all to itself as it raced to make its rendezvous before the sun went down. It bounced over the rough terrain beneath a gloomy, overcast sky that was almost the same gray color as the hills. A keening wind whipped through the desolate peaks and canyons.

A bad omen, Dr. Leonid Pavel thought. The middle-aged scientist sat tensely in the middle of the vehicle, flanked by grim-faced men armed with automatic weapons. More soldiers guarded the prisoners in the rear of the cruiser: three silent figures with hoods over their heads. They sat rigidly, their hands cuffed, under the watchful gaze of the guards.

Pavel squirmed uncomfortably, feeling more like a prisoner than a passenger. He ran an anxious hand through a mop of unruly white hair. Sweat glued his shirt to his back. *Am I doing the right thing?* he fretted. *What if I'm making a terrible mistake?*

Other sounds began to be heard. Just when he had convinced himself that he should never have accepted the Americans' offer, the cruiser arrived at its destination—a remote airstrip overlooking a war-torn city. Artillery fire boomed in the distance, the reverberations echoing off the desolate hillsides. Sirens blared. The sounds of the conflict, which had been going on for months now, reminded Pavel why he had been so eager to flee the country for a safer, more civilized location. This was no place for a man of his intellect—not anymore.

The cruiser squealed to a stop, and the guards hustled him out of the vehicle. An unmarked turbojet airplane waited on the runway, along with a small reception committee consisting of a bland-looking man in a suit and a small escort of armed guards. Although the soldiers bore no identifying uniforms or insignia, Pavel assumed they were US Special Forces, probably from the CIA's own secretive Special Activities Division. The elite paramilitary teams specialized in sabotage, assassination, counter-terrorism, reconnaissance...and extractions. Pavel hoped he could trust them to keep him safe, especially after his recent narrow escape.

His driver shoved him toward the man in the suit.

"Dr. Pavel?" The man smiled and held out his hand. "I'm CIA." He did not volunteer his name, not that Pavel would have believed him if he had. The anonymous American agent handed a leather briefcase over to the driver of the land cruiser, who accepted it eagerly. The briefcase contained more than enough funds to make this risky delivery worth the driver's while. He gestured behind him.

"He was not alone," the driver announced.

The CIA man spotted the hooded men in the back of the cruiser. He frowned at Pavel.

"You don't get to bring friends."

"They are not my friends!" the scientist protested. Indeed, he wanted to get as far away from the hooded men as possible. *You don't know what they're capable of doing!*

"Don't worry," the driver told the CIA agent. "No charge for them."

The American contemplated the prisoners dubiously.

"Why would I want them?"

"They were trying to grab your prize," the driver explained, smirking. "They work for the mercenary. For the masked man."

A look of excitement came over the CIA agent's nondescript, unmemorable features. He gave the prisoners a closer look.

"Bane?"

The driver nodded.

"Get 'em on board," the CIA agent ordered his men, swiftly revising his plans. Clearly this was an opportunity he wasn't about to pass up. He extracted a cell phone from his jacket. "I'll call them in."

Pavel swallowed hard. He didn't like the way this was going. He shuddered at the memory of the attempted kidnapping, and at the very mention of his attackers' infamous commander. Bane had become synonymous with atrocities, at least in this part of the world. Had it not been for the militia's timely intervention, he would now be in the killer's clutches.

Given a choice, he would have left Bane's men far behind them.

Within minutes, they were in the air, flying low over the remote mountains in an attempt to avoid detection. Special Agent Bill Wilson checked on Dr. Pavel, who was safely tucked into a passenger seat, before turning his attention to their prisoners. Beneath his cool, professional exterior, Wilson was thrilled at the prospect of finally getting some reliable intel on Bane. To date, the notorious mercenary had defied the Agency's best efforts to neutralize or even co-opt him. They didn't even know what he looked like beneath that grotesque mask of his. The man was a mystery— with a body count.

Forget Pavel, Wilson thought. *If I can get the 411*

on Bane, that would be quite the feather in my cap. There might even be a promotion in it for me. Maybe a post in Washington or New York.

The hooded men knelt by the cargo door, their wrists cuffed behind them. Special Forces commandoes stood guard over the prisoners. Wilson grabbed the first captive at random.

"What are you doing in the middle of my operation?" he demanded.

The prisoner kept his mouth shut.

Fine, Wilson thought. *We'll do it your way.* He hadn't expected the man to crack without a little persuasion. He pulled a semiautomatic pistol from beneath his jacket and placed the muzzle against the man's head. The prisoner flinched, but remained silent. Wilson decided to up the ante. He raised his voice so that all three prisoners could hear him even through their hoods.

"The flight plan I just filed with the Agency lists me, my men, and Dr. Pavel here. But only *one* of you."

He threw open the cargo door. Cold air invaded the cabin as the wind outside howled like a soul in torment. Wilson grabbed onto a strap to anchor himself. He nodded at the Special Forces guys, who seized the first prisoner and hung him out the cargo door. The wind tore at his hair and clothing, threatening to yank him out of the paramilitaries' grip. Wooded peaks waited thousands of feet below.

"First to talk gets to stay on my aircraft!" Wilson

shouted over the wind. He cocked his weapon. "So...
who paid you to grab Dr. Pavel?"

The men remained silent. Bane's goons were loyal,
Wilson would give him that. He would have to push
harder.

Time for a little sleight of hand...

He fired his weapon out the door, the sharp report
of the gun blasting through the wailing wind. The
SAD guys yanked the stubborn prisoner back into
the plane, and then clubbed him with a baton before
he could make a sound. In theory, the other two
prisoners would think that their comrade was dead
and thrown overboard.

Maybe that would loosen their tongues.

"He didn't fly so good," Wilson lied. "Who wants
to try next?"

The Special Forces men shifted to the second hooded
prisoner. Moving with practiced efficiency, they hung
the would-be kidnapper out the door, high above the
mountains. The drop was enough to put the fear of
God into just about anyone.

"Tell me about Bane!" Wilson demanded. "Why
does he wear the mask?"

Only the wind answered him.

Frustrated, Wilson placed his gun against the second
man's head. He was getting fed up with the prisoners'
stubborn refusal to cooperate. Did they think he was
just joking around here? He cocked his gun again, but
still...nothing.

"Lot of loyalty for a hired gun!"

"Or," a new voice interrupted, "maybe he's wondering why someone would shoot a man before throwing him out of an airplane."

The muffled voice came from the third prisoner, who appeared larger and better built than the other two. Muscles bulged beneath his black leather jacket and weathered fatigues. He had the build of a bouncer or professional wrestler, and held his head high despite the hood.

Giving up on the second man, Wilson had the soldiers haul the useless waste of flesh back into the plane, and then slammed the cargo door shut to keep out the howling wind, making it easier to conduct an interrogation. It was time for some answers.

"Wise guy, huh?" He examined the third captive. "At least you can talk. Who are you?"

"We are nothing," the man replied. "We are the dirt beneath your feet. And no one cared who I was, before I put on the mask."

Whoa, Wilson thought, caught off guard. A peculiar mixture of excitement and apprehension got his heart racing. *Did he just say what I think he said?*

He approached the prisoner warily, holding his breath, and yanked off the man's hood, exposing a disturbing visage that Wilson immediately recognized from captured spy photos and combat footage. It was a face—and mask—that inspired nightmares in the bloodier corners of the globe.

Dark eyes gleamed above an intimidating dark blue mask that concealed the bottom half of the man's face, covering his nose, mouth, and chin. The mask, made of rubber with riveted metal components, was held there in part by a thick vertical strap that bisected the mercenary's brow and hairless cranium. Two rows of coiled steel breathing tubes ran above and below some sort of built-in inhaler that covered the man's mouth. It gave his face a vaguely skull-like appearance. Pipes ran along the edges of the mask to a pair of miniature canisters at the back of his skull. Air hissed as he breathed. No sign of fear showed in the man's piercing eyes. He spoke calmly, and with complete assurance.

"Who we are does not matter," Bane said. "What matters is our plan."

Wilson was fascinated by the man's elaborate headwear, which resembled a specialized gas mask. Was it there purely for effect, or did the breathing apparatus serve some vital function? He gestured at it.

"If I pull this off, will you die?"

"It would be extremely painful," Bane answered.

Good to know, Wilson thought. He had no sympathy for the ruthless mercenary. Bane was a bad guy who deserved to suffer. "You're a big guy."

"For you," Bane clarified.

A chill ran down Wilson's spine, but he tried not to show it. It was important to remain in control of the interrogation.

"Was being caught part of your plan?"

"Of course," Bane said. "Dr. Pavel refused our offer, in favor of yours. We had to know what he told you about us."

"Nothing!" the scientist shouted from his seat. He sounded absolutely terrified by Bane's presence, even though the mercenary was safely in custody. Pavel's eyes were wide with fright. He called out frantically, as though he was pleading for his life. "I said nothing!"

Wilson ignored Pavel's hysterics.

"Why not just ask him?" he said, nodding his head in the scientist's direction.

"He would not have told us."

"You have methods," Wilson said.

"Him, I need healthy," Bane explained. "You present no such problems."

The man's utter confidence was unnerving. Wilson laughed, mostly for his men's benefit, then glanced up as a deep bass tone rumbled somewhere above them. The unexpected sound penetrated the plane's fuselage, competing with the sound of the engines.

Thunder? The weather report hadn't predicted any storms.

A massive transport plane, many times larger than the small turbojet aircraft, descended from above. Its dull gray hull gave no indication of its loyalties as it drew dangerously close to the smaller plane. A ramp opened beneath the transport and four men dropped down, hanging from cables—two on either side of their target. They were armed and ready.

The rumbling grew louder by the moment. Turbulence rattled the plane, causing it to lurch to one side. Wilson struggled to hang on to to his balance. He exchanged a puzzled look with the leader of the Special Forces Group, a sergeant named Rodriguez, who peered out of one of the plane's small windows. The soldier squinted into the fading sunlight.

"Sir?"

Wilson didn't know what was happening, but he wasn't about to show it. He still had an interrogation to conduct.

"Well, congratulations," he taunted Bane. "What's the next step of the master plan?"

"Crashing this plane." Bane rose slowly to his feet. "With no survivors."

An armed man suddenly appeared outside a window, thousands of feet above the ground. Startled, one of the guards spun toward the window, but not quickly enough. Shots rang out from opposite directions as a pair of snipers fired through windows. Glass shattered and Wilson's men dropped to the floor. Blood and chaos spilled throughout the cabin. Death amended the flight plan.

No! Wilson thought. *This can't be happening! I'm in charge here!*

* * *

Outside the plane, the other two men attached sturdy steel grapples to the fuselage. Thick, industrial-strength cables connected the two aircraft as one of the men signaled the crew aboard the big transport. Powerful hoists activated, tugging on the tail of the smaller plane that flew below. Groaning winches exerted tremendous pressure on the captured turbojet. Its tail was yanked upward.

The entire cabin tilted forward at an almost ninety-degree angle, throwing the CIA agent and his men off balance. Loose baggage and debris tumbled toward the front of the plane.

The CIA man clutched onto a seat to keep from falling, but dead and wounded soldiers plunged through the upended cabin, plummeting past Dr. Pavel, who remained strapped to his seat. The frantic scientist tried to process these unexpected disasters, but things were happening too fast.

I knew it, he despaired. *I shouldn't have tried to flee. There was no escape for me. Not from Bane.*

Only the masked man seemed prepared for the sudden change in orientation. Falling forward, he wrapped his thick legs around the back of a nearby seat and seized the CIA agent's head with both hands. His wrists were still cuffed together, but that didn't stop him from cracking the American's neck as easily as someone else might tear open a candy wrapper.

The nameless operative died instantly, far from home.

Bane turned the corpse into a weapon, dropping it onto a young sergeant, who was slammed into the cockpit door with a heavy thud. The sergeant's own body went limp. Pavel couldn't tell if he was dead or simply unconscious. Not that it truly mattered—the panicked scientist was too frightened for his own life to worry about some unlucky American soldier.

Bane will kill us all to get what he wants.

He stared down at the front of the cabin, which was now the bottom of what felt like an endless roller coaster. Gravity pulled on Pavel, and he propped his feet against the back of the seat in front of him, pushing away from it.

The plane shook violently—it was tearing itself apart. He could feel the destructive vibrations through the floor, the seat, and his spine. He was a physicist, not an aeronautics engineer, but even he knew the plane couldn't take much more of this.

The wind howled through the shattered windows. Staring through the broken glass, he saw the right wing shear off before his eyes. The plane lurched to one side.

This is it, he realized. *We're all going to die.*

* * *

Outside, the four men climbed the tail of the dangling aircraft. They moved briskly and efficiently, carrying out their mission. The second wing sheared off, plummeting toward the unforgiving peaks below. A cloud of smoke and debris erupted where the severed wing hit the mountains.

The men quickened their pace. They attached explosives to the tail of the plane. Leaving little margin for error, they jumped away from the aircraft, swinging out on their tethers...

Bane snapped the handcuffs as though they were cheap plastic toys. Opening his legs, he released his grip on the chair and dropped with remarkable agility down the cabin, somersaulting through the air until he reached Pavel, at which point he thrust out his arms to halt his controlled descent. He clearly knew just what he was doing—and what he wanted.

Pavel's eyes widened in fear.

A deafening explosion tore off the rear door of the cabin, nearly giving him a heart attack. Acrid white smoke instantly filled the cabin. Bane's men dropped into the plane through the smoke, suspended on cables. Pavel watched anxiously, uncertain what was happening.

Was Bane here to kill him—or save him?

A heavy object was lowered into the cabin. A body bag, Pavel realized. Bane laid it out atop the backs of the seats next to Pavel. *Is that for me?* the scientist wondered.

Then he realized that the ominous black plastic bag was already occupied. Bane unzipped the bag to reveal the body of a stranger, who nonetheless looked vaguely familiar. It took Pavel a moment to realize that the dead man was roughly the same size and age as himself, with the same swarthy complexion and unruly white hair. There was even a distinct resemblance to their faces.

I don't understand, he thought. *What does this mean?*

Bane didn't waste time explaining. He tore open Pavel's sleeve, then reached into a hidden pocket in his own jacket's lining, removing a length of surgical tubing. Hollow needles sprouted from both ends of the tubing. Bane kept a firm grip on Pavel's arm. He palpated a thick vein at its crook.

Wait, Pavel thought. *Don't...*

But it was no use. Bane jabbed the needle into his arm, expertly threading the vein on the first try. Pavel winced in pain. He had never liked needles.

What are you doing?

Swiftly taping the first needle in place, Bane inserted the other end of the tube into the arm of the corpse. Dark venous blood began to flow through it toward the dead man. Confused and horrified, Pavel watched aghast as Bane performed compressions upon the dead man's chest, *drawing the blood into the lifeless body.*

The scientist felt sick to his stomach.

Less than a pint later, the obscene transfusion was over. Bane withdrew the needle from Pavel's arm and gestured for him to apply pressure to the wound to keep it from bleeding out.

Meanwhile, an armed mercenary plucked the hoods from his comrades' heads, then took hold of the first captive and hooked him to a cable. He hung on tightly as it pulled them both up through the cabin toward freedom. Within moments, they had disappeared from sight.

So there is *a way out*, Pavel realized. Maybe there was still hope for him—if Bane didn't kill him first. *I need to get off this plane before it crashes!*

The second prisoner, no longer bound, started to clip himself to a cable.

Bane shook his head.

"Friend," he said gently. "They expect one of us in the wreckage."

The other man nodded in understanding. Without a word of protest, he unhooked himself from the life-saving cable. He clambered down toward Bane and clasped his leader's arm. His eyes glowed with the fervor of a true believer.

"Have we started the fire?" the man asked.

Bane squeezed his arm in return.

"The fire rises."

Evidently that was good enough, for the man handed Bane the line. He clipped it around Pavel, checking to make sure it was secure, and then produced a knife that he must have taken from one of his men— or perhaps one of the murdered American soldiers. Pavel gulped at the sight of the gleaming steel blade, imagining it slicing across his throat, but Bane merely slashed through Pavel's seat belt, cutting him loose.

Gravity seized Pavel as he began to fall forward at last. He flailed in panic, searching for something to grab onto before he plunged to the bottom of the cabin. *Help me!* he thought. *I'm falling...!*

They slipped free of the seats, hanging in the chaos, several feet above the cockpit doors and the bodies heaped there. Smoke and blood filled the cabin. Pavel wondered if the pilot was still vainly trying to regain control of the wingless aircraft. Loose bits of ash and debris blew against his face. His ears still rang from the explosion. His legs dangled in the air.

Bane took out a small hand-held detonator, and looked him in the eyes.

"Calm, doctor. Now is not the time for fear. That comes later."

He pressed the firing button. Pavel couldn't hear the click over the roar of the wind, but he definitely heard the explosions that released the CIA plane from the grapples. All at once, the entire cabin dropped away, leaving them hanging thousands of feet above the mountains. The man who had sacrificed his life fell with what was left of the plane, along with the pilots and the dead bodies.

Pavel stared down at the heart-stopping drop beneath them. The wingless cockpit and cabin crashed into the rugged wilderness, throwing up a huge geyser of dust and rubble. Fuel tanks ignited, triggering a fiery explosion. Smoke and flames rose from the wreckage.

Leonid Pavel, distinguished scientist and engineer, screamed in utter terror as he was hoisted into the sky.

CHAPTER TWO

"Harvey Dent Day may not be our oldest public holiday," Mayor Anthony Garcia declared, "but we're here tonight because it's one of the most important. Harvey Dent's uncompromising stand against organized crime and, yes, ultimately, his sacrifice, have made Gotham a safer place than it was at the time of his death, eight years ago." Behind him stood a large mounted photo of Dent.

A fashionable crowd filled the moonlit grounds of the Wayne estate. Elegant men and women, representing the cream of Gotham society, listened politely to the mayor's speech as they mingled and chatted amongst themselves. Bright lights dispelled the shadow of the looming manor in all of its restored Gothic splendor, revealing not a hint that the entire edifice had burned to the ground several years before.

Expensive jewelry glittered on women in designer evening gowns, who were escorted by men in tailored silk suits and tuxedos. Champagne glasses clinked. Waiters wove through the party, offering fresh drinks and refreshments. It was a beautiful fall night, and the weather was perfect.

"This city has seen a historic turnaround," the mayor continued from his position at the podium. He was a lean man whose slick black hair and photogenic good looks had survived several years in office. "No city is without crime. But this city is without *organized* crime, because the Dent Act gave law enforcement teeth in its fight against the mob.

"Now people are talking about repealing the Dent Act. And to them I say...not on my watch!"

An enthusiastic round of applause greeted his words. Everyone in the crowd had benefited from the city's improved climate. One could confidently invest in Gotham again, and expect to reap a handsome profit. Small wonder the mayor had been re-elected to a third consecutive term.

"I want to thank the Wayne Foundation for hosting this event," he continued, humbly accepting the applause. "I'm told Mr. Wayne couldn't be with us tonight, but I'm sure he's with us in spirit."

Or maybe he's closer than we think, Jim Gordon thought. The commissioner sat alone at an open bar not far from the dais. He was an ex-Chicago cop in his late fifties, with graying brown hair and a mustache.

World-weary blue eyes gazed out from behind a pair of horn-rimmed glasses. Glancing up at the stately marble façade of the manor house, he spotted a solitary figure gazing down on the festivities from one of the upper balconies. The figure was so still and silent that he might have been mistaken for a chimney, or a gargoyle, but Gordon knew a lurker when he saw one. He suspected that this particular lurker owned everything in sight.

"Now I'm going to give way to an important voice," the mayor promised, snagging Gordon's attention away from the lonely shadow on the balcony. The commissioner's heart sank, and he wished he had time to fortify himself with another stiff drink. He fumbled unenthusiastically with the sheets of paper laid out in front of him, reviewing his handwritten speech one more time. He'd sweated blood over every word, but still wasn't sure he had the nerve to read them out loud.

Then he braced himself for what was to come.

Am I really going to go through with this? he asked himself. *After all these years?*

"Commissioner."

A hearty voice intruded on his reverie. Gordon looked up to see Congressman Byron Gilly muscling his way toward the bar. Judging from the man's ruddy complexion, Gordon guessed that Gilly had already tossed back a drink or two…or three. He was a stocky man, flush with prosperity. His haircut probably cost more than a beat cop's weekly salary.

"Congressman."

Gilly glanced around the sprawling grounds. Manicured lawns and gardens, adorned with tasteful stone fountains and statuary, played host to the annual celebration.

"Ever lay eyes on Wayne at one of these things?"

Gordon chose not to mention the figure on the balcony. He shook his head.

"No one has," a third party cut in. "Not for years."

Peter Foley, Gordon's deputy commissioner, joined them at the bar. A real up-and-comer, he was half a decade younger than Gordon, but was already making a name for himself downtown. Dapper and well-groomed, with thick brown hair as yet untouched by gray, he wore his tailored suit more comfortably than Gordon, whose attire was already rumpled despite his halfhearted efforts to dress up for the occasion.

Gordon glanced down at his clothes and grimaced. There had been a time when his wife made sure he was presentable at these affairs. But, then again, times had changed.

The mayor's voice continued from the podium.

"He can tell you about the bad old days," he continued, apparently in no hurry to surrender the spotlight. "When the criminals and the corrupt ran this town with such a tight grasp that people put their faith in a murderous thug in a mask and cape. A thug who showed his true nature when he betrayed the trust of this great man." He turned toward the large color portrait of Dent. "And murdered him in cold blood."

Ignoring the mayor's speech, Gilly grinned as he spotted an attractive young server who breezed by bearing a tray of canapés. A black maid's uniform, complete with a pressed white apron, cuffs, and collar, flattered the brunette's slender figure. She froze as the congressman rudely grabbed her derrière.

"Sweetheart," he scolded her. "Not so fast with the chow."

She turned to face him, deftly extricating herself from his grasp. A tight smile belied the indignation lurking behind her large brown eyes. She held out a tray.

"Shrimp balls?"

Gordon repressed a smirk.

The dig flew over Gilly's well-coifed head as he snatched a pair of the snacks and stuffed them into his mouth. The maid quickly made her escape, not that Gordon could blame her. Congressman or not, Gilly needed to keep his hands to himself.

"Jim Gordon," the mayor said, "can tell you the truth about Harvey Dent—"

Talking with his mouth full, Gilly nodded at the sheets of paper Gordon had been reviewing.

"Jesus, Gordon, is that your speech?" he said, spewing crumbs. "We're gonna be here all night." Gordon hastily covered the papers.

"Maybe the truth about Harvey isn't so simple, congressman."

"—so I'll let him tell you himself," the mayor concluded. He stepped away from the podium. "Commissioner Gordon?"

Another round of applause rose from the assembled partygoers.

That's my cue, Gordon thought glumly. He gulped down the last of his drink and made his way to the dais, feeling like a convicted felon approaching the gallows. He stepped up to the mike and took out his speech, even as a battery of doubts assailed him.

"The truth?" he began.

Unwanted, an ugly memory flashed before his mind's eye. He saw Harvey Dent as he truly remembered him. The left half of Dent's face had been burnt away, leaving behind a hideous expanse of charred muscle and scar tissue. A bloodshot eye, ablaze with madness, bulged from a naked socket. A ragged gap in his cheek offered a glimpse of exposed jawbone, while a strip of raw gristle stretched vertically across what remained of Harvey's smile.

By contrast, the right side of his face remained just as handsome as ever.

No longer the crusading district attorney, Harvey menaced a small boy with a loaded handgun. The boy, Gordon's own precious son, trembled in the madman's clutches, trying bravely not to cry, even as Gordon pleaded desperately for his child's life.

Unmoved, Dent flipped a coin...

Gordon forced the ghastly memory from his mind.

He gazed out at the audience, wondering if they were finally ready to hear what he had to say. Harvey's portrait, the portrait of a hero, loomed silently behind him. Gordon pondered his options—and his motives. Was clearing his own conscience worth risking all that had been accomplished in Harvey's name?

"I *have* written a speech telling the truth about Harvey Dent," Gordon admitted, making up his mind. He folded up his papers and stuffed them inside his jacket, close to his chest. "But maybe the time isn't right."

"Thank Christ for that," Gilly muttered at the bar, a tad too loudly.

"Maybe all you need to know," Gordon said, "is that there are a thousand inmates in Blackgate Prison as a direct result of the Dent Act. These are violent criminals, essential cogs in the organized crime machine that terrorized Gotham for so long. Maybe for now all I should say about Harvey Dent's death is this—it has not been for nothing."

The crowd clapped enthusiastically—all except for the figure on the balcony, who silently turned away and disappeared into the upper reaches of the mansion. Watching him out of the corner of his eye, Gordon saw him vanish.

Can't blame him, Gordon thought. *I didn't say anything worth hearing.*

Feeling like a coward, he retreated from the dais. Doubts followed him, as they had every day for eight long years. Had he done the right thing? Or had he simply chickened out?

He found Foley at the bar.

"The second shift reports in?" Gordon asked.

"On your desk," Foley assured him. "But you should put in more time with the mayor."

Gordon snorted.

"That's your department." Foley was better at working City Hall, and stroking the egos of politicians. Gordon preferred the nuts-and-bolts of old-fashioned police work.

With one last, rueful glance at the portrait on the dais, he decided he'd done his part for Harvey Dent Day this year. So he headed for the gravel driveway in front of the mansion, where a long row of spotless town cars waited for their powerful and/or affluent passengers. He couldn't wait to get out of here.

This got harder every year.

Back at the bar, the congressman shook his head at Gordon's abrupt departure. He couldn't believe the dumb schmuck was actually abandoning this fancy spread to go back to work, especially now that the war against crime had already been won.

"Anyone shown him the crime stats?" he said.

Foley shrugged.

"He goes by his gut, and it's been bothering him lately, whatever the numbers."

"Must be popular with the wife," Gilly cracked. His own ball-and-chain was conveniently home with a migraine.

"Not really," Foley replied. "She took the kids and moved to Cleveland."

"Well, he'll have plenty of time for visits soon." Gilly lowered his voice to a conspiratorial whisper. He leaned in toward the younger man. "Mayor's dumping him in the spring."

"Really?" Foley was surprised by the revelation— or at least seemed to be. "He's a hero."

"*War* hero," Gilly said. "This is peacetime." He poked Foley in the chest. "Stay smart, the job's yours."

While he let Foley mull that over, Gilly glanced around the party. It was picking up, now that the speeches were finally over and done with. Unlike Gordon, he had better things to do than burn the midnight oil.

Say, the congressman thought, *whatever happened to that cute piece of ass in the maid outfit?*

She could still feel the congressman's grabby fingers on her butt. Her ire rose at the memory. *He's lucky I didn't teach him a painful lesson in manners.*

The mansion's kitchen offered a temporary refuge from the demanding partygoers out on the lawn. A small army of waiters, caterers, and cooks were deployed throughout the spacious area, working overtime to keep the guests lavishly fed and watered. Discarding her empty tray, she dived into the bustling activity, blending in with the rest of the wait staff. Nobody gave her a second look.

Forget the congressman for now, she reminded herself. *Focus.*

She overheard a small cluster of maids gossiping in the corner.

"They say he never leaves the east wing."

"I heard he had an accident, that he's disfigured."

Another maid hurriedly signaled them to shut up. All chatter died as a distinguished older gentleman in a butler's uniform entered the kitchen. His silvery hair complemented his gentle, careworn features.

Alfred Pennyworth, she identified him. *The faithful family retainer.*

"Mr. Till," he said, addressing the chief caterer. A cultured British accent betrayed his roots. "Why are your people using the main stairs?"

Mr. Till murmured an apology that she didn't bother to hear. Instead she watched carefully as Pennyworth placed a glass of fresh water on a tray beside an assortment of covered plates and dishes. The butler glanced around the kitchen.

"Where's Mrs. Bolton?"

Briskly the maid stepped forward.

"She's at the bar, sir," she said. "Can I help?"

He sighed, as though not entirely happy with the situation, but handed her the tray and an old-fashioned brass key.

"The east drawing room," he instructed. "Unlock the door, place the tray on the table, lock the door again." He paused for emphasis. "Nothing more."

She nodded meekly, keeping her head down, and accepted the key.

Slipping out of the kitchen before anything could go awry, she made her way through the gigantic mansion toward the east wing. Austere white walls and heavy draperies gave the house a cold, unwelcoming feel. The hubbub of the party gradually died away as she left the celebration behind. She couldn't help noticing the valuable antiques, tapestries, and paintings gracing the halls, as well as how hushed and lifeless the place seemed. Less like a home than a museum.

A large oak door barred the entrance to the wing. She tried the key, and the door swung open before her, revealing a richly appointed drawing room that was probably twice the size of her crummy apartment back in Old Town. Hand-turned mahogany furniture had begun life as trees in the Wayne plantations in Belize, she knew. Pricy china, vases, and other knick-knacks adorned the mantle of a large unlit fireplace. Despite its opulence, the room was dimly lit and quiet as a tomb.

Not exactly the Playboy Mansion, she noted. *All this tired old money—just going to waste.*

She glanced around, but didn't see anybody, not even the famously reclusive master of the house. Placing the tray down on a polished walnut table, she did *not* exit the chamber as instructed. Instead her eyes locked on an inner door at the other side of the room. It had conveniently been left ajar.

She grinned mischievously.

How perfect was that?

CHAPTER THREE

"I'm sorry, Miss Tate, but I've tried. He won't see you."

Alfred lingered in the hallway to converse with the stylish younger woman who had attempted to enlist his assistance. Miranda Tate—a member of the board of directors of Wayne Enterprises—was probably the most attractive business executive Alfred had encountered in his many decades of service. Lustrous dark hair framed a classically beautiful face. Striking gray–blue eyes shone with intelligence and determination.

"It's important, Mr. Pennyworth," she insisted. Her voice held a faint accent that, despite his extensive travels throughout Europe and elsewhere, he couldn't quite place.

"Mr. Wayne is as determined to ignore important things as trivial ones," he replied wryly.

A derisive chuckle interrupted their conversation. John Daggett strolled up to them, looking smug and obnoxious—as usual. The business tycoon, who had inherited a thriving construction company, boasted a head of sculpted brown hair that would put Donald Trump to shame. His bespoke suit could barely contain his self-importance.

"Don't take it personally, Miranda," he told her. "Everyone knows Wayne's holed up in there with eight-inch fingernails, peeing into Mason jars." Turning, he added belatedly, "Alfred...good of you to let me on the grounds."

The butler did nothing to conceal his distaste. Daggett was the epitome of greed and vulgarity—quite unlike the Waynes, who had always used their wealth to better the world around them.

"The Dent Act is about Gotham," Alfred replied evenly. "Even you, Mr. Daggett." He bowed his head politely toward Miranda. "Miss Tate, always a pleasure." He took his leave of them, but could not help overhearing their voices as they echoed down the hall. Alfred stopped some distance away and turned to look.

"Why waste your time," Daggett asked Miranda, "trying to talk to the man who threw away your investment on some save-the-world vanity project?" His voice was thick with derision. "He can't help you get your money back.

"But I can."

She replied coolly.

"I could try explaining that a save-the-world project, vain or not, is worth investing in, whatever the return. I could try, Mr. Daggett, but you understand only money and the power you think it buys, so why waste my time, indeed." She spun about and left him standing in the hall. Scowling, he watched her go.

Bravo, Miss Tate, Alfred thought. *Bravo.*

Bruce Wayne had grown up in Wayne Manor, at least in its original incarnation, so he barely noticed the drawing room's sumptuous decor as he limped toward his dinner. The sole remaining heir to the Wayne fortune leaned heavily upon a single wooden cane, favoring his injured left leg.

His face was gaunt and drawn. Dark circles haunted his eyes. Traces of gray had infiltrated the dark hair at his temples. A rumpled silk dressing gown was draped over his slumped shoulders. His slippered feet padded noiselessly across the floor.

A tempting aroma rose from the dinner tray. Bruce lifted a lid, mildly curious to see what Alfred had come up with this evening, only to freeze in mid-motion. His gaze shifted from the tray to the open door leading to the sitting room. Was it just his imagination or was the door slightly more ajar than he had left it before?

Cool brown eyes narrowed suspiciously.

Interesting, he thought. *What do we have here?*

* * *

The sitting room was just as expensively furnished as the rest of the mansion. Despite the urgency of her mission, she couldn't resist taking a moment to snoop around.

Careful, she warned herself. *Don't dawdle too long.*

A set of framed photos, some noticeably singed around the edges, occupied a place of honor upon a table. She recognized Thomas and Martha Wayne, tragically murdered in an alley more than three decades ago. A third frame held a portrait of an attractive brunette who somehow managed to look serious, even when she was smiling for the camera.

Rachel Dawes, realized the maid, who had done her homework. *Harvey Dent's dead girlfriend. Killed by the Joker—or so they say—shortly before Dent was killed by the Batman.*

The row of pictures was like a miniature cemetery, complete with headstones. The maid ran her fingers over the gilded frames before moving on to the most conspicuous oddity in the room—a full-sized archery target mounted to a large wooden cabinet. More than a dozen arrows were stuck in the target, clustered around the bulls-eye. Intrigued, she reached out to inspect one of them, only to yank her hand back as a new arrow *thwacked* into place, only inches from her fingers.

Startled, she spun around to see Bruce Wayne

himself, looking rather more haggard than the dashing billionaire playboy the world remembered. He stood at the other end of the room, clutching a large compound bow. She was impressed, despite herself.

She couldn't remember the last time someone had snuck up on her.

Bruce lowered the bow. He put it aside and picked up his cane.

"I'm...I'm terribly sorry, Mr. Wayne," the maid stammered sheepishly. She struck him as very young and embarrassed. "It is Mr. Wayne, isn't it?"

He nodded and limped toward her.

"Although you don't have any long nails," she babbled nervously, "or facial scars..." Her voice trailed off.

Bruce inspected the inquisitive young intruder. He didn't recognize her as one of the regular maids. *Must be a temp taken on for tonight's festivities*, he figured. *Couldn't resist snooping around.*

"Is that what they say about me?" he asked. She shrugged.

"It's just that...nobody ever sees you."

That's the idea, he thought.

A flawless pearl necklace graced her slender neck. Bruce came closer.

"That's a beautiful necklace," he commented. "Reminds me of one that belonged to my mother. It can't be the same one, though. Her pearls are in this safe—"

A large mahogany bureau rested against a wall. He used his cane to press down on a recessed wooden panel, which slid aside to reveal a hidden compartment.

"—which the manufacturer assured me was uncrackable."

The door of the safe swung open.

"Oops," the maid said. "Nobody told *me* it was supposed to be uncrackable."

Her whole attitude changed in an instant. She dropped the coy, girlish act and took on a cockier, more confident posture. It reminded him of the way he had once discarded the role of a careless, immature playboy, whenever it was time to let his true self out. He was impressed, despite himself.

Bruce nodded at the pearls.

"I'm afraid I can't let you take those." They had been a gift from his father, which his mother had worn on the night they were both murdered. In a very real sense, they had cost his parents their lives. He wasn't about to let anyone walk away with them.

"Look," she said, smiling, as she stepped toward him, acting not at all concerned about being caught red-handed. She sized him up with a look. "You wouldn't hit a woman any more than I would beat up a cripple…"

Without warning, she kicked the cane out from under him. A karate chop to his shoulders dropped him to the floor. His bad knee screamed in protest as he hit the carpet. He clutched the injured joint.

"Of course," she added, "sometimes exceptions have to be made."

With a move worthy of an Olympic gymnast, she vaulted onto the bureau, taking the pearls with her. A high window provided a ready egress. "Good night, Mr. Wayne," she said teasingly, before flipping backward out the window. Bruce heard her touch down lightly in the gardens outside.

Gathering himself, he chuckled, amused by the woman's nerve. Ignoring the usual aches and twinges, he rocked forward on his good leg and rose smoothly to his feet. But his brow furrowed as he took a closer look at the violated safe.

Was that *powder* on the door?

Fun's fun, she thought, *but let's not overstay our welcome.*

The party was starting to break up. Having made her escape from the building, she wasted no time heading for the line of town cars waiting in the driveway. Along the way, she deftly peeled off her servile white apron, cuffs, and collar, discarding those previously handy bits of camouflage in various leafy mounds of shrubbery.

By the time she reached the drive, what the valets saw was a breathtaking young woman wearing a little black dress and pearls. One of the young men rushed forward to assist her.

She quickly scanned the row of limos and found just the one she was looking for. She pointed it out to the valet, who obligingly opened the door for her. Thanking him, she slid into the car beside Congressman Gilly, who looked both startled and delighted by her unexpected entrance. Exactly as she had planned from the moment they had met.

"Can I have a ride?" she purred.

He leered at her like she was just another tasty morsel for his consumption. Deep in his cups, he slurred his response.

"You read my mind."

The car pulled away from the house and toward the front gate.

Alfred found Bruce kneeling before the hidden safe, his cane lying on the floor a few feet away. The butler wondered what his troubled employer was looking for.

"Miss Tate was asking to see you again," he said.

Bruce did not look up from the safe.

"She's very persistent."

"And quite lovely," Alfred observed. "In case you were wondering."

"I wasn't."

Alfred sighed. It was precisely the response he had anticipated. *I'm sorry, Miss Tate*, he thought. *I tried.*

His obligation to Miranda Tate discharged, albeit

to no avail, he turned his attention to his employer's current preoccupation.

"What are you doing?"

"Examining print dust," Bruce said tersely. "We've been robbed."

Alfred was startled by the news. Wayne Manor's security was state-of-the-art, and then some. They had never been burgled before.

"And this is your idea of raising the alarm?" he asked. Wayne just shrugged.

"She took the pearls," he answered. "Tracking device and all."

Alfred recalled the precautions Bruce had taken to protect his late mother's pearls. Poor Mrs. Wayne had been wearing those pearls the night she and her husband had lost their lives. It would be tragic if they were not recovered.

Then he realized...

"She?"

"One of the maids." Bruce gave Alfred a wry look. "Perhaps you should stop letting them into this side of the house."

"Perhaps you should learn to make your own bed, then." He bent to look over Bruce's shoulder. "Why are you dusting for prints?"

"I'm not," Bruce said. "She was."

CHAPTER FOUR

The rooftop of police headquarters had become Commissioner Gordon's personal refuge, away from the nonstop phone calls, emails, faxes, meetings, and bureaucracy that came with the job. He liked to think he did his best detective work here, where he could actually concentrate without being interrupted—at least some of the time.

On clear nights like this one, the roof offered a good view of midtown, the bridges, and the adjoining islands. The city appeared quiet, but Gordon knew that looks could be deceptive. Who knew what was going on behind closed doors and in the murky back alleys? Let the politicians brag that Gotham had been cleaned up for good. Gordon had been a cop too long to take anything for granted. Crime never slept, so he couldn't afford to, either.

Especially now that he didn't have a certain Dark Knight backing him up.

He yawned. It was late, but he was in no hurry to return to his depressingly empty apartment. Sometimes he wondered why he even bothered keeping it—he practically lived at Police HQ anyway, or so Barbara had always complained. Smacking a thick stack of files against a nearby air duct to shake off the dust, he settled back against the railing to read. A shattered searchlight, rusted over and corroded, sat neglected a few yards away. Gordon had personally smashed it with a sledgehammer almost eight years ago. But he had never had the heart to remove it.

Maybe someday…

"Sir?" A young uniformed officer joined him on the rooftop. He approached Gordon tentatively. "I didn't want to bother you up here, but they're looking for you."

Gordon glanced up from the reports.

"What's the problem, son?"

"Congressman Gilly's wife has been calling. He hasn't made it home from the Wayne Foundation event."

Gordon remembered Gilly pawing that poor maid. Maybe he had found a more cooperative plaything.

"That's a job for the police?" he asked.

"Sir," the rookie said, "I've been a cop for a year, and I've only logged half a dozen arrests. When you and Dent cleaned up the streets, you cleaned them up good." He shrugged. "Pretty soon we'll be chasing overdue library books."

Gordon smiled. He appreciated the young officer's candor.

"But here you are, sir." He indicated the large stack of files Gordon held in his hands. "Like we're still at war."

"Old habits," Gordon said.

"Or instinct?"

Gordon heard something in the younger man's voice. He gave the rookie a closer look. He was a husky young man with short, neatly cropped dark brown hair. He seemed shockingly young and fresh-faced, but Gordon recognized a hungry look in the youth's eyes and the set of his jaw—an eagerness and curiosity Gordon remembered from his own early days as a beat cop in Chicago.

"What's your name, son?"

"Blake, sir."

Gordon put down the files.

"You have something you want to ask me, Officer Blake?"

Blake hesitated, then spit it out.

"It's that night," he said eagerly. "*This* night, eight years ago. The night Dent died."

"What about it?"

"The last confirmed sighting of the Batman," Blake said. He shook his head as if something didn't add up. "He murders those people, takes out two SWAT teams, breaks Dent's neck, and then just vanishes?"

Officially, the masked vigilante known as Batman had been blamed for the murders of five people, including two cops and a prominent mob boss. Only Batman and Gordon knew who was truly responsible for those killings. Or how Harvey Dent had really fallen to his death.

"I'm not hearing a question, son."

Blake shifted uneasily, but stuck to his guns.

"Don't you want to know who he was?"

"I know *exactly* who he was." Gordon walked over to the broken searchlight. He ran his finger over its rusty frame. Once upon a time, the lens had been capable of projecting an ominous bat-winged silhouette onto the night sky. It had been a signal that let the good people of Gotham City know that someone was watching out for them—and that kept the bad people spooked. "He was Batman."

Blake looked disappointed by Gordon's answer, but was smart enough not to argue with his boss. Gordon couldn't blame him for wanting answers. The mystery of the Batman had gone unsolved for close to a decade now. Blake had probably grown up hearing the legend—and its ugly conclusion.

Time to change the subject, Gordon thought. He walked past Blake and toward the stairs. "Let's go see about the congressman's wife."

* * *

Sunlight crept through the thick curtains over the bedroom windows. Alfred entered, bearing breakfast on a tray, and was surprised to find the bed unoccupied. In fact, it appeared as if it had not been slept in at all.

"Master Bruce?"

No answer. Puzzled, he explored the east wing, but found no sign of his elusive employer. It dawned on him that there was one other place Bruce might be, although it had been many months—at the very least—since Bruce had ventured down there. Alfred frowned, and wondered if this was a good sign or not.

Wooden bookcases lined the walls of the study. An antique globe rested atop a polished mahogany table, not far from a grand piano that resembled the one Bruce's mother had often played before her tragic demise. Alfred glanced at one particular bookcase before walking over to the piano.

He tapped out a specific, rather difficult sequence of three notes on the black-and-white keys. In response, a door-sized segment of the bookcase swung outward, exposing a hidden elevator. Concealed hinges, long unused, squeaked slightly. He made a mental note to oil them later.

Could it be that Bruce had gone…below?

Alfred rode the elevator down, concerned about what he might find at the bottom. He had long hoped for something that might shake Bruce out of his malaise, and induce him to re-enter the world, but he wasn't at all certain that the answer to his prayers was to be found down here.

In the Batcave.

The vast caverns had once been used to shelter runaway slaves escaping to the North. Damp limestone walls glistened beneath the subdued interior lighting that Bruce had installed years ago. A shallow, slow-moving river was all that remained of the underground waterway that had carved out the caverns in ages past. Massive wooden arches, high overhead, helped to support the mansion's foundations.

Scores of North American brown bats roosted amidst the jagged stalactites hanging from the ceiling. Towering calcite columns rose hundreds of feet in height. The bats squeaked and rustled overhead.

Filthy animals, Alfred thought.

He descended a stone ramp to the concrete floor of the main grotto, where a series of dark slate obelisks loomed directly ahead. A footbridge led across the river to where Bruce was seated at the main computer station, atop a large slate cube. A large, high-definition flatscreen monitor dominated the wall before him. Seven linked Cray supercomputers hummed softly, providing him with enough data storage and computing power to put the NSA to shame. Bruce's gaze was glued to the screen even as his fingers danced over the keyboard. His cane rested against his seat.

He did not shift his attention as Alfred came up behind him.

"You haven't been down here for a long time," the butler observed.

"Just trying to find out more about our jewel thief," his employer replied. "I ran her prints from the photos she handled." With that, he pulled up a mug shot. The face in the photo belonged to a scowling armed robbery suspect with a receding hairline, double chins, and a bad case of five o'clock shadow. It bore little resemblance to the larcenous "maid" they had briefly encountered the night before.

"She was wearing someone else's fingerprints," Bruce explained, with a hint of grudging admiration in his voice. "She's good."

"That she may be," Alfred conceded. "But we still have a trace on the necklace."

"Yes, we do, so I cross-referenced the address she went back to, with the police data on recent high-end B-and-Es."

Breaking and entering, Alfred translated mentally. It troubled him that Bruce had become so familiar with law-enforcement jargon. That was not a field of study he would have chosen for the sweet young boy Bruce had once been. *Your father was a doctor.*

Bruce hit another key and a new photo appeared. This time Alfred recognized the young lady, although she appeared rather less demure than he remembered. What appeared to be a long-distance surveillance photo captured an alluring face graced with striking brown eyes and sleek brown hair. It was a face worth remembering.

"Selina Kyle," Bruce said. "No convictions yet, but the databases are full close calls, tips from fences."

A montage of newspaper headlines flashed across the screen:

THE CAT STRIKES AGAIN

POLICE SUSPECT 'CAT' BURGLAR
IN JEWELRY HEIST

PENTHOUSE ROBBER LEAVES
FEW CLUES BEHIND

ART MUSEUM LATEST VICTIM OF 'THE CAT'?

Alfred nodded. He recognized some of the headlines from the morning papers. The string of high-profile heists had been notable for their daring and execution. He had thought Wayne Manor was burglar-proof, but this Miss Kyle had proven otherwise.

"She's good," Bruce repeated, "but the ground is sinking beneath her feet."

Our crimes always catch up with us, Alfred thought. The smell of a burning letter wafted across his memory, reminding him that he had a few guilty secrets of his own. "We should send the police before she fences the pearls."

"She won't," Bruce said. "She likes them too much. And they weren't what she was after."

Alfred didn't understand.

"What *was* she after?" he inquired.

"My fingerprints," Bruce stated. "There was printer toner mixed with graphite on the safe. Gives you a good pull, and it's untraceable."

"Fascinating," Alfred said dryly. "Perhaps you could trade notes over coffee."

Bruce finally looked away from the screen.

"Now you're trying to set me up with a jewel thief?"

"At this point, sir, I would set you up with a chimpanzee if I thought it would bring you back to the world."

Bruce's expression darkened. Any trace of levity vanished from his voice.

"There's nothing out there for me."

"And that's the problem," Alfred said, hoping he could get through for once. "You hung up the cape and the cowl, but you never moved on. You won't get out there and find a life. Find someone—"

"I did find someone, Alfred." The memory of Rachel Dawes hung over him like a shroud. She had been the only woman Bruce had ever truly cared for— until the Joker cruelly ended her life. Her death in that explosion had haunted him ever since.

"I know," Alfred said gently. "And then you lost her. That's part of living, sir. But you're not living, you're waiting. Hoping for things to go bad again."

For a chance to let the Dark Knight loose once more.

Bruce didn't deny it. He just sat silently at the computer. Bats rustled overhead.

"Remember when you left Gotham?" Alfred persisted. "Before all this. Before Batman. Seven years you were gone. Seven years I waited, hoping that you wouldn't come back."

Bruce looked up in surprise. Confusion showed upon his face.

"Every year I took my holiday," Alfred said, trying to explain. "I'd go to Florence. There's a café by the Arno. Any fine evening I would sit there and order a *Fernet-Branca*. I had a fantasy I indulged in often. I liked to imagine that one day I'd look across the tables and see you. Sitting there with your wife, perhaps some children. You wouldn't say anything to me, but we'd both know—that you'd made it. That you were happy."

A poignant memory surfaced briefly. There had been a time, Alfred recalled, when he had spotted a happy couple a few tables away and—just for a moment or two—he had truly thought that the man might be Bruce, at large and at peace. But then the man had turned toward him, revealing the face of a stranger.

He vividly recalled the bitter disappointment he had felt at that moment.

"I never wanted you to come back to Gotham," he confessed. "I knew there was nothing here for you but pain and tragedy. And I wanted more for you than that." He paused to let his heartfelt word sink in. "I still do."

There was nothing more to say. He turned and quietly left the cave, leaving Bruce alone with his obsessions—and the ceaseless rustling of the bats.

CHAPTER FIVE

The sewage treatment plant was on the outskirts of Gotham, near the river. Officer John Blake had expected it to smell, but the odor was more chemical than putrid. Thick pipes and other conduits linked various tanks, pumps, and basins. Squat, ugly buildings were painted a dull industrial green. The whole complex was intended to purify the fetid output of Gotham's sewers before discharging the excess effluent into the river.

Or at least that was the theory. Blake didn't want to think about how effective the process was, or wasn't.

He and his partner, Tyler Ross, got out of their patrol car. Ross was a twenty-something Asian–American, only a few years older than Blake. They had been partners for nearly a year now, with Ross showing him the ropes. Blake knew he could count on his partner to watch his back.

It was early in the morning and they had a long shift ahead of them. Although fall had only just arrived, a nip in the air warned that winter was coming. The plant's supervisor, a middle-aged guy named Jenkins, led them to a long concrete trough filled with foul-looking water. A greasy film coated the surface—and the lifeless body stretched out on a rusty metal grate above the basin. The body looked young.

"They wash up a couple times a month," Jenkins explained. "More when it gets colder. Homeless, sheltering in the tunnels. We had to pull him out to clear the basin, but other than that we didn't touch him." He kept back, letting the cops approach the corpse. "They come out by the catchment basin."

Blake knelt to inspect the body, which appeared to belong to a teenage boy, seventeen years old at most. Ragged, well-worn clothes looked like they had seen hard use even before the body had ended up in the sewers. One sneaker had come off the dead kid's foot. Dead, glassy eyes gazed up into oblivion. Blake took a closer look at the face—and froze.

Oh crap, he thought.

Ross didn't miss his partner's reaction.

"What?"

"Name's Jimmy," Blake said, feeling sick to his stomach. "He's from St. Swithin's, the boy's home where I...coach ball sometimes." That wasn't the full story, but Blake didn't feel like getting into it right now. Not even with Ross. His throat tightened.

He resisted the temptation to close Jimmy's eyes for him.

St. Swithin's Home for Boys was housed in a shabby, four-story building that had seen better days. If anything, it seemed even more rundown than Blake remembered. Getting out of his car, he gazed up at the home's crumbling façade. Memories, both good and bad, flooded over him. He shook his head to clear his mind before heading inside. He was off the clock now, having ditched his partner back at the station.

This was something he wanted to do on his own.

He found Father Reilly in the same cluttered office the old priest had occupied for years. Like the building, Reilly was showing his age. He was a hefty, broad-faced Irishman, whose receding white hair had all but surrendered to baldness. Orphaned and abandoned children, ranging in age from toddlers to teens, roamed the halls outside the office, jostling and joking with one another. Shrill laughter was interspersed with the occasional noisy squabble. Second-hand clothing had been passed down from one generation of orphans to another. Curious eyes peered in the doorway.

Reilly closed the door to cut down on the hubbub and give the two men a degree of privacy.

"Jimmy hadn't been here for months," the priest said.

Blake scribbled in his notepad. "Why?"

"You know why, Blake. He aged out. We don't have the resources to keep on boys after sixteen." The cop gave Reilly a puzzled look.

"The Wayne Foundation gives money for that."

Reilly shook his head.

"Not for two years now."

I hadn't heard that, Blake thought. He was disturbed by the news, but had more pressing matters to deal with at the moment. "He has a brother here, right?" Reilly nodded sadly.

"Mark. I'll tell him."

"I'd like to, if that's okay."

After wrapping things up with Father Reilly, and promising to visit again soon, Blake located Mark out in the playground. Jimmy's little brother was only ten years old, but he took the news of his brother's death with the shut-down, stony-faced resignation of someone who had already stopped expecting life to be fair.

He bit down on his lip, refusing to cry.

"I'm sorry," Blake said. The words felt completely inadequate.

Mark just nodded and stared at the ground.

"What was he doing in tunnels?" the cop asked.

"Lots of guys been going down the tunnels when they age out," the boy said flatly. "Say you can live down there. Say there's work down there."

Blake scratched his head.

"What kinds of work you gonna find in the sewers?"

"More than you can find up here, I guess."

Blake didn't like the sound of that. Whatever Jimmy had been doing in the sewers, it obviously hadn't turned out well for him.

And Blake wanted to know why.

CHAPTER SIX

The bar was a real dive, like so many others in this part of Gotham. A jukebox blared in the background, competing with harsh laughter and dirty jokes. Ceiling fans fought a losing battle against the smoky haze, which reeked of tobacco and other controlled substances. Tough-looking ex-cons, hoodlums, and bikers played pool and quarreled over darts. A worn-out waitress, old beyond her years, dodged grabby hands. Cigarette butts and peanut shells littered the floor.

A television, its volume muted, was mounted over the grimy mirror behind the bar. Nobody was paying it much attention.

Ordinarily, Selina wouldn't be caught dead in a sleazy gin mill like this, but she had important business to conduct. She strolled boldly into the place, where her slinky black dress and lithe figure drew appreciative leers and catcalls. She was accompanied by a reeling drunk in a loud Hawaiian shirt. Barely able to stand under his own power, he sagged against her and mumbled incoherently. She batted away his sweaty paws, which apparently hadn't learned their lesson yet. His ruddy face was unshaven. His drooping eyes were bloodshot and unfocused. She deposited him on a barstool before sauntering over to a nearby table to keep her appointment.

"You brought a date?" Philip Stryver asked incredulously. He was a waxy-faced creep in a three-piece suit who seemed distinctly out of place in the dingy establishment, not that anyone appeared inclined to make an issue of it. His unsavory reputation preceded him, even in this den of thieves and cutthroats. He looked askance at the drunk at the bar.

"I like having someone to open doors for me," she offered by way of explanation.

She glanced around, scoping out the scene. Hired muscle was scattered all around the bar, just as she had expected. They weren't even pretending not to be watching her. Opening her purse, she extracted an unmarked envelope and handed it over to Stryver.

"Right hand," she said. "No partials."

Not taking her word for it, he opened the envelope and took out a flexible acetate transparency. Held up to the light, the transparency showed four perfect fingerprint transfers.

"Very nice," he pronounced, before pocketing the envelope.

"Not so fast, handsome," she said. "You got something for me?"

A smirk lightened his typically phlegmatic expression.

"Oh, yes."

He signaled a thug, who moved to lock the front door. Another bruiser joined them at the table. A gun bulged beneath his cheap sports jacket. He glowered at her in an obvious attempt at intimidation.

She wasn't impressed—or surprised.

"I don't know what you're going to do with Wayne's prints," she said, "but I'm guessing you'll need his thumb."

Stryver blinked in surprise. Flummoxed, he took out the merchandise and checked it again. His reaction was priceless.

"You don't count so well, huh?" she added.

"I count fine," he snarled. He nodded at his flunky, who drew his gun and pressed it against her head. "In fact, I'm counting to ten right now."

They faced off across the table. The thug cocked his gun. Nobody in the bar showed a hint of coming to her rescue, not even her tipsy companion.

So much for chivalry, she thought. *I guess it's true. Gotham's last knight in shining armor died years ago.*

"Okay, okay."

She reached for her purse, only to be blocked by

the bruiser, who insisted on reaching in and taking out her phone himself. He slid it across the table to his boss.

"My friend is waiting outside," she promised. "Just hit 'send.'"

Stryver toyed with the phone, eyeing her suspiciously, before finally doing as she instructed. Then they waited in silence. Within minutes, there was a knock at the door. The goon at the door peered out cautiously before unlocking it to admit a petite blonde who looked like she belonged in high school. Flaxen curls tumbled past her slight shoulders. A halter-top and miniskirt practically screamed *jailbait*. Hazel eyes lit up as she spotted Selina at the table. She scampered over and pulled out an envelope.

A tense hush fell over everyone, like the calm before a storm. The girl glanced around cluelessly.

"Place is a little dead," Jen said as Selina took the envelope.

"It will liven up in a minute, trust me."

Jen picked up on the tension in the room.

"Everything okay?"

"Great," Selina lied. "See you later."

To her relief, Stryver let the girl depart, perhaps to avoid any unnecessary complications. Or maybe he just had a soft spot for blondes. Taking the envelope from Selina, he inspected a second transparency. This one bore the flawless image of a single thumbprint.

He nodded in satisfaction.

"It would have been a lot easier," she pointed out, "to just give me what we agreed on."

He shook his head.

"We can't have any loose ends." He looked her over appreciatively. "And, even in that dress, no one is going to miss you."

"No," she agreed. "But my friend over there?" She cocked her head toward the bar, where her oblivious "date" was drooling into a bowl of cocktail peanuts. "Every cop in the city's missing him."

As if on cue, a news update flashed across the screen of the muted television set. A headline scrolled beneath a campaign photo of a certain prominent local politician.

MANHUNT FOR MISSING CONGRESSMAN

Stryver's startled gaze darted between the TV and the drunk, and then back again.

"Cute," he said, recovering quickly. "But they're not going to be looking for him in a place like this."

"I don't know," she countered. "You did just use his cell phone."

Stryver stared in horror at the phone in his hand. He hastily wiped it down with a silk handkerchief, even as—all at once—the entire Gotham City Police Department seemed to converge upon the bar. Sirens blared outside, drowning out the jukebox. The noisy whirr of helicopter blades came from above, growing louder by the moment. Spinning red gumball lights could be glimpsed through the drawn window shades.

Brakes squealed.

Boots pounded toward the door.

Stryver's face blanched. He glanced toward the window. Clearly, this wasn't part of his plan.

She seized the moment. Moving quickly, she cracked his head against the table, then grabbed the big bruiser's gun hand and flipped over the table with feline grace and dexterity. Before the baffled thug even knew what was happening, she used his gun and opened fire on the other hoods. Winged henchmen yelped and dropped to the floor.

Selina pistol-whipped the gunman, knocking him senseless, and dived beneath the table. Just in time...

A SWAT team, each member in full body armor and a faceless black helmet, battered down the door. They fanned out through the bar, the lasers on their automatic rifles sweeping the premises, vivid in the smoke-laden air.

Right on schedule, she thought.

Cowering beneath the table, she screamed as though terrified. A helmeted trooper came to her rescue.

"It's all right, miss," he said gruffly. "Just stay down."

The SWAT team stampeded past her, chasing Stryver and his remaining thugs into a back alley, even as wounded hoodlums groaned and writhed upon the floor. Making sure the coast was clear, she got up and strolled toward the door. A whimper caught her ear and she spied Congressman Gilly crouching beneath the bar, clutching his leg. The pathetic figure was a far cry from the smug politician in the campaign photo— no wonder the SWAT boys hadn't ID'd him yet.

"Keep some pressure on that, sweetheart," she advised him. She took a moment to adjust her dress.

Bleary eyes watched her leave.

"Call me?" he pleaded.

Blake chased after the SWAT guys, eager to get in on the action. A pretty girl in a black dress, rushing out of the bar, ran right into him. She looked terrified.

"There's a man in there!" she said frantically, sounding scared out of her wits. "He's bleeding!"

He did his best to calm her.

"It's okay, miss," he said. "It's okay."

Impatient to get into to the bar, and frustrated by the delay, he nonetheless took the time to guide the distraught young woman to safety, leaving her on the tailgate of one of the parked SWAT vehicles. There would be time enough for someone to take her statement...later. Right now, the congressman was still missing—and the perps might be getting away.

Gun drawn, he raced into the bar, where his fellow officers were already rounding up a bunch of confused and injured lowlifes. A sloppy-looking bum was sprawled by the bar, blood soaking through his soiled trousers. His hair was disheveled and he reeked of booze. Stubble dotted his jowls.

"Help me," he whimpered.

It took Blake a moment to recognize the missing congressman.

"I've got him," he reported into the radio on his shoulder. He gave the injured politician a quick once-over. "Bullet to the leg, but he's okay."

In his excitement, he forgot all about the girl in the black dress.

A firefight broke out in the alley behind the bar. Vicious hoodlums, desperate to get away, opened fire on the SWAT teams, who returned fire with extreme prejudice. The sound echoed off the grimy brick walls of the alley. Bullets ricocheted off rusty trash bins and dumpsters. Frightened rats scurried for safety. Broken glass, cigarette butts, syringes, crack vials, and other debris crunched beneath the heels of the racing cops and criminals.

Laying down a blistering volley of cover fire, a group of the crooks darted into an even narrower passage.

A cop car, its bubble light spinning wildly, squealed to a halt, blocking the mouth of the alley. Jim Gordon emerged from the car, brandishing his trusty Smith & Wesson pistol. A rumpled brown trench coat protected him from the night's chill. He hurried to take charge of the situation. Anyone who would brazenly abduct a congressman deserved his personal attention.

SWAT troopers converged on the murky passage,

massing on both corners, just out of the line of fire. They exchanged hand signals and counted down silently before rounding the corner, their rifles aimed high and low. Gordon sprinted after them.

He half-expected to find the armed felons waiting in ambush, but instead the dead end appeared to be completely empty. Only heaps of trash and obscene graffiti greeted his eyes. A high brick wall, topped with razor wire, blocked the other end of the passage.

What the devil? Gordon thought. *Where did they go?*

Searching for the hostiles, the troopers looked upward, raising their rifles toward the rickety fire escapes overlooking the scene. Laundry hung like flags, flapping on makeshift clotheslines.

But Gordon had another idea. He scanned the filthy, litter-strewn pavement.

"Manhole!" he shouted.

A cast-iron manhole cover, about midway down the passage, appeared slightly off-kilter. Responding to Gordon's summons, two armored SWAT troopers wrenched the heavy disk free and rolled it aside, exposing a deep, shadowy cavity. Gordon snatched a flashlight from the nearest SWAT guy.

The beam probed the open shaft. A rusty ladder descended deep beneath the city streets. A pungent odor wafted up from the sewers. Gordon thought he heard footsteps splashing through the tunnels below. A shredded cobweb, recently disturbed, hung in tatters.

"You three," he ordered the nearest men, "down with me." He glanced over at the remaining troopers. "You two, head down to the next exit."

The men looked around uncertainly.

"Where?"

The hell if I know, Gordon thought. "Get the DWP down here...now!" He wished he could wait for somebody from the Department of Water and Power himself, but there wasn't any time. For all he knew, the men behind the congressman's abduction were making their escape. He had to go after them.

Taking a deep breath to steady his nerves, he led the way down into the gloom, scrambling down the ladder as swiftly as his aging bones could manage. The three SWAT men hustled after him.

Gordon hoped they wouldn't end up lost down in the tunnels.

Congressman Gilly had been safely delivered into the hands of medics, leaving Blake free to join in the pursuit. He rushed through the alleys behind the bar until he found a large circle of cops crowded around an open manhole. Deputy Commissioner Foley was already on the scene. He glared at his watch.

"Where's the DWP guy?" Foley grumbled impatiently.

Blake shouldered his way into the group. He peered into the gloomy shaft.

"They went down there?" he asked.

Foley nodded.

"And Gordon took SWAT in after him."

The sewers were dank and dark and difficult to navigate. Slime coated the crumbling brick walls. Rats, lizards, and other vermin scurried in the shadows. Gordon and his men crept warily through the claustrophobic tunnels, watching their steps as they trod upon slippery maintenance walkways. Rusted, rickety guardrails couldn't be trusted. Raw sewage coursed through the endless drains, the putrid odor turning Gordon's stomach. Bile rose at the back of his throat.

He kept his gun drawn and his flashlight low. His eyes probed the Stygian darkness. His ears strained to hear which way the suspects had gone. For a few, frustrating moments, he was afraid that that the fleeing kidnappers had given them the slip, but then he thought he heard some furtive footsteps ahead, just around a corner.

He signaled the men behind him to be on their guard. Adrenalin rushed through his veins, keeping him sharp. He welcomed the extra edge. It had been a long time since he had led a raid like this.

Maybe too long.

Sure enough, the minute they rounded the corner, they were met with a furious hail of gunfire. Muzzles flared in the shadows. Bullets sparked off the walls, chipping away at the stonework and pelting Gordon's face with bits of rock and mortar. The cramped tunnels amplified the deafening report of the guns, hurting his ears. The acrid smell of cordite competed with the stench of the sewers. Gordon and his men pulled back, seeking shelter while returning fire. In the oppressive darkness, he couldn't even see who was shooting at them. Suddenly he envied the SWATs their body armor.

Where the hell are our reinforcements?

A sudden explosion lit up the tunnels behind them, sending the SWAT men flying. They smashed against the walls before splashing into the sewers. Staggered but still standing, Gordon felt a scorching heat at his back and turned to see bright orange flames engulfing the tunnels and spreading toward him. Dashing into the intersection up ahead, he fled through the tunnels, frantic to get away from the inferno.

The smoke and flames chased after him.

Putting another turn between himself and the flames, he paused to get his bearings. On his own now, he held on tightly to his pistol. He sagged against a damp wall, breathing hard, and checked to make sure he hadn't lost his glasses in the confusion. His ears rang from the explosion.

Loose gravel crunched somewhere behind him. He spun around, but not swiftly enough. A heavy blow struck him in the head.

* * *

A fireball erupted from the open shaft. Blake and the other cops jumped back to avoid being scorched. Startled shouts and curses escaped their lips. Blake felt the heat of the flames against his face.

"Come on!" he blurted, realizing that Gordon was in trouble. "We gotta get down there!"

An older cop snorted.

"That was a gas explosion, kid."

"Gas?" Blake challenged him. "This is a sewer!"

Foley stepped forward to take charge. He wiped the soot from his face.

"No one goes in until we know what's down there."

"But we know what's down there, sir! The police commissioner!"

Foley shot Blake a dirty look, visibly annoyed by the young cop's outburst.

"Somebody get the hothead out of here," he ordered. "And get me a DWP guy!"

Realizing there was no point in arguing, Blake backed off and retreated from the passage. He couldn't believe that Foley and the others weren't rushing to find Gordon, fire or no fire. There were miles of tunnels underneath Gotham. Gordon could be anywhere now.

Maybe even…

An idea occurred to him. He ran for his patrol car.

CHAPTER SEVEN

Dazed from the blow, Gordon struggled to hang on to consciousness. Rough hands took his gun and rolled him over onto his back. Playing possum, he cracked his eyelids open just enough to make out two blurry figures leaning over him. The rank odor of unwashed hair and clothing invaded his nostrils. A foot kicked him in the ribs, eliciting a gasp of pain.

"This one's alive," a raspy voice pronounced. The man bent over to take a closer look. "Jesus, it's the police commissioner!"

His accomplice scratched his head.

"What do we do?"

They stood there for a moment, uncertainty flickering across their faces. Then the first one spoke again.

"Take him to Bane."

They half-carried, half-dragged Gordon through a bewildering maze of tunnels. Despite his groggy state, he tried to note the route, but soon lost track of the numerous twists and turns. They moved deeper beneath the city, the temperature dropping noticeably as they traveled lower and lower.

Hanging lanterns and glowing naked bulbs provided just enough light by which to navigate. He was surprised—and troubled—to glimpse all sorts of activity going on in the tunnels. Beefy men, their bodies gleaming with sweat, attacked the walls and ceiling with drills and jackhammers. Scowling guards equipped with automatic weapons stood watch over the workers. Ragged street kids who looked like they still belonged in school hauled away buckets of loose debris, squeezing through narrow cracks. Bags of powdered cement were piled high in the corridor.

A major excavation appeared to be underway, but Gordon suspected that the city's planning department hadn't authorized any of this. He doubted they even knew about it.

This is bigger than just a kidnapping, he realized. *Much bigger.*

The workers stopped briefly to watch as Gordon was dragged past, only to resume their labors after a moment. The din of the jackhammers echoed off the dripping stone walls of the tunnels before receding into the distance. Gordon wondered where his captors were taking him—and just who this "Bane" was.

Another level below twin cataracts of clear run-off water gushed down into an underground river. A catwalk led between the spraying waterfalls, and his ambushers hauled Gordon across the walkway onto a recessed platform hidden behind curtains of falling water. The cavernous space appeared to have been converted into an ad hoc command center, complete with living quarters. Desks and file cabinets were crammed into the corners. Maps and blueprints papered the desks. A faded quilt of exotic design, spread out atop a large cot, provided an incongruously homey touch.

Armed guards in military fatigues eyed the new arrivals suspiciously, but let them pass. An imposing, bare-chested figure, the size of a professional wrestler, stood before an open furnace, his broad back turned toward Gordon and his captors. Firelight cast a hellish glow over his muscular frame. A jagged line of rough scar tissue ran down his spine. A dark rubber headpiece was strapped to his skull.

"Why are you here?" the man asked. Gordon guessed this was Bane.

The thugs tossed Gordon at his feet.

"Answer him!" one of them demanded.

Bane turned toward them. Gordon's eyes widened at the sight of the elaborate apparatus concealing the giant's nose and mouth. Some sort of gas mask? The commissioner sniffed the air, but detected only the stale atmosphere of the tunnels.

"I'm asking *you*," Bane said, turning toward the two men.

"It's the police commissioner," one of them volunteered. Hearing this, Bane did not look pleased.

"And you brought him down here?" he asked.

"We didn't know what to do," the other man said, trying to explain. "We—"

"You panicked," Bane said, cutting him off. "And your weakness cost three lives."

The flunky looked around in confusion.

"No, he's alone—"

Bane lunged forward with surprising speed. Before the man could even complete his sentence, Bane seized his head and twisted it sharply. An unmistakable crack ended the unlucky henchman's life. His lifeless body dropped to the floor.

Good Lord, Gordon thought. He stared at Bane in horror. *What kind of monster is this?* The masked killer turned toward the remaining thug. Then he nodded in Gordon's direction.

"Search him," he ordered. "Then I will kill you."

His intended victim gulped. All the blood drained from his sallow features. His knuckles tightened on the grip of Gordon's captured pistol. He glanced around anxiously, no doubt searching for a way out, only to see Bane's guards hefting their weapons. The soldiers had the battle-hardened look of professional mercenaries.

Escape was not an option.

The man held onto Gordon's gun for a moment

longer before meekly surrendering. He put it down, and a look of mournful resignation came over his face. Rummaging through the prone officer's pockets, he took out Gordon's wallet, badge, and several folded sheets of paper.

My speech, Gordon realized with alarm. *Dear God, no…*

The doomed felon handed the items over to Bane, who briefly examined them, one by one. They appeared to be of little interest to him, until he came to the papers. He skimmed the pages quickly, then paused and read through them more carefully. His eyes narrowed.

No one spoke. All eyes were on Bane and the poor stooge who was slated for execution. Nobody was paying any attention to Gordon as he lay sprawled on the floor of the chamber, not far from the edge of the platform. He could hear the water surging by several feet below. The spray from the twin cataracts rose up to spatter him.

He cautiously lifted his head to make sure no one was watching.

This is it, he realized. *This could be my only chance.* Adrenaline cut through the cloudiness fogging his brain, and he rolled frantically over the edge of the platform, splashing into the churning waters below.

Instantly he sank beneath the surface. He tried to hold his breath, but the cold water gushed into his mouth and nose. The current caught hold of him and started to carry him away.

Startled guards shouted and cursed, the sound muffled by the water. Automatic weapons blared loudly. Bullets slammed into Gordon's body, tearing through flesh and bone. Searing jolts of pain rocked him from head to toe. He screamed beneath the water.

No! Gordon thought. *I have to get away...sound the alarm.*

Crimson foam spread atop the water. The current cleared it away.

Bane gazed down into the flowing river. His unworthy minion, who had been imprudent enough to bring Gordon into their base of operations in the first place, stared at the channel, as well.

"He's dead," the fool insisted, as though that might somehow excuse his poor judgment. The smell of gunfire hung in the air. The body of his comrade still rested on the ground, just a few feet away. "He has to be."

Bane tucked Gordon's papers into his belt, so that he could examine them at his leisure. His mind raced with ways he might put these revelations to use.

He spoke to the terrified man.

"Then show me his body."

"That water flows to any one of outflows," the man protested. "We'd never find him."

Bane considered the problem. He turned to his lieutenant, Barsad. The loyal soldier had fought beside

THE DARK KNIGHT RISES

him in so many conflicts over the years, all around the world. He owed Bane his life a dozen times over.

"Give me your GPS," the masked leader demanded.

Barsad handed over the unit, and Bane tucked it into the terrified stooge's leather jacket. He zipped the jacket up like a doting mother sending a child off to school. He patted the jacket to make sure the GPS unit was secure.

"Follow him," he said.

The worthless fool stared at him with an utter lack of comprehension.

"Follow?"

Bane drew his gun and shot the man between the eyes.

The body dropped to the floor. Bane kicked it over the edge of the platform and into the turbulent water, then watched as the current carried the corpse in the same direction as Gordon. He turned and again addressed Barsad.

"Track him," Bane instructed him. "Make sure both bodies will not be found. Then brick up the south tunnel."

Barsad hurried to carry out his orders. Bane took out Gordon's papers and leafed through them again. If the pages were to be believed, they were easily worth the lives of any number of men. He welcomed the fortuitous turn of events that had brought them into his possession.

Fate, it appeared, was on his side.

* * *

The sewage treatment plant looked uglier by night. Blake pulled up to the gate and flashed his badge at the puzzled security guard, who let him through. Ross was off-duty, at home with wife and kids, but Blake was putting in some unpaid overtime. Playing a hunch, he parked his vehicle and raced for the basin where Jimmy's body had washed up earlier.

This was a long shot, Blake knew, and he was already dreading the prospect of finding Gordon's body in the same state as Jimmy's, but anything was better than standing around wondering if the commissioner was still alive. He had to believe that Gordon had survived the underground explosion. Gotham still needed him.

Moonlight rippled atop the water that flowed beneath the metal grate. Bracing himself for the worst, Blake thought he spotted something that poked up briefly through the grille before sinking back into the currents below. Something pale groped for the air.

Fingers?

He ran forward and thrust his hand down into the basin. He groped frantically until—his heart pounding—he caught hold of what felt like another man's wrist.

Yes! It was Gordon.

Straining, he tugged the commissioner up through an opening in the grille and hauled him onto the concrete pathway. His breathing ragged, the commissioner looked barely alive. His face was gray, and his glasses were missing. Dripping clothes were soaked with blood and water. Crimson swirls streaked the puddle that began pooling beneath his trembling body.

Blake could tell at once that Gordon had been shot more than once. He shouted anxiously for help.

"Man down!" Then he realized the commissioner was trying to speak.

"Bane," Gordon whispered urgently, almost too softly to hear. "Under the city. Warn Gotham, warn—"

Blake leaned in closer, trying to make out what he was saying. The cop felt torn between fear and relief.

At least he's still alive, he thought.

But for how much longer?

CHAPTER EIGHT

Blake had never been to Wayne Manor before. Its stately stone walls and towers made it look more like a castle than a house. High lancet windows and marble columns added to the grandeur. Gargoyles gazed down from the upper stories. An elegant parapet circled the roof. Stone spires stabbed at the sky. All that was missing was a moat and drawbridge. The mansion belonged in some far-off European kingdom, not mere miles away from downtown Gotham.

He found it hard to believe that the whole place was home to just one guy, even if that guy was Bruce Wayne. You could move an entire orphanage into it, and still have room for a small army.

An elderly butler greeted him at the door. Based on his research, Blake recognized Alfred Pennyworth, a man who had served the Wayne family for at least two generations. He wondered how much the old servant knew about his master's secrets.

"I need to see Bruce Wayne," Blake said.

"I'm sorry," the butler said. "Mr. Wayne doesn't take unscheduled calls. Not even from police officers."

"And if I go to get a warrant, in the investigation of Harvey Dent's murder?" Blake asked. "Would that still count as 'unscheduled'?"

The butler frowned and gave the young policeman a closer look.

Minutes later, Blake found himself waiting in an opulent study, surrounded by antiques and heirlooms he was almost afraid to touch. He fidgeted upon a well-upholstered couch, still wondering if he was doing the right thing. He had rehearsed this visit a thousand times in his head, but it was one thing to imagine it, and another thing to actually go through with it. What if he was making a tremendous mistake?

Maybe some secrets should stay buried…

Bruce Wayne entered the room, hobbling on a cane. Blake was startled by how much the once-dashing playboy had changed, but tried not to show it. He looked older and scruffier these days, better suited to retirement than a red-carpet gala. Wearing a rumpled dressing gown and slippers, he made Blake feel overdressed.

The one-time prince of Gotham City did not sit down. Blake wondered how he had injured his leg.

"What can I do for you, officer?" Wayne asked.

Blake got straight to the point.

"Commissioner Gordon's been shot."

"I'm sorry to hear that—"

"He chased some gunmen down into the sewers," Blake elaborated, cutting him off. "When I pulled him out, he was babbling about an underground army and a masked man called Bane."

Wayne maintained a neutral expression.

"Shouldn't you be telling this to your superior officers?"

"I did," Blake admitted. "One of them asked if he also saw any giant alligators down there." He shook his head, remembering how Foley and the others had brushed him off, once Gordon was safely delivered to the hospital. Only hours had passed since the commissioner had been shot, but it already felt like ages. They needed to do something!

"He needs you." Blake took a deep breath before going on. "He needs the Batman."

There, he thought. *I said it.*

If Wayne was shocked by his implication, the reclusive billionaire gave no sign of it. He merely chuckled wryly.

"If Commissioner Gordon thinks I'm the Batman, he *must* be in a bad way—"

"He doesn't know or care who you are," Blake

said. "But we've met before…when I was a kid. At the orphanage."

Wayne gave him a quizzical look.

"See, my mom died when I was small," Blake continued. "Car accident, I don't really remember it. But a couple years later my dad was shot over a gambling debt. I remember that just fine." He looked into Wayne's eyes. "Not a lot of people know what that feels like, do they? To be angry, in your bones. People 'understand,' foster parents 'understand'—for a while. Then they expect the angry kid to do what he knows he can never do. To move on, to *forget*."

He spat out the word.

"So they stopped understanding and sent the angry kid to a boys' home, St. Swithin's. Used to be funded by the Wayne Foundation." Blake paused to let that register. "See, I figured it out too late. You have to hide the anger. Practice smiling in the mirror, like putting on a mask." The words—and memories—tumbled out of him. "You showed up one day in a cool car, pretty girl on your arm. Bruce Wayne, billionaire orphan. We made up stories about you. Legends. The other boys' stories were just that. But when I saw you I knew who you really were.

"I'd seen that look on your face. That mask. Same one I taught myself."

Blake stopped. He wasn't sure what else there was to say. He waited for Wayne to respond, to deny or confirm, but the other man just stood there silently, looking lost in thought. The young cop wondered what was going through his mind.

"I don't know why you took the fall for Dent's murder," he said finally, "but I'm still a believer in the Batman. Even if you're not."

Wayne looked at him.

"Why did you say your boys' home *used* to be funded by the Wayne Foundation?"

"Because the money stopped." Blake could tell Wayne was surprised by the news. He rose to his feet, disappointed by what he had had found at the mansion. "Might be time to get some fresh air, and start paying attention to details. Some of those details might need your help."

He showed himself out.

Bruce and Alfred watched from the front hall as the patrol car drove away.

"You checked that name?" Bruce asked. He assumed Alfred had been listening in on his meeting with the young police officer. "Bane?" The word had sinister connotations. A cause of ruin, disaster, and death, at least according to Webster. Bruce wondered what kind of man would choose such a name for himself.

A man who wished to instill fear in others?

He understood the reasoning.

"Ran it through some databases," Alfred said. The faithful butler had once served as an operative for

British Intelligence, before going into service. His skills at garnering information still came in handy. "He's a mercenary. No other known name. Never been seen or photographed without a mask. He and his men were behind a coup in West Africa that secured mining operations for our friend John Daggett."

Wayne raised an eyebrow. Daggett was the kind of shark that gave rich tycoons a bad name.

"Now Daggett's brought them here?" he asked.

"It would seem so," Alfred replied. "I'll keep digging."

The butler turned to leave, but Wayne had another question.

"Why did the Wayne Foundation stop funding boys' homes in the city?"

"The Foundation is funded from the profits of Wayne Enterprises," Alfred reminded him. "There have to be some."

Bruce's expression fell. Recent years had taken their toll on the company Bruce's ancestors had founded, but he hadn't realized that Wayne Enterprises' financial reverses had hurt the charities that depended on its largesse. He rebuked himself for not paying closer attention.

"Time to talk to Mr. Fox, I think," Bruce declared.

Lucius Fox was the chief executive officer of Wayne Enterprises, and had been for several years now. Bruce trusted him almost as much as he trusted Alfred.

"I'll get him on the phone," Alfred said.

"No." Bruce glanced out the front door. Marble steps led down to the gated front drive. "Do we still have any cars around the place?"

Alfred smiled.

"One or two."

Good, Bruce thought. "And I need an appointment at the hospital. About my leg," he added.

The leg had been bothering him for eight years now, ever since he'd fallen several stories. The fall had killed Harvey Dent. Bruce had merely injured his left knee. Perhaps for good.

"Which hospital, sir?"

"Whichever one Jim Gordon is in."

Wayne Enterprises occupied a gleaming glass-and-steel skyscraper in downtown Gotham. The city's monorail system and utilities were routed through the building, making it the unofficial center of the city.

A board meeting was just breaking up on the top floor of the tower. Worried executives rose from their positions around a large polished oak table, gathering up their notes and reports. Picture windows looked out on the thriving city below. Half-empty pitchers of fresh water waited to be picked up by the service staff. Marble busts of company's founders, Solomon and Zebidiah Wayne, gazed down from their perches as the board members exited the room.

Miranda Tate lingered behind, hoping for a

private word with the CEO.

"Mr. Fox," she said, "I believe in what Mr. Wayne was trying to do. I'm only asking for explanations because I think I can help."

"I'll pass along your request," Fox said. "Next time I see him."

A dignified African–American gentleman in his sixties, Lucius Fox sat at the head of the table. His neatly trimmed hair and mustache were now more salt than pepper. An old-fashioned bow tie gave him a courtly air. He had started out as a research scientist and engineer, before assuming control of the company nearly a decade ago.

"He doesn't talk to you either?" Miranda inferred.

"Let's just say that Bruce Wayne has his... eccentricities."

To put it mildly, Fox thought.

"Mr. Fox," she persisted. "Are you aware that John Daggett is trying to acquire shares of Wayne Enterprises?"

"I was not," he admitted. "But it wouldn't do him any good. Mr. Wayne retains a clear majority." At that he fell silent, indicating that the conversation was at an end.

Miranda departed, clearly disappointed not to have learned more about the company's current prospects. Fox sighed. He appreciated the woman's energy and conviction, but certain information could not be shared with anyone other than Bruce Wayne himself.

Miss Tate needed to remain in the dark, along with the rest of the world.

Returning to his own office, he found an unexpected visitor.

"Bruce Wayne," he intoned. "As I live and breathe."

Bruce rose to greet him, leaning on his cane. Fox couldn't remember the last time the hibernating heir had visited Wayne Tower.

"What brings you out of cryo-sleep, Mr. Wayne?" he asked. Bruce chuckled.

"I see you haven't lost your sense of humor—even if you *have* lost most of my money."

Fox just dismissed the accusation.

"Actually, you did that yourself," he replied. "See, if you funnel the entire R&D budget for five years into a fusion project that you then mothball, your company is unlikely to thrive."

"Even with—"

"A wildly sophisticated CEO, yes." He leaned forward, and gave Bruce the cold, hard truth. "Wayne Enterprises is running out of time. And Daggett is moving in."

Bruce accepted the gloomy prognosis without complaint.

"What are my options?"

"If you're not willing to turn your machine on—"

Bruce cut him off.

"I can't, Lucius."

"Then sit tight," Fox advised. "Your majority

keeps Daggett at arm's length while we figure out a future for the energy program with Miranda Tate. She's supported your project all the way, incidentally. She's smart, and quite lovely."

Bruce rolled his eyes.

"You too, Lucius?"

"We all just want what's best for you, Bruce." It pained Fox to see such a remarkable man, who had already overcome so much tragedy, cut himself off from any hope of happiness. Bruce deserved better than the self-inflicted purgatory to which he had condemned himself. "Show her the machine."

"I'll think it over," Bruce said. That was more than Fox had expected, so he chose to leave it at that.

"Anything else?" Lucius asked.

"No, why?" Bruce responded. Fox smiled nostalgically.

"These conversations used to end with some... unusual requests."

"I retired," Bruce said tersely.

Neither man needed to clarify. They had always understood each other with regard to Bruce's former...pursuits, even if they seldom spoke of them directly. Plausible deniability had its advantages, at least as far as Fox was concerned.

Nevertheless, he wasn't finished.

"Let me show you some stuff anyway."

CHAPTER NINE

Wayne Enterprise's Applied Sciences Division was hidden away in a hangar-sized bunker deep beneath the tower, many stories below the business offices. When Bruce had first visited the facility, nearly a decade ago, it had become a graveyard for discarded prototypes and forgotten projects, left to gather dust out of sight, and out of mind.

Only he and Lucius had seen the potential in the division's extensive collection of high-tech castoffs. Together, they had turned the mothballed relics into an arsenal.

Before it all went wrong.

Now the bunker was a graveyard again. Bruce limped uncomfortably through the vast, cavernous chambers, inspecting Lucius's growing collection of high-tech toys. A brilliant mechanical engineer as well as a savvy businessman, Lucius had designed or overseen practically every item hidden away in the facility. He had been with Wayne Enterprises for decades, ever since helping to build Gotham's citywide monorail system for Bruce's father a generation earlier.

Thomas Wayne had been a philanthropist devoted—along with his beloved wife—to making Gotham City a better place to live for all its citizens. Bruce sometimes feared that the city had never truly recovered from their senseless murders.

They passed a row of tank-like vehicles painted for desert camouflage. Squat and angular, with wide racetrack tires, the heavily armored "tumblers" had been designed for the US military, but cost overruns and technical difficulties had scuttled the project. Bruce had once put a similar model to good use, before it was destroyed while he was chasing the Joker. He had never bothered to replace it.

"I figured you'd have shut this place down," Bruce said.

"It was always shut down, officially," Lucius reminded him.

"But all this new stuff?"

"After your father died," Lucius said, "Wayne Enterprises set up fourteen different defense subsidiaries." That had been under the ethically dubious leadership of one William Earle, whom Bruce had ousted several years ago. Fox had proven to be a much more conscientious and socially responsible CEO.

"I've spent years shuttering them, and consolidating all the prototypes under one roof. My roof."

Bruce marveled at the sheer size of the stockpile.

"Why?"

"Stop them from falling into the wrong hands," Lucius said. "Besides, I thought *someone* might get some use out of them—"

Bruce shook his head. What part of "retired" did the other man not understand?

"Sure I can't tempt you with something?" Lucius pressed. "Pneumatic crampons? Infrared contact lenses?" He eyed Bruce's cane. "At least let me get you something for that leg."

Bruce appreciated the offer, but no. His bad knee kept him grounded, more or less.

"It's fine for the use its gets these days."

Lucius shrugged.

"Well, I have just the thing for an eccentric billionaire who doesn't like to walk."

He moved to a thick metal door that guarded an adjacent chamber. Lucius entered a code into a keypad mounted next to the door and the security barrier rolled upward, exposing the hangar beyond. Bruce's eyes widened at the sight of a sleek, state-of-the-art vehicle that appeared to be all folding metal planes and panels. Enormous rotors waited to lift the intimidating craft into the air.

"Defense Department project for tight-geometry urban pacification," Lucius said proudly. "Rotors configured for maneuvering between buildings without recirculation."

Bruce was impressed.

"What's it called?"

"It has a long and uninteresting Wayne Enterprises designation," Lucius stated, "so I took to calling it the Bat." He turned toward Bruce with a sly smile on his face. "And, yes, Mr. Wayne, it does come in black."

Bruce couldn't resist taking a closer look. He limped forward and ran his hand over one of the prototype's many angled and overlapping elevons. The cockpit was sheltered beneath the wings in a sturdy armored module. The empty pilot's seat called out to him. Instinctively he wondered how the Bat handled in the air.

"Works great," Lucius said, as though reading his mind. "Except for the autopilot."

Bruce stepped back from the machine.

"What's wrong with that?"

"Software-based instability," Lucius said with a sigh. "Might take a better mind than mine to fix it."

Bruce eyed him skeptically.

"Better mind?"

"I was trying to be modest. A less busy mind," he amended. "Yours, perhaps."

But Bruce refused to let the older man entice him. He turned his back on the aircraft with an undeniable twinge of regret.

"I told you," he said firmly. "I retired."

* * *

"I've seen worse cartilage in knees," the doctor commented, examining an X-ray.

Bruce sat on an examination table in Gotham General Hospital. It was already dark outside, but Alfred had managed to arrange an after-hours appointment. The Wayne name still opened doors in Gotham, no matter what the latest financial reports said.

"That's good," Bruce responded absently, only half-listening. He had other things on his mind.

"Not really," the doctor said. "That's because there is *no* cartilage in your knee. And not much of any use in your elbows and shoulders. Between that and the scar tissue on your kidneys, residual concussive damage to your brain tissue, and the general scarred-over quality of your body, I simply cannot recommend that you go heli-skiing." He *tsk*ed at the map of old scars criss-crossing Bruce's bare back and chest. "About the only part of your body that looks healthy is your liver, so if you're bored, I recommend you take up drinking, Mr. Wayne."

"I'll take that under advisement, doctor."

The physician left to attend to his rounds, leaving his patient alone in the exam room.

Finally, Bruce thought. He quickly dressed and pulled a wool ski mask over his head. Moving rapidly, before anyone remembered to check on him, he hobbled over to the window and climbed onto the sill. Twisting the head of his cane, he drew out a length of unbreakable monofilament wire and clipped it to his belt, then wedged the cane securely behind the window frame. The glass pane slid open easily. A crisp autumn wind blew into the room. Bruce leaned out to inspect the view.

The exam room was on one of the topmost floors of the hospital, facing a dark alley. Litter blew across the floor of the alley, hundreds of feet below. A metal dumpster was filled with non-biological waste. Bruce had specifically requested this room—for privacy's sake, he had claimed. It wouldn't do, after all, for Bruce Wayne's medical issues to be splashed all over the tabloids.

As cover stories went, it had the ring of plausibility.

He didn't linger on the sill. Although he hadn't attempted a stunt like this in years, he threw himself out the window into the night. Gravity seized him and he plunged toward the alley below, the wire unspooling behind him. The night wind whipped past his face.

One, two... He counted off the floors as he plummeted past them, accelerating at nine-point-eight meters per second squared. He waited until just the right moment to trigger the braking mechanism. *Three!*

He came to a halt directly outside a private room on the eleventh floor. Dim lights penetrated the curtains as he stealthily raised the window and slipped inside the room. Trained in the arts of the ninja, he made not a sound as he crossed toward the haggard figure in the bed. His heart sank at the sight.

Bruce had first met Jim Gordon on the worst night of his life. As a young police officer, freshly transferred from Chicago, Gordon had attempted to comfort an eight-year-old child mere hours after the boy's parents had been murdered by a mugger in what would someday be known as Crime Alley. Although traumatized by the murders, which had taken place right before his eyes, Bruce had never forgotten the young officer's kindness. One of the few honest cops in a town that liked being dirty, Gordon had proven a valuable ally in Batman's war against crime.

Over the years, the Dark Knight had come to depend on Gordon's integrity and courage.

Now Gordon lay helpless in a hospital bed, hooked up to machines. Blinking medical equipment monitored his vital signs, which were alarmingly weak. An oxygen mask was affixed to his face. An IV fed fluids into his arm. Gordon's face was ashen. His skin looked clammy. Bruce felt a long-buried anger building in his chest.

Gordon was his friend.

Whoever did this to him needed to pay.

Bane.

A low growl escaped Bruce's lips, rousing Gordon, whose eyes fluttered open. For a moment, Bruce feared that the commissioner might panic at the sight of a masked man standing at the foot of his bed, yet somehow the injured man seemed to recognize him. Gordon tried to speak, but the oxygen mask muffled his words. Wincing in pain, he tugged the mask away from his mouth.

"We were in this together," he said hoarsely. "Then you were gone—"

"The Batman wasn't needed anymore," Bruce responded, disguising his voice. "We won."

"Built on a lie," Gordon croaked. "Our lie." He moaned weakly, in obvious distress. "Now there's an evil rising from where we tried to bury it. Nobody will listen." Anxious eyes pleaded with his visitor. "The Batman must come back."

Does he know what he's asking? Bruce wondered. "What if he doesn't exist anymore?" he replied aloud.

"He must," Gordon murmured, gasping for breath. "He must."

CHAPTER TEN

Gotham's Old Town had once been a prestigious place, but the neighborhood had never fully recovered from a series of economic downturns over the last few decades. Affluent families had abandoned it, only to be replaced by successive waves of struggling immigrants, welfare recipients, and squatters.

Elegant townhouses had been subdivided into shabby apartments and left to decay, neglected by absentee landlords who pocketed their rent checks but seldom laid eyes on their rundown properties. Graffiti blemished the buildings' sooty brick walls. Prostitutes and drug dealers loitered openly on the stoops and street corners. Iron bars guarded the first floor windows. The police and politicians claimed to have cleaned up Gotham, but the view from Selina's apartment told another story.

Looking away from the window, she admired herself in the mirror of her cramped, closet-sized bathroom. Her new pearls went nicely with the slinky black dress she had picked out for the night's excursion. She was looking forward to getting out of the dingy apartment for a few hours.

A disturbance in the hall outside interrupted her thoughts.

"I told you!" Jen shouted, loud enough for all their neighbors to hear. "Money first!"

Selina rolled her eyes. *Here we go again.*

Moving quickly to the door, she stepped out into the hall, where she found Jen backed up against a wall by a smarmy yuppie type who looked twice her size and way too old for her. His face was flushed with anger. "Goddammit!" he swore. "You took my wallet!"

He drew back his fist. An expensive gold watch glittered on his arm.

Intent on bashing Jen, he didn't even hear Selina pounce. She grabbed onto his wrist, her nails digging into his flesh.

"Get out," she hissed.

Startled, he glared angrily at her.

"She took my wallet!"

Probably, Selina admitted to herself, but that didn't matter. Nobody was turning Jen into a punching bag—not while she was around. She twisted the jerk's arm behind his back and propelled him toward the stairwell. He grunted in pain.

"*Now*," she insisted.

The guy got the message. Muttering obscenities under his breath, he retreated down the stairs, glancing back furiously over his shoulder on his way out. Selina waited until she heard the front door slam shut downstairs before checking on Jen. Her reckless young protégé was already rifling through the guy's thick wallet.

Selina sighed.

"I've told you not to try it with the assholes, Jen."

"They're all assholes," Jen replied. She was dressed to entice, all slutted out in a micro-miniskirt, midriff-baring halter top, and high heels. Her makeup was about as subtle as a porn film. The guy with the fist was hardly the first jerk to take the bait.

Selina conceded the point.

"Okay, the assholes who hit."

Jen had already been hit enough in her young life. She had been a runaway, living on the streets when Selina had first taken her under her wing. They had gone through a lot together, doing what they had to in order to survive. Selina just wished Jen showed better sense sometimes.

"I don't know what he's so upset about." Jen pulled a handful of bills from the wallet. "He only had sixty bucks here."

"Probably the watch," Selina guessed.

"Watch?"

Selina held out her wrist. A brand-new Rolex

gleamed against her bare arm. Smirking, she peeled it off and gave it to Jen.

"Don't wait up for me," she said.

A silver Lamborghini was parked in the shadows across from the converted townhouse. Although slightly out of place in this low-rent district, the deluxe sports car only attracted a few curious glances. It wasn't uncommon for the upper classes to go slumming in Old Town, looking for drugs and other illicit diversions. Like the yuppie who had just followed a young girl into the apartment building, only to storm out in a rage minutes later.

Looks like he didn't get what he wanted.

Bruce crouched inside the automobile. A hand-held tracking device informed him that his mother's pearls were just across the street. He was weighing his next move when Selina Kyle emerged from the townhouse and hailed a cab. She looked as if she was dressed for a fancy date, or a party. The pearls hung elegantly upon her neck.

He had to admit that she wore them well.

He gave the cab a slight head start before pulling away from the curb. The tracker beeped on the dashboard.

Let's see where she's going with those pearls, he thought.

The cab dropped her off in front of the Gotham

Museum of Art, where some sort of lavish celebration was being held. Spotlights splashed across the museum's graceful neoclassical façade as limos disgorged elegant men and women in formal attire. Throngs of paparazzi lined the red carpet, snapping shots for tomorrow's society columns and websites. Flashes went off incessantly, practically blinding the arriving guests. Bruce couldn't help wishing that Selina Kyle had chosen a somewhat less public venue for her night on the town.

Good thing I put on a decent suit tonight, he mused.

He pulled up to the curb and turned the Lamborghini over to a valet, who appeared suitably impressed by the sweet ride. Gritting his teeth in anticipation of the attention he was about to receive, Bruce removed his cane from the back seat.

"Look at that," a paparazzo chortled nearby. "Another rich stiff too out of shape to climb out of his sports car."

"No, that's Bruce Wayne!" another photographer said excitedly. He pushed forward to capture a shot of the famous recluse. "Hey, Mr. Wayne! Where you been hiding?"

Dozens of lenses swung toward Bruce, who quietly pressed a button on his key fob. All at once, every camera in the vicinity went dead. Frustrated paparazzi clicked uselessly and cursed their equipment. Bruce repressed a smile.

Climbing the steps, he approached the front entrance.

"I'm not sure my assistant put me on the guest list," he said to a man who stood in the doorway.

"Not a problem," the awestruck greeter assured him. "Right through here, Mr. Wayne."

Bruce entered to find a tasteful charity masquerade underway. Twinkling white party lights were strung upon the walls and ceilings. Rose petals fell like confetti. Gotham's A-list, wearing colorful masks along with the rest of their finery, mingled and massed throughout the gallery. The main exhibition hall, located below the mezzanine, had been converted into a dance floor. A live band performed on a stage in front of an exhibit of sixteenth-century Dutch oils.

Thirsty revelers congregated at an open bar. Champagne fizzed in crystal flutes. Marble sculptures posed on their pedestals. Oddly enough, Bruce was the only person *not* wearing a mask.

Too bad I left my cowl at home, he thought.

But where was Selina Kyle?

Nodding politely to anyone who tried to engage him in conversation, Bruce wove through the crowd with ease, searching for the elusive thief. He eyed the priceless masterpieces hanging on the walls. Was the "cat" planning another elaborate heist?

Of course, he thought. *That's her M.O.*

Taking the stairs up to the mezzanine, he leaned upon the railing and scanned the main hall below. A sea of masked partygoers, at least a quarter of them wearing little black dresses, made locating a single woman challenging. It took him a moment, but he soon spotted Selina on the dance floor, sharing a slow dance with a well-fed older gentleman wearing a simple white domino mask. She sported a lacy black mask of her own, complete with velvet cat ears. The stolen pearls still gleamed around her neck.

He stepped away from the banister, moving to intercept her. But before he could reach the stairs, a voice called out to him.

"Bruce Wayne? At a charity ball?"

He turned to find an attractive brunette in a red gown gazing at him in surprise. A frilly Venetian mask was her only concession to the theme. Her striking blue–gray eyes looked vaguely familiar. It took him a moment to recognize her from various business articles and profiles.

"Miss Tate, isn't it?" he said.

She seemed amazed to find him here. When she spoke, it was with a hint of an exotic accent.

"Even before you became a recluse, you never came to these things..."

"True." He looked around with disdain. "Proceeds go to the big fat spread, not the cause. It's not about charity, it's about feeding the ego of whichever bored society hag laid it on."

"Actually, this is my party, Mr. Wayne," she said.

Bruce seldom blushed, but for once he came close.

"Oh."

"And the proceeds will go where they should,

because I paid for the fat spread myself."

He had no reason to doubt her.

"That's very generous of you."

"You have to invest, if you want to restore balance to the world," she continued, lowering her mask. "Take our clean energy project, for instance."

Alfred and Lucius were right, Bruce noted. She *was* lovely.

"Sometimes the investment doesn't pay off," he responded blithely. "Sorry."

She regarded him thoughtfully.

"You have a practiced apathy, Mr. Wayne. But a man who doesn't care about the world doesn't spend half his fortune on a plan to save it—and isn't so wounded when it fails that he goes into hiding."

Bruce felt as if his own mask was slipping. Miranda Tate was clearly a woman to be reckoned with. He would have to be on guard around her.

"Have a good evening, Mr. Wayne," she said as she turned to leave.

He watched her walk away, almost forgetting about Selina Kyle for a moment. Then he recalled what had brought him here, and hurried down the stairs as quickly as his bad leg would allow. To his relief, Selina was still waltzing in the arms of her gray-haired companion, whom Bruce recognized as Horace Gladstone, a rich old twit if ever there was one.

As they spun, she pretended to laugh at his jokes.

"Mind if I cut in?"

Annoyed, Gladstone turned. Bruce thrust his cane into the other man's hand and took Selina by the waist. Without missing a beat, he swept her away from the fuming old gent.

She glared at him as they danced.

"You don't seem very happy to see me," he observed.

She glided gracefully atop her high heels, letting him lead.

"You were supposed to be a shut-in."

"Felt like some fresh air."

She eyed him curiously, more irked than alarmed.

"Why didn't you call the police?"

"I have a...powerful friend who deals with this kind of thing." He admired the tufted ears sprouting from her sleek brown hair. "Brazen costume for a cat burglar."

"So?" she challenged him. "Who are you supposed to be?"

"Bruce Wayne, eccentric billionaire." He glanced back at Gladstone. "What about your date?"

"His wife's in Ibiza, but she left her diamonds behind." Selina smirked. "Worried they might get stolen."

I should have known, he thought. *Why else would a woman like Selina waste time with a pompous old boor like him?*

"It's pronounced 'I-*beetha*,'" he said, correcting her. "You wouldn't want these nice people realizing you're a crook, not a social climber."

She bristled at the suggestion. Her eyes flashed angrily.

"You think I care what anyone in this room thinks of me?" He caught a hint of Gotham's East End in her voice, although she had obviously worked hard to eradicate her accent. He admired her skill and intelligence, if not her fondness for appropriating other people's property.

"I doubt you care what anyone in *any* room thinks of you," he countered.

"Don't condescend, Mr. Wayne," she replied. "You don't know a thing about me."

"Well, Selina Kyle, I know you came here from your walk-up in Old Town. Modest place for a master jewel thief. Which means either you're saving for retirement—or you're in deep with the wrong people."

It was the only plausible explanation for why such a high-end burglar—who had already scored big several times over—was slumming in Old Town. She had to be trying to stay off someone's radar, even if this gala—and Mrs. Gladstone's jewels—had lured her out of hiding.

She frowned at that.

"You don't get to judge me because you were born in the master bedroom of Wayne Manor."

"Actually, it was the Regency Room."

"I started off doing what I had to do," she said unapologetically. Then a hint of regret entered her voice. "But once you've done what you had to, they'll never let you do what you want to."

"Start fresh?" he guessed.

She laughed bitterly.

"There's no fresh start in today's world. Any twelve-year-old with a cell phone could find out what you did. Everything we do is collated and quantified. Everything sticks. We are the sum of our mistakes."

"Or our achievements," he argued.

"The mistakes stick better. Trust me."

Bruce knew all about mistakes...and regrets. He eyed the pearls around her neck.

"You think that justifies stealing?"

"I take what I need from those who have more than enough," she said, a tad defensively. "I don't stand on the shoulders of people with less."

"Robin Hood?" He couldn't quite imagine her in forest green. Black suited her better.

"I'd do more to help someone than most of the people in this room," she insisted. "Including you."

"Maybe you're assuming too much," he said.

"Or maybe you're being unrealistic about what's really in your pants other than a fat wallet."

"Ouch."

Still gliding in his arms, she glanced around at the ostentatious display of wealth and extravagance.

"You think all this can last?" She shook her head dubiously. "There's a storm coming, Mr. Wayne. You and your friends better batten down the hatches, because when it hits you're all going to wonder how you ever thought you could live so large...and leave so little for the rest of us."

"Sounds like you're looking forward to it," he said.

"I'm adaptable," she promised.

But maybe not for much longer, Bruce thought. He recalled the damning accumulation of tips and clues filling her files. The net was closing in on her, even if she didn't want to admit it. Small wonder she yearned for a fresh start.

"Those pearls look better on you than they did in my safe." He rolled her into his shoulder and reached up to unclasp the necklace. "But I still can't let you keep them."

The pearls slid off her neck into his other hand. She glared at him again, then surprised him by lunging forward and kissing him hard. Breathless, he let her slip away into the crowd. By the time he recovered from the kiss, she already had a decent head start on him. He tried to limp after her, but his bad knee slowed him down.

Within moments, she had vanished from sight.

What was that all about? he thought. *Not that I'm complaining.*

Exiting the dance floor, he retrieved his cane from Gladstone.

"You scared her off," the old man complained.

"Not likely," Bruce said. "But if I were you, I'd keep an eye on your wife's diamonds."

Tucking the pearls safely into his pocket, he headed for the exit. The taste of her kiss lingered on his lips.

Maybe Alfred is right, he thought. *Perhaps I do need to get out more.*

The fall air outside was bracing after the sweltering heat of the party. He approached the valet to reclaim his car. He patted his pockets. "I seem to have misplaced my ticket."

It wasn't an act. He really had lost his ticket somehow.

The valet looked puzzled.

"Your wife said you were taking a cab home, sir."

"My wife?"

The Lamborghini zoomed away from the museum. Behind the wheel, Selina grinned and gunned the engine.

Alfred picked him up in the Rolls-Royce an hour later. Bruce climbed into the back of the car.

"Just you, sir?" the butler asked dryly.

Bruce gave him a withering look. He wasn't used to being outsmarted.

"Don't worry, Master Bruce," Alfred assured him, clearly enjoying the situation. "Takes a little time to get back into the swing of things."

Bruce ignored the butler's teasing. He was in no mood to exchange banter right now. Instead he took out his phone and hit a number on speed dial.

Lucius Fox answered on the second ring.

"This is Fox."

"Remember those unusual requests I used to make?"

"I knew it," Fox said. Bruce could easily imagine the other man's amused expression. *Am I really that predictable?*

Up front, Alfred's smile faded. Bruce glimpsed the butler's careworn face in the rear-view mirror. Alfred looked distinctly troubled now, like he knew what was coming next, and wasn't at all happy about it.

Bruce couldn't blame him, but he had made up his mind.

It was time to come out of retirement.

CHAPTER ELEVEN

The experimental carbon-fiber brace arrived at Wayne Manor the very next morning. Bruce tried it out in the cave, away from the prying eyes of everyone except Alfred and the bats roosting overhead. He had gotten only a few hours of sleep since the masquerade, but wasn't about to take time out for a nap. He had slept enough these last eight years.

He clamped the brace onto his right leg and pressed a blinking button on its side. The pivoted orthotic toned up at once, tightening around the joint. A thin layer of padding cushioned the brace. Bruce stood up and worked the knee, attempting deep bends and stretches. It took some effort, but the brace moved with him smoothly, without chafing or riding up and down his leg.

So far so good, he thought.

Alfred put down a thermos of hot coffee.

"You've got the wrong leg, sir."

Bruce shook his head.

"You start with the good limb," he explained, "so the brace learns your optimum muscle patterns." He sat down on a slate cube and swapped the brace to his bad left knee. He rose cautiously, putting his weight on it, and grunted in satisfaction as the reinforced leg appeared to support him. He bent slowly, then rose again, more confidently this time. He threw a kick at the empty air.

A rare smile lifted his lips. He was liking this.

"Now we tighten it up."

He pressed harder on the button, clicking it again. The brace contracted against his leg, the unyielding carbon fibers digging into his flesh. Grimacing, he gritted his teeth against the increased pressure.

Alfred looked on with concern.

"Is it terribly painful, sir?"

"You're welcome to try it, Alfred."

"Happy watching, thank you, sir."

Bruce let out a howl as the brace clicked home. He took a moment to get used to the discomfort before rising to his feet again. Despite the pain, the leg felt more solid than it had in years. Than it had since the night Batman fell.

"Not bad," he said.

A stack of bricks waited a few feet away. Bruce spun and delivered a furious roundhouse kick to the bricks, which went flying across the cave. Overhead, startled bats screeched in alarm. They flapped wildly among the stalactites.

"Not bad at all."

Alfred appeared somewhat less enthusiastic about the success of their experiment. Picking up a brick, he turned it over slowly in his hands. A pensive look came over his face.

"Master Bruce, if you're truly considering going back out there, you need to hear some worrisome rumors about this Bane individual."

Bruce gave Alfred his full attention.

"I'm all ears."

"There is a prison," Alfred began grimly, "in a more ancient part of the world. A pit where men are thrown to suffer and die. But sometimes a man rises from that darkness. Sometimes the pit sends something back."

Bruce nodded, understanding.

"Bane."

"Born and raised in a hell on earth," Alfred said. Bruce's brow furrowed.

"Born in a prison?"

"No one knows why," Alfred reported. "Or how he escaped. But they know who trained him once he did." Alfred took a deep breath before speaking the name. "Rā's al Ghūl. Your old mentor."

Bruce stared back at him in dismay. Rā's al Ghūl, who had also gone by the alias "Henri Ducard," had been the ruthless leader of the League of Shadows, an ancient order of assassins and crusaders dedicated to waging war on crime and corruption—by any means necessary. Rā's had trained Bruce to carry on in his footsteps, and had been largely responsible for shaping the orphaned billionaire into the Dark Knight he had become.

But when Rā's had turned his sights on Gotham City, convinced that the embattled city was beyond saving, Batman had been forced to fight back against the League—with fatal results. Rā's had died, incinerated in a fiery monorail crash. Batman hadn't killed him, but he hadn't tried to save him either.

"Rā's plucked Bane from a dark corner of the Earth," Alfred continued, "and trained him in the blackest disciplines of combat, deception, and endurance. Just as he did with you."

Bruce was stunned by the news. He had thought Bane merely a vicious mercenary, but the truth was far worse.

"Bane was a member of the League of Shadows."

"Until he was excommunicated," Alfred said. "And a man considered too extreme for Rā's al Ghūl is not to be trifled with."

But Bruce refused to be intimidated.

"I didn't know I was known for 'trifling' with criminals."

"That was then," Alfred said gravely. "And you can put the cowl back on, but it won't make you what you were."

"Which was?"

"Someone whose anger at death made him value all life," the servant replied. "Even his own."

My own life doesn't matter, Bruce thought. Then he spoke. "If this Bane is all the things you say he is, then this city needs me."

"Yes," Alfred seemed to agree. "Gotham needs Bruce Wayne. Your resources, your knowledge. Not your body—not your life. That time has passed."

"I tried helping as Bruce Wayne," the billionaire protested. "And I failed."

Just ask Miranda Tate, he thought. But Alfred did not give in.

"You *can* fail as Bruce Wayne," he said. "As Batman, you can't afford to."

"Is that what you're afraid of?" Bruce asked indignantly. "That if I go back out there, I'll fail?"

"No," Alfred said. "I'm afraid you *want* to."

I can't listen to this, Bruce thought. Gordon was depending on him. Gotham was depending on him. *I have to go back out there.*

He crossed the Batcave, no longer needing his cane, and unlocked a rectangular metal closet the size of an upright sarcophagus. Inside the cabinet, hidden away for eight years, was a suit of matte-black body armor made of reinforced Kevlar bi-weave fabric and fire-retardant Nomex. The silhouette of a winged nocturnal predator was emblazoned upon the broad chest piece, which was capable of resisting anything except a straight shot at close range.

Adjacent shelves held steel-tipped black boots, gauntlets with scalloped metal fins, a hanging cloak, a golden Utility Belt, and—last but not least—a pointy-eared cowl. Its mere shadow had once struck terror into the hearts of Gotham's criminal element.

He took the cowl off the shelf.

CHAPTER TWELVE

The Gotham City Stock Exchange was a scene of frenzied activity. Buyers and sellers, wearing jackets and wide suspenders, crowded the trading floor, shouting out orders and keying them into their hand-held wireless devices. The latest stock prices and interest rates scrolled across the countless flat-screen monitors mounted all around. It was pretty much impossible to look in any direction without seeing a flood of financial data.

Computer terminals facilitated electronic trading. Canvas banners extolling the GCSE hung above the busy traders. Sweat mixed with expensive cologne, which in turn mixed with the greed in the air. It was nearly closing time, but the trading was still going strong.

"You can't short a stock just because Bruce Wayne

THE DARK KNIGHT RISES

goes to a party."

A pair of traders, taking a break from the commotion, exchanged notes at a shoeshine stand just around the corner from the main floor. They paid no attention to the nameless peon who was polishing their handmade Italian leather shoes.

"Wayne coming back is change," the second trader insisted. "Change is either good or bad. I vote bad."

"On what basis?"

The other trader shrugged.

"I flipped a coin."

At the market's grandiose front entrance, overlooking Castle Street, a hungry trader haggled with a delivery guy. It was already getting dark outside, and he hadn't eaten in hours. He scowled at his sandwich.

"No, *rye*, he insisted. "I told them rye."

Bad news from the west coast flashed across one of the ubiquitous monitors. A major Silicon Valley product launch had just been hacked. Suddenly, his sandwich was the least of his concerns. He thrust a ten at the vendor.

"All right. I'll take it."

A motorcycle pulled up to the rear entrance. Unlike the front of the building, which saw a constant stream of traders going in and out, the rear entrance was only used for deliveries. Bored security guards watched as a courier entered the building. A messenger pouch was slung over his shoulder. A ruby-red crash helmet concealed his features.

"Hey, rookie!" An exasperated female guard moved to block him. "Lose the helmet. We need faces for the camera."

He reached for his helmet.

In the men's room, a janitor mopped the floor. Toilets flushed in the background. Crumpled paper towels littered the floor. He paused to peek at his wristwatch.

Almost time, he thought.

He reached into his bucket and extracted a sealed Ziploc bag. A micro-Uzi machine pistol waited inside the bag.

The janitor tossed away his mop.

The brokers' shoes shone like new. They paid the shoeshine guy, stiffing him on the tip, and headed back toward the trading floor, still debating the significance of Bruce Wayne's return to the spotlight.

The shoeshine man, whose name was McGarrity, put down his brush. A bulging gym bag rested at the foot of the stand. Glancing about, he unzipped the bag and inspected a loaded sub-machine gun. Smuggling the gun into the building had not been easy, but the time for stealth was almost over.

He hoisted the bag over his shoulder and trotted after the unsuspecting brokers.

The delivery guy drew a pistol from beneath his jacket and brained his unhappy customer. The hungry trader collapsed onto the floor, just inside the front entrance. His pastrami sandwich—on white bread—slipped from his fingers.

The food vendor kicked it aside as he stormed into the building.

The motorcycle courier took off his helmet. The female guard gasped out loud at the sight of the freaky rubber gas mask beneath the helmet. She fumbled for her taser.

Bane was too fast for her. Lunging forward without hesitation, he lifted her above his head and hurled her into the other guards, who tumbled to the floor in a tangle of limbs. They tried to scramble to their feet, but Bane was already among them, dispatching the outmatched men and women with ruthless efficiency. His boot stamped on one guard's throat, crushing his windpipe, while he caught another guard in a headlock, snapping her neck, even as his fist slammed into a third guard's face, driving shards of bone and cartilage into his brain.

His goal was simple: inflict as much damage as he could as quickly and efficiently as possible. Despite his muscular frame, Bane moved with the speed and ferocity of a wild animal. Bones shattered beneath his expert blows. Ribs cracked, shins and knees and collars snapped. Blood spurted.

The guards never had a chance.

The shoeshine man charged onto the trading floor. He pulled out the sub-machine gun and opened fire on the monitors, which exploded in a shower of sparks and shattered plastic. A different kind of chaos erupted. Horrified traders hit the floor or else raced for the exits, only to find their way blocked by yet more gunmen. The janitor and the sandwich guy joined their compatriot, herding the hostages into the center of the room. Smoke and the smell of burning circuitry pervaded the air. Desperate traders pleaded for their lives.

Bane strode onto the floor like a conqueror.

"This is a stock exchange!" one hostage called out. He was the same trader who had neglected to tip the shoeshine man earlier. "There's no money you can steal!"

Bane regarded the man scornfully.

"Why else would you people be here?"

He seized the outspoken trader by the neck and dragged him over to one of the many automated trading terminals. Taking hold of the man's hand, he placed the broker's thumb on the fingerprint reader. The scanner hummed briefly before recognizing the thumbprint. The screen lit up helpfully.

"Enter your password," Bane said, "or I send these men to your home."

The blood drained from the hostage's face. He hastily typed his password into the machine.

By now, sirens could be heard outside, growing louder by the minute. Bane wasn't concerned. He had expected as much.

The shoeshine man, McGarrity, came forward to do his part. He plugged a portable USB drive into the terminal. An antenna on the drive established a link with his laptop. Figures raced across the terminal's monitor.

Bane stood by silently, watching his plan unfold.

Patrol cars screeched onto Castle Street, the narrow avenue in front of the stock exchange building. Blake and Ross were among the first to arrive on the scene. Blake swore out loud as he spotted a large cement mixer blocking their way. He jumped out of the car and ran up to the mixer, where a burly construction worker was busy pouring cement for a new sidewalk.

"Move it now!" Blake ordered. "We've got a situation!"

The construction guy indicated the tight squeeze, made worse by the fleet of cop cars swarming the scene. Then he smirked at Blake.

"Where can I move it?"

"That way!" the cop shouted, pointing to the nearest intersection, but by now the SWAT vans had arrived in force, blocking every avenue. He cursed silently. "Get in your vehicle," he ordered the civilian. "And stay there!"

Foley piled out of a SWAT van, accompanied by Commander Allen of the special anti-terrorism unit. A frantic-looking man in a suit ran toward the police officers, holding up a laminated ID. Blake gathered that he was in charge of security for the stock exchange. He was having a very bad day.

"You've gotta get in there," the man pleaded. But Foley was reluctant to charge in with guns blazing.

"This is a hostage situation."

"No!" the security chief exclaimed. "It's a robbery. They've got direct access to the online trading desk!"

Foley sounded unimpressed.

"I'm not risking my men for your money," he insisted.

"It's not our money," the other man countered. "It's everyone's!"

Allen snickered.

"Really?" he said. "Mine's in my mattress."

Frustrated, the security chief struggled to make the cops understand.

"If you don't shut these guys down, the stuffing in that mattress might be worth a whole lot less, pal!"

Foley got the message.

"Cut the fiber line, shut down the cell tower." He scowled at the looming building, which was the nerve center of Gotham's booming economy. Blake wondered if he was thinking of his 401K. "That'll slow them down."

Blake hoped it would be enough.

McGarrity looked up from his laptop.

"They cut the fiber," he reported, "but the cell's still working—"

"For now," Bane said. "How much longer does the program need?"

McGarrity consulted the progress bar on his screen. "Eight minutes."

Bane glanced up at a clock on the wall. Under ordinary circumstances, the closing bell would have rung minutes ago.

"Time to go mobile."

McGarrity nodded and stuffed the laptop into his bag.

"Get the barriers up!" Allen shouted. "No more in and out on this street!"

Wedge-shaped metal barricades, installed after the Joker's reign of terror, rose up at the mouth of the street. The barricades were intended to stop any truck bombs from crashing into the stock exchange.

SWAT teams fanned out around the building's front entrance. A police sniper peered through a thermal scope, watching the door. Four large heat signatures bloomed, too large to be people.

"I've got something!" the sniper called out.

A ferocious roar came from inside the stock exchange. The front door blew open, causing the nearest SWAT troopers to duck from the blast, as four high-speed motorcycles leapt from inside the building, jumping the front steps to touch down on the pavement in front of Allen and his men.

Terrified hostages could be seen strapped to the rear of the bikes, their silk ties blowing in the wind. Revving their engines, the bikes zoomed straight for the raised barricades—which, designed to stop vehicles speeding *toward* the stock exchange, proved to be highly effective ramps for bikes heading in the opposite direction.

The bikes vaulted over the heads of the surrounding police officers before speeding away into the night. Flustered cops scrambled into their cars to give chase, even as the failed barriers retracted back into the pavement.

Allen swore loudly.

Breaking every speed limit in the book, the bikes wove through the packed evening traffic. Horns honked angrily as they ran red lights with abandon, causing startled drivers to slam on the brakes and get rear-ended for their trouble. A taxi swerved onto the sidewalk to avoid being hit, knocking over an outdoor pretzel stand. Pedestrians scrambled for safety. A city bus pulled to the side to let a speeding patrol car race by.

A black-and-white cruiser fell in behind the fleeing bikes. A gumball light flashed atop the car. Its siren screamed like a banshee.

A rookie, Officer Simon Jansen had never been in a high-speed chase before. He gripped the steering wheel tightly while flooring the gas pedal. As far as he could tell, he and his partner were leading the chase. His heart pounded with excitement. If they were lucky, they might even be the ones to capture the fugitives.

"Shoot the tires!" he shouted.

His partner, a twenty-year veteran named Kelly, drew his gun and leaned out the passenger-side window. He tried to get a bike in his sights, but balked at the expression of the petrified trader clinging to the rear of the bike. The terrified hostage, who was wearing wide suspenders, stared back at him. Kelly shook his head.

"No shot!"

The deputy commissioner's voice blared from the cruiser's radio.

"*Back off*," he ordered. "*They've got hostages.*"

The bikes vanished into a midtown tunnel. The cruiser followed them into the tunnel, maintaining a safe distance. Fluorescent lights, mounted in the ceiling, lit up the tunnel—at least at first. To his surprise, Jansen saw his rear-view mirror go dark.

He glanced back.

"What's going on with the lights?"

A wave of darkness seemed to be advancing through the tunnel, extinguishing every light it encountered. Not just the overhead lights, but also the headlights of every oncoming vehicle blinked out abruptly. A chill ran down the rookie's spine as the encroaching darkness—which instilled an almost superstitious dread—caught up with the speeding cruiser. Their headlights burned out, the gumball blacked out, and the siren went silent.

The car's engine sputtered and died.

What the—?

Out of the inky blackness, a shadowy shape roared past at high speed. An ebony cape flapped behind it.

Kelly's jaw dropped.

"It can't be…"

"The hell was that?" Jansen exclaimed. He had no idea what was happening.

"Oh, boy," the veteran cop said. "You're in for a show tonight."

CHAPTER THIRTEEN

The bikes shot out of the tunnel onto the highway. Bane led the way while the sandwich guy, Petrov, took up the rear.

Looking back over his shoulder, past his squirming hostage, the mercenary saw the streetlights exploding behind him, one by one, throwing the highway into darkness. The night was cloudy and starless—Petrov couldn't see what was chasing them.

He frowned. This wasn't part of the plan.

All at once, the bike's engine choked and died. Swearing, he worked the throttle, but it was no good. Though he still sped forward, through sheer momentum, he was falling behind the rest of his team. Seeing a chance, the hostage behind him undid his straps and leapt from the back of the bike. Hitting the concrete, the capitalist parasite rolled to the side of the highway and clambered to his feet.

"Help!" he shouted. "Somebody, help me!"

As he continued to glide forward on the silent machine, Petrov drew his pistol. He wouldn't be taken without a fight.

Show yourself, he thought. *I am ready for you.*

The darkness swept over him like a tidal wave. Something grabbed onto his collar and yanked him off the seat. He was thrown to the ground hard enough to be knocked senseless. His gun slipped from his grasp. His bike toppled over, throwing up sparks as it skidded across the lanes.

Petrov lifted his head, on the verge of passing out. His blurry eyes widened.

Speeding away from him, in pursuit of Bane and the others, was an armored figure leaning low atop a customized black motorcycle. His midnight cloak spread out behind him, flapping in the wind like the wings of an enormous bat.

"Let's roll," Foley shouted. "They've spotted Batman!"

Abandoning the armored SWAT van, which was too heavy for a high-speed pursuit, he piled into the back of Blake's patrol car. The young officer couldn't believe his ears.

Is he really back? he wondered. *After all these years?*

He hit the accelerator, and the cruiser sped away from the stock exchange.

* * *

The bikes, one short now, split up as they reached a highway intersection. Two of them stuck together, while the third veered off in a different direction. A high overpass loomed above the crossing—as did Batman.

The Bat-Pod rumbled beneath him as he pulled up to the guardrail. He was stretched out belly down atop the cycle, steering it with his shoulders instead of his hands. The prototype's unique design kept his head low and his gloved hands free. Bulletproof shields protected his arms.

Grappling hooks, mini-cannons, and machine-gun muzzles protruded from the chassis. High-performance, single-cylinder engines were embedded in the hubs of both of the cycle's huge twenty-inch wheels. The cycle had once been built into a larger four-wheeled tumbler as an emergency escape pod, but functioned perfectly well on its own. Batman hadn't ridden it in years.

He sat up and drew out a futuristic-looking rifle. The muzzle glowed a luminous shade of blue as he took aim at one of the fleeing bikes on the roadway below.

An electronic tone sounded.

The glowing muzzle pulsed.

The janitor had traded his mop for a pistol and sports bike. Breaking away from Bane and the others, he thought he had a good chance of eluding the police—until his engine suddenly sparked and died.

Instinctively he hit the brake, and then cursed himself for doing so. The speeding bike slowed dramatically even as a slew of police cars, their sirens blaring, closed in on him. A frightened trader jumped from the bike, choosing a nasty tumble over the prospect of being caught in a crossfire.

Enjoy what little time you have left, the janitor thought. He did not bother chasing after the hostage. *Your days are almost over.*

He brought his bike to a full halt, stoically resigned to being captured by the authorities. His own freedom was of no consequence—not as long Bane got away. The cause was all that mattered.

The fire rises, he thought.

Batman frowned as the last two bikes disappeared under another overpass, out of range. He holstered the electromagnetic pulse rifle, which had taken out the first two fugitives. Then he gunned the engine. He would have to eliminate the remaining criminals the old-fashioned way.

Works for me, he thought grimly. *I'm coming for you, Bane.*

The Bat-Pod hurled down the highway.

* * *

"Call everyone in," Foley barked into the radio, turning the back of Blake's patrol car into a mobile command center. The cord was stretched taut between the dashboard and the back seat. "Every patrol car, beat cop—off-duty, too. Call 'em all them in. Close every street. Now!"

The city rushed past them as Blake pushed the patrol car to its limits. The speedometer crept toward three digits. Foley stared out the windows impatiently. He drummed his fingers against the seat cover.

"I'm gonna do what Gordon never could," he predicted.

"What's that?" Blake asked.

"I'm going to take down the Batman."

Blake just remained silent. Batman wasn't a danger to Gotham, no matter what people said. He was more worried about the felons who had just pulled off such an ambitious strike on the stock exchange.

"Sir, what about the armed robbers?" he asked.

Foley ignored the question.

Reports poured in over the radio. All around the city, the GCPD was mobilizing in force. Police cars, vans, and motorbikes flooded the streets, joining the chase. Choppers whirred overhead, their spotlights sweeping the highways below. Even the canine units were being activated.

But to capture whom?

* * *

The highway stretched in front of Bane. He pulled up alongside McGarrity's bike. The computer hacker glanced inside his bag, which was stowed up by the handlebars. He held up his fingers to signal that the program still had two minutes to run.

His was the only bike not weighed down with a hostage.

Bane glanced behind him, seeing the spreading darkness that had already brought down two of his men. He recognized the effects of a localized EMP generator. He could think of only one individual in Gotham who might employ such a device.

The Batman.

So he made a decision. He reached back and plucked a whimpering hostage off his own bike and swung him over onto McGarrity's. The hacker's vehicle wobbled under the increased load, losing speed. The displaced trader clung desperately to its driver.

No longer saddled with a worthless waste of flesh, Bane's bike accelerated. He peeled away from the other rider, making his escape. He glanced back once more. As he had anticipated, Batman chose to pursue the bike with the hostage. Compassion had always been his weakness.

Bane smiled behind his mask. The time would come when he would face Rā's al Ghūl's greatest mistake— but not tonight. He had other business to address.

Another day, betrayer.

* * *

A police chopper reported in to Foley.

"*One bike's veered off, no hostage.*"

Foley listened without responding.

"*Should we pursue?*" the spotter asked via the radio.

"Negative," Foley ordered. "Stay on Batman."

Blake spoke up.

"But the perp's getting away!"

"Who do you want to catch?" Foley scoffed at Blake as if the young rookie was an idiot. "Some robber, or the son of a bitch who killed Harvey Dent?"

Ross kept his mouth shut.

Blake bit down on his tongue.

John Daggett's luxury penthouse occupied the top floor of a skyscraper in a ritzy uptown neighborhood overlooking the park. Flashy gold trim and black leather furniture advertised his wealth. He paced restlessly back and forth across the king-sized living room while Stryver stood nearby, in case his boss needed him. Every television in the penthouse was tuned to the breaking news story.

"—police aren't saying much," a blonde anchor-woman reported. "Frankly, they're too busy. But all signs suggest that what we're seeing is in, in fact, the return of the Batman."

Daggett glared at the screen.

* * *

Only a room away, behind the closed door to Daggett's home office, Catwoman crouched in front of a safe, working the combination lock. Her lithe figure was wrapped tightly inside a sleek black body suit designed for stealth. Avid brown eyes gazed out from behind a thin black mask. High-tech goggles, raised away from her eyes, cast a shadow that bore a distinct resemblance to the ears of a cat. A black Utility Belt hung low on her hips. Knee-high boots boasted serrated steel heels.

The glow from a spare television set lit up the dark room. She glanced up from her labors in time to catch an aerial shot of a cloaked figure racing down the highway astride the coolest motorcycle she had ever seen. A news copter briefly captured the cycle with its searchlight. The masked cyclist was crouched low upon the wheels, tearing up the highway at high speed. Even from a distance, the rider looked an awful lot like a certain legendary Dark Knight.

"Well, well," she whispered. "What do you know?"

Ordinarily, she would have enjoyed watching the live coverage herself, but unfortunately she had urgent business to attend to. Assuming that Daggett and his slimy second-in-command were busy watching the news, she cracked the lock and opened the safe. A thick steel door swung open. She reached inside.

There was nothing there.

She frowned, glaring angrily at the empty safe.

It's not fair, she thought. *It was supposed to be here!*

CHAPTER FOURTEEN

Lights flashing, sirens blaring, two black-and-white police cruisers zipped past Bane as he rode between them, racing in the opposite direction. Intent on joining the chase for Batman, the patrol cars paid no heed, and he appreciated the unexpected diversion. The Dark Knight's return had only made his own escape easier.

Welcome back, Bane thought. *I've been waiting for you to emerge from hiding.*

Jumping onto a concrete barrier, Bane sped down the rail, leaving the increasingly hectic highway behind. An open drainage tunnel waited at the bottom of the slope. Bane glanced behind him, where it appeared that the entire Gotham City Police Department was closing in. Fleets of police cars screamed down the highway. Choppers tilted across the night sky. Searchlights and sirens disturbed the darkness.

Bane chuckled inwardly. He would have to remember to thank Batman later. When the time came.

Without bothering to decelerate, he disappeared into the tunnel.

McGarrity was on his own now. He accelerated down the highway, trying to stay ahead of the Batman. The laptop in his bag beeped, and a quick glance confirmed that the program had finished running. He sighed in relief. His mission was complete.

Now he just needed to get away...if possible.

The sobbing hostage, bouncing on the rear of the bike, slowed him down. Gleaming skyscrapers rose on either side of the highway, the light from the buildings allowing McGarrity to glimpse the Dark Knight's own cycle gaining on him. Remembering what had happened to his comrades, he ducked his head as the Bat-Pod came along beside him, but, to his surprise, the vehicle appeared to be missing its rider.

Batman was no longer astride the cycle.

What the hell? McGarrity thought. *Where—?*

A dark shape came swooping down from the sky, casting a fearsome shadow over the hacker and his hostage. Batman's scalloped black cape extended outward like the wings of a glider. Strong hands ripped the kidnapped trader off the back of the bike, jarring McGarrity, who lost control of his vehicle, laying it down across the highway in a shower of sparks.

The driver rolled away from the bike. Bruised and bleeding, he reached desperately for his laptop.

Batman was on him in an instant. The cloak falling back over his shoulders, he grabbed McGarrity and yanked him to his feet. His masked face was only inches away from the hacker's.

He shouted at his prisoner.

"*What were you stealing?*"

McGarrity gulped, but held his tongue. He owed his allegiance to another masked man, one even more dreadful than the infamous Batman.

I do not fear you, he thought defiantly. *I fear only Bane.*

There was no time to try to sweat the truth out of the thief. He smacked the man's head into a concrete divider, knocking him out so the police could pick him up. An electronic chirp caught Batman's ear and he turned his attention to a gym bag that had been thrown clear of the crash. A battered laptop rested inside the bag, a message on its screen.

APPLICATION COMPLETE

In the next moment a blinding light from above left him exposed on the highway. A police chopper descended from the sky. Glancing around, Batman saw a veritable host of cops closing in on him from all directions. Thousands of cars, vans, bikes, and dogs. Multiple sirens screamed along, adding to the din caused by the whirr of the helicopter rotors. Bloodhounds bayed and strained at their leashes.

The Bat-Pod rolled to a stop nearby, just as Batman had programmed it to do.

The freed hostage, dropped off by the side of the road, ran toward the oncoming police presence. The hapless trader was safe enough now.

Time to go, Batman realized.

A USB drive was plugged into the laptop. He plucked it out of the slot and placed it into a pouch in his Utility Belt, even as a loudspeaker boomed overhead.

"STEP AWAY FROM THE BIKE!"

He scanned the vicinity, mindful as ever of his surroundings. Rā's al Ghūl had taught him that. Stopped traffic packed the highway. A large car transporter, its racks empty, idled below a nearby onramp.

Jumping back onto the Bat-Pod, he activated the cycle's twin 40mm blast cannons. The front-mounted weapons unleashed their firepower, and a well-aimed blast struck the back of the transporter, causing its rear ramp to crash onto the concrete.

The Bat-Pod raced toward the truck, mounted the ramp, and used it to jump directly to the onramp above.

Weaving through the stalled traffic, Batman fled his pursuers. But the GCPD remained hot on his heels.

* * *

"Eight years!" Daggett exclaimed angrily. He tossed down a drink from the bar. The fifty-year-old Scotch did little to calm him. He paced back and forth in his apartment. "After eight years, he has to pick *tonight* to come back!"

Stryver pointed out the bright side.

"He's drawing the cops off Bane."

That's true, Daggett conceded. *What do I care about Batman? He's not connected to me. Unlike Bane.*

Maybe things were actually working out in his favor. *That* calmed him down.

"How did you let him go?" Foley demanded.

The radio squawked in his grip.

"He's got a lot of firepower."

"And you don't?" Foley wasn't accepting any excuses. "We're not letting one nut with a bad attitude and some fancy gadgets run this town again, you hear me?"

"He's heading back downtown."

Foley grinned.

"Then he's as dumb as he dresses." SWAT teams were already in place downtown following the attack on the stock exchange. He got on the horn to Allen. "Close it down, gentlemen."

Blake turned the cruiser around, joining the thousands of other cops converging on the downtown area. He'd never seen this many units chasing after a single suspect. Jockeying for position amidst the swarm of vehicles, he managed to get out ahead of the other patrol cars.

His eyes widened as he spotted Batman up ahead. He recognized the vigilante's one-of-a-kind cycle from grainy news footage of Batman's confrontation with the Joker years ago. Batman had once flipped over a speeding semi-trailer using the vehicle's built-in grappling hook and cable. Despite his visit to Wayne Manor, Blake had never really expected to see it with his own eyes.

Is this my fault? he wondered. *Did I drag him out of hiding?*

Batman zoomed down a wide boulevard, only to find another wave of cop cars charging at him from the other end of the street. Soaring choppers caught him in their searchlights, exposing him to the world. He was trapped in a vise made up of two oncoming walls of cars.

But he didn't slow down. His cycle did a sharp ninety-degree turn, flipping over in the process, and darted into the sheltering darkness of large blind alley. Cops cars squealed to a halt, blocking the entrance. The choppers hovered above them, providing air support. It looked like Batman had nowhere left to go.

Blake hit the brakes at the perimeter of the police lines, sealing the bottleneck. Foley jumped out of the cruiser and stalked toward the narrow opening between the buildings.

The young cop hurried after him.

"Like a rat in a trap," Foley said confidently. He reached out for a bullhorn which was thrust into his hand. He started to raise it to his lips.

VAROOOOM.

A deafening roar, coming from the alley, drowned out whatever the deputy commissioner intended to say. The assembled cops exchanged puzzled looks. None of them, including Blake, knew what sort of machine could produce such a roar.

That's no motorcycle, Blake realized.

"You may have the wrong animal there, sir," a nearby cop said aloud.

The copters' spotlights blew out and a massive dark cyclone roared out of the narrow roadway, high above the street level, spinning the choppers sideways. Blake stared in awe at an intimidating matte-black aircraft like nothing he had ever seen before. Overlapping wings caught the air, while shielding grilled metal vents. A transparent windshield offered a glimpse of Batman seated inside a heavily armored cockpit. Dual rotors produced a powerful downdraft, forcing the cops to the ground. Flying dirt and litter were whipped about by artificial winds.

The craft thundered over the assemblage of GCPD, taking off into the sky.

Blake couldn't resist.

"You sure it was him?" he asked.

Foley glared at him, and thrust the bullhorn into his hands.

Gordon sat up in his hospital bed, still hooked up to machines. The TV in his room was tiny and had lousy sound, but he could make out the aircraft rocketing out of the alley. His heart soared with it.

For the first time in days, he smiled.

"—police are keeping quiet about the prospect of a return by the Batman, but eyewitnesses accounts seem to clearly suggest the type of—"

Daggett watched the huge flatscreen TV intently. Stryver put down his cell phone.

"Bane says the Batman interfered, but the task was accomplished."

Nevertheless, Daggett was still worried.

"What about the men they arrested?"

"He says, and I quote, 'they would die before talking.'"

At that, Daggett relaxed a little. Bane could probably be trusted where his men were concerned. Lord knows they had pulled off that operation in West Africa without a hitch.

"Where does he find these guys?" he wondered aloud.

Stryver just shrugged. Daggett figured they didn't want to know.

"Open the champagne," he instructed, his spirits continuing to rise. After all, a celebration was in order. He headed for his office to click off the TV in there. He'd had enough of Batman tonight. He was in the mood for a different kind of entertainment. "And can we get some girls up here?"

"Careful what you wish for."

A woman in tight black leather leapt through the doorway. Grabbing him, she threw him across the living room, slamming his back into a wall. He reached for the gun he kept holstered under his jacket, but she threw up her leg, impossibly high, and used her heel to trap his wrist to the wall at shoulder height. He whimpered in pain as she leaned in toward him, her face hidden behind a mask.

"Cat got your tongue?" she purred.

Startled, it took him a moment to recognize Selina Kyle. Or as she was known in some circles, the Catwoman. He had never seen her in full gear before. It was a sight to savor—unless she had you pinned against a wall...and not in a good way. Her taut leg kept his wrist pinned at an uncomfortable angle.

She plucked the gun from his trembling hand and flung it across the room.

"You dumb bitch," he muttered. He couldn't believe her nerve, confronting him here on his own turf. Did she really think he didn't have protection?

His bodyguards would be here in minutes.

"Nobody ever accused me of being dumb," she replied.

"Dumb to show up here tonight."

She dug her heel in, grinding his wrist against the wall.

"I want what you owe me."

Stryver finally got around to earning his paycheck. He placed a gun against her head.

Daggett smirked. He could see that his henchman was enjoying the view, keeping his gun in place as his eyes traced the contours of her leather-clad figure.

"'I want' never gets—" Daggett began, and then he stopped as she began to lower her leg.

"Nice outfit," Stryver commented. "Those heels make it tough to walk?"

"I don't know," she replied. "Do they?" Without warning, she drove a six-inch steel stiletto heel into his calf. He let out an agonized scream even as she spun around and twisted his wrist, forcing him to release his gun. Stryver staggered backwards, clutching his leg. Selina stuck the gun in her belt and threw Daggett up against the wall again, with even more force than before.

"Where is it?" she demanded.

"Where is what?" Daggett replied, playing dumb.

"The program. The 'Clean Slate.'"

"Oh, yeah," he said. "The ultimate tool for a master thief with a record." He shrugged. "I don't have it."

Catwoman hissed, but before she could lash out at him again, there was a commotion in the hallway and more bodyguards rushed into the room, guns drawn.

About time they got here! Daggett fumed.

Catwoman spun Daggett around, using him as a human shield, and kicked at the plate glass window behind her. The serrated steel heel made contact, and the glass shattered loudly, spilling out onto the rooftops below. Then she tumbled backwards, dragging Daggett with her. The terrified tycoon shrieked in terror.

Ohmigod, the crazy bitch is going to kill us both!

They fell through the night—landing on a suspended window cleaning platform ten feet below. Without missing a beat, she sliced through a knot with her heel, releasing the platform, which plunged down the side of the building.

Daggett started screaming again, until the platform halted just above the flat rooftop of an adjacent building. She tossed him there, and then sprang nimbly onto the roof herself.

Catwoman towered over Daggett, who lay sprawled on the rough, tar-papered surface. Furious brown eyes flashed menacingly, and when she lifted her hands, he saw claws. Unbidden, the thought occurred to Daggett that some men would pay good money to be in his position right now. All she needed was a whip.

"Where is it?" she repeated.

"The 'Clean Slate?'" he said, trying to make it sound derisive. His heart was still going a mile a minute, but he wasn't going to let this crazy woman get the better of him. "Type in a name and date of birth, and within a couple of hours that person ceases to exist in any database." He snickered at the tantalizing notion. "Little too good to be true."

"You're lying," she hissed. "Rykin Data took it to beta-testing."

"That's why I bought them," he admitted. "But they had nothing. It was just a gangland myth."

She stepped back, mulling it over. He could tell she was troubled by the idea that she'd been chasing a mirage.

Chew on it, he thought acidly. *You get what you deserve, you psycho bitch.*

Just wait 'til I sic Bane on you.

CHAPTER FIFTEEN

Selina was taken aback by Daggett's claim.

Was he telling the truth?

Before she could react, armed men joined them on the rooftop, coming from several directions. Sporting guns, military fatigues, and surly expressions, they dropped down on bungee cables and came scrambling up the fire escapes. She was impressed by the speed of their response. She couldn't fault Daggett's goons for their persistence.

Let's hope they're just as concerned for his safety, she thought, yanking the tycoon up onto his feet. She held onto his throat, her claws digging into his flesh.

"Stay back!" she warned the newcomers. But to her surprise, they kept on coming. A scowling gunman, who had the stone-cold eyes of a professional, screwed a silencer onto his Glock. She tightened her grip, eliciting a gasp of pain from the shaking tycoon.

Blood trickled onto his collar.

"I'm not bluffing," she insisted.

"They know." A gravelly voice came from the shadows. "They just don't care."

All eyes moved to the source. Selina spotted a cloaked figure crouching atop the roof of a luxury apartment complex, one building away. The unmistakable silhouette of bat-like ears rose from the newcomer's ebony cowl. A winged emblem was embossed upon his chest.

It's him, she realized. *Batman.*

The Dark Knight's startling presence distracted her adversaries. The goon with the silencer spun in surprise. Seizing the moment, she tossed Daggett aside and pounced on the gunman, wresting the pistol from his grasp. None of the other men rushed to Daggett's aid, proving that Batman was right. These weren't his men at all.

So who?

But there was no time to worry about that now. Batman jumped effortlessly across the intervening space, landing immediately behind her even as the other men charged at them from all sides. Back to back, they took on her anonymous attackers, lashing out with boots and fists. Batman was a flurry of lightning-fast strikes and dodges, not a move wasted. A bat-shaped boomerang disarmed one attacker, while he caught a knife blade between the fins on his gauntlet and butted another man in the head with his cowl.

Grateful for his timely assistance, she fired the "borrowed" Glock, clipping an overeager goon, who dropped like a stone. She targeted a second man, aiming right between his eyes, but, before she could squeeze the trigger, Batman yanked her arm down, spoiling her shot.

He took out the goon with a well-placed kick to the gut instead.

"You've got to be kidding," she protested.

"No guns," he growled. "No killing."

She was both annoyed and amused by his scruples. "Where's the fun in that?"

He didn't reply as more men poured onto the roof. Catwoman recognized some of them from Bane's underground militia. She was almost flattered by all this attention, but it was clearly time for a strategic retreat. Batman evidently felt the same way. He ran for the edge of the roof.

"Come on!" he gritted.

She watched in confusion as he flung himself off the top of the building, and hesitated momentarily before chasing after him.

Doesn't he know that cats can't fly?

A bullet whizzed past her, spurring her on. Hoping that Batman knew what he was doing, she ran across the roof and peered over the edge. Her eyes widened behind her mask.

A stealth aircraft hovered just below the edge of the

roof, several stories above the street below. Batman waited in an open cockpit, surrounded by a complex array of matte-black elevators, vents, and ailerons.

Shots rang out behind her as she leapt. Landing nimbly on one of the smooth, aerodynamic panels, she slid into the passenger seat beside him.

Okay, she thought. *Consider me impressed.*

Powerful engines roared to life. A steel canopy hissed shut above the cockpit, taking gunfire from above. Bullets pinged off the armor plating. She tried not to let her relief show.

"My mother warned me about getting into cars with strange men."

"This isn't a car," he pointed out.

The fantastic aircraft thundered into the sky. The downdraft forced all but one of the gunmen down onto the roof. The sole exception was an imposing masked figure who advanced slowly into the wind, refusing to be brought to his knees by a mere blast of air. His massive fists clenched at his sides.

Bane watched the Bat escape into the night.

Batman put a safe distance between themselves and Selina's attackers before landing the Bat on the empty helipad of a midtown skyscraper. An EMP pulse took out any inconvenient lights and security cameras, ensuring their privacy for the moment.

He wanted to know what she had been up to at Daggett's penthouse—and why Bane's men were after her.

The canopy slid open above them, letting in the crisp night air. Selina sprang from the passenger seat.

"See you around," she said breezily.

He followed her onto the roof, where he took a moment to admire her skintight outfit—which struck him as both practical and flattering. He of all people had to appreciate a flair for the dramatic.

"You're welcome," he said.

"I had it under control," she insisted.

He disagreed.

"Those weren't street thugs," he asserted grimly. "They were trained killers." He fixed his dark eyes on her. "I saved your life. In return, I need to know what you did with Bruce Wayne's fingerprints."

She looked him over thoughtfully, putting the pieces together.

"Wayne wasn't kidding about a 'powerful friend.'" She hesitated before coming clean. "I sold his prints to Daggett—for something that probably doesn't exist."

He caught a note of bitterness in her voice.

"I doubt many people get the better of you," he said. But she shrugged her shapely shoulders.

"Hey, when a girl's desperate—"

"What were they going to do with them?" he persisted. He was careful to use his "Batman growl."

She seemed to have a way of putting two-and-two together, and he didn't want her to recognize him—especially after that kiss.

"I don't know," she admitted, "but Daggett seemed pretty interested in that mess at the stock exchange."

He didn't like the sound of that. He already knew there was a link between Daggett and Bane—forged by the West African coup—but what exactly were they trying to accomplish? And why had they needed Bruce Wayne's fingerprints?

A police chopper swept past overhead, continuing the manhunt. Batman stepped back into the shadows, evading its searchlight until the aircraft had passed. Then he turned back to continue the questioning.

But she was gone.

"Miss Kyle?"

She had disappeared, as silently as a cat.

Batman grunted. The irony of the situation did not escape him.

"So that's what that feels like."

CHAPTER SIXTEEN

Truth to tell, Alfred had never liked the Batcave. He found it dank, gloomy, unsanitary, difficult to dust, and more than a little depressing.

Still, Master Bruce had spent a fortune converting the ancient caverns—which had once been a stop on the Underground Railroad—into a state-of-the-art forensic laboratory, garage, armory, and communications center. So it would be foolish not to avail oneself of the cave's sophisticated technology, even if it meant keeping company with a plague of winged rodents.

At least that's what he told himself.

Alfred was seated at the computer, studying captured security footage of the assault on the stock exchange, when a booming roar and the glare of high-intensity landing lights penetrated the waterfall that hid the mouth of the cave. A bright white glow shone through the curtain of water, heralding the arrival of Bruce's newest toy.

A wet spray sprinkled Alfred's face as, rotors spinning, the Bat flew into the cave. A pair of slate cubes rose to form a landing pad. The Bat touched down on the cubes.

The canopy opened and Batman emerged from the cockpit. Alfred was relieved to see that he was still in one piece, and in no immediate need of first aid, despite being out of commission for eight long years. He had been worried about that.

"Very inconspicuous," the butler observed, brushing water from his suit. "Shall I tell the neighbors that you got yourself a new leaf blower?"

Batman shed his cape and cowl, becoming Bruce Wayne once more.

"We bought all the neighbors."

So we did, Alfred recalled. He took Bruce's cloak as they walked away from Lucius Fox's latest contribution to "the cause." The Bat was an impressive aircraft, he had to admit. Perhaps too impressive.

"From the look of the television coverage, you seem to have your taste for wanton destruction back."

Bruce ignored the gibe. He plucked a USB drive from his Utility Belt.

"I retrieved this."

"Shouldn't the police be gathering the evidence?" Alfred suggested.

"They don't have the tools to analyze it."

Alfred glanced around at a high-tech apparatus filling the cave. It was enough to make the FBI envious.

"They would if you gave it to them." But Bruce shook his head.

"One man's tool is another man's weapon."

"In your mind, perhaps," Alfred said. "But there aren't many things that you couldn't turn into a weapon."

"Alfred, *enough*," Bruce said impatiently. "The police weren't getting it done."

"Perhaps they would have," the butler persisted, "if you hadn't made a sideshow of yourself."

Bruce refused to even consider the possibility.

"Perhaps you're just upset that you were wrong."

Alfred looked puzzled.

"Wrong?"

"You thought I didn't have it in me anymore," Bruce said.

Alfred returned the cape and cowl to the closet where they belonged. He wished he could lock them away for good.

"You don't," he said. "You led a bloated, overconfident police force on a merry chase with some fancy new toys from Fox." He called Bruce's attention to the ghastly security footage on the main monitor. "What about when you come up against *him*. What then?"

On the screen, Bane murdered a roomful of security guards with terrifying speed and brutality. His lethally effective fighting technique was eerily similar to Batman's, but much more final. Bruce's jaw tightened as he contemplated the footage.

"I'll fight harder," he said. "Like I always have."

"When you had something to fight for," Alfred argued. "What are you fighting for now? Not your life."

Bruce frowned and moved to switch off the screen. Alfred stopped him.

"Take a good look," the butler said. "At his speed, his ferocity, his training. I see the power of belief...of the fanatic. I see the League of Shadows resurgent."

Bruce stared at Bane.

"You said he was excommunicated."

"By Rā's al Ghūl," Alfred said. "Who leads them now?"

"Rā's al Ghūl *was* the League of Shadows," Bruce insisted. "And I beat him." He sat down at the computer and killed the security footage. "Bane's just a mercenary, and we have to find out what he's up to." He plugged the USB into the computer, then pecked at the keyboard and streams of text scrolled across the screen. He scrutinized the data.

"Trades of some kind," he realized. "Coded."

The text vanished, replaced by a scanned image of a thumbprint. Bruce scowled.

"Is that—?" Alfred began.

"Mine," Bruce confirmed. "Courtesy of Selina Kyle." He'd tell Alfred about his run-in with

Catwoman later. Right now he had more pressing concerns. He rose from the computer and unplugged the USB drive.

"Get this to Fox," he instructed. "He can crack the code and tell us what trades they were executing."

Alfred took the USB and left the cave. Bruce changed into his civilian garb and followed him up to the manor. He found the butler in the main hall, at the foot of the grand stairway. He was already on his way out.

"I'll get this to Fox," Alfred said gravely. "But no more." Something in the older man's tone got Bruce's attention. He turned away from the stairs and looked toward Alfred.

"I've sewn you up and set your bones," the butler continued, "but I won't bury you.

"I've buried enough members of the Wayne family."

Is he serious? Bruce wondered. Alfred was the one person who had never given up on him. "You'd abandon me?" he said quietly.

"You see only one end to your story," Alfred said. "Leaving is all I have left to make you understand. You aren't Batman anymore. You have to find another way."

There is no other way, Bruce thought. *Not for me. Not anymore.*

"You used to talking about finishing," Alfred reminded him. "About life beyond that awful cave."

Bruce shook his head. That dream had ended eight years ago.

"Rachel died knowing that we'd decided to be together," he said bitterly. "That was my life beyond the cave, so I can't just move on. She didn't. She *couldn't*."

Because Batman failed to save her.

"What if she had?" Alfred asked. "What if she wasn't intending to make a life with you?"

Bruce didn't see the point in speculating.

"She was," he said. "I can't change that."

Alfred shifted uncomfortably, and a strange look came over his face, as if he was wrestling with something.

"What if," he said finally, "she'd written a letter? Explaining that she'd chosen Harvey Dent over you." Alfred sighed wearily, as though releasing a heavy load. "And what if, to spare you pain, I'd burnt that letter?"

Realization dawned, and Bruce stared in shock. He felt his entire world—everything he'd believed for the last eight years—come apart beneath him.

"Why would you say such a thing?" he asked.

"Because I have to make you understand," Alfred said. "Because you're as precious to me as you were to your own mother and father, and I swore to them that I would protect you...and I haven't."

"You're lying," Bruce accused him.

"I've never lied to you," he replied. "Except when I burned Rachel's letter."

The hell of it was, Bruce believed him.

A cold fury erupted inside him, very different from the righteous anger he had directed at crime and criminals for so long. This was much more personal.

"How dare you use Rachel to stop me?" he growled.

"I'm using the truth, Master Bruce. Maybe it's time we all stopped trying to outsmart the truth, and just let it have its day." He gazed at Bruce sadly. "I'm sorry."

"Sorry?" Bruce rasped. "You expect to destroy my world, then shake hands?"

"No," Alfred said. "I know what this means." But Bruce forced him to say it.

"What does it mean, Alfred?"

"It means your hatred. It means losing the person I've cared for since I first heard his cries echo through this house." He paused. "But it might also mean saving your life. And that is more important."

Bruce glared at him. Calmly, coldly, he said the worst thing he could say.

"Goodbye, Alfred."

The butler nodded, looking older and more tired than he had just moments ago. His shoulders slumped.

"Goodbye, Bruce."

Bruce turned his back and marched up the stairs.

CHAPTER SEVENTEEN

The doorbell woke him. Bruce rolled over in bed, waiting for Alfred to answer it.

Then he remembered.

He rose and threw on a dressing gown. No breakfast awaited him, and the house somehow seemed colder than it had before. Moving down the corridor toward the front, he called out tentatively.

"Alfred?"

The answering silence confirmed that last night had really happened. Bruce's face hardened. Knotting his robe shut, he hurried down the stairs and threw open the door.

Lucius Fox gazed at him with surprise.

"Answering your own door?"

"Yes," Bruce said tersely. He didn't feel like explaining. "Could you decode the trades on that drive?"

Instead of answering, Fox handed him the morning paper. The front page headline was in huge type.

BATMAN BACK TO FOIL OR MASTERMIND STOCK RAID

The headline was accompanied by a blurry photo of the Bat in flight. A sidebar displayed a chronology of Batman's career, beginning with his capture of mobster Carmine Falcone, so many years ago.

"I didn't need to," Fox said. "Page three."

Puzzled, Bruce flipped past the coverage on Batman's alleged return until he stumbled onto another, significantly smaller headline.

WAYNE DOUBLES DOWN—AND LOSES

Bruce scanned the article in growing dismay.

"It seems you made a series of large put options on the futures exchange. Verified by thumb print." Fox shook his head grimly. "The options expired at midnight last night."

Bruce looked up from the paper, reeling from the news. He had always preferred crime-fighting to high finance, but he grasped the implications of what he had just read. And the consequences were devastating.

"Long term, we may be able to prove fraud," Fox said, spelling it out. "But for now...you're completely broke. And Wayne Enterprises is about to fall into the hands of John Daggett."

"The weapons." Bruce instantly zeroed in on what mattered most. "We can't let Daggett get his hands on Applied Sciences."

"Applied Sciences is shut up tight and off the books," Fox assured him. "But the energy project is a different story."

Then it sunk in, that it was the worst of all possible worst-case scenarios—the prospect of a man like John Daggett, with his connections to Bane, taking control of the mothballed project.

Bruce realized he needed help.

"Miranda Tate," he said, thinking aloud. "We need to convince the board to get behind her, instead of Daggett." He knew what that meant. "Let's show her the reactor."

Fox was way ahead of him.

"We're meeting her in thirty-five minutes," he said. "You better get dressed."

The recycling plant was located across the river from Gotham. Acres of abandoned scrap metal, surrounded by a barbed-wire fence, enjoyed a scenic view of the city's imposing skyline. Gulls and pigeons scavenged in the garbage. Bins of discarded car batteries and electronics equipment waited to be disposed of. Rust ate away at the accumulated refuse.

Miranda Tate glanced around dubiously as Fox led her from the car. She stepped lightly amidst the piles of junk, avoiding a greasy puddle.

"You brought me out here to show me a rubbish dump, Mr. Fox?" she said as he unlocked the front gate. Then he turned.

"Bear with me, Miss Tate."

A derelict-looking portacabin was hidden deep within the junkyard, behind towering heaps of scrap metal. Nothing but a glorified aluminum shed, with poorly maintained siding, the one-story building hardly seemed worth her time.

Wearing a cryptic smile, Fox invited her inside.

"Keep your hands and feet inside the car at all times," he commented.

An empty office was tucked away inside the cabin. Dust covered the desk and file cabinets. A pinup calendar on the wall was more than a year out-of-date. Beat-up office equipment looked as if it belonged in the heaps of recyclables outside. Fox flipped a concealed switch beneath the desk and, all at once, the entire office turned into an elevator, sinking into the floor. The room tilted like a funhouse ride as it slid diagonally into a massive concrete tunnel that angled beneath the junkyard and toward the river.

Miranda gasped out loud. Her eyes widened in excitement.

"This is it, isn't it?" he asked. Fox nodded.

"The reactor is beneath the river, so it can be

instantly flooded in the event of a security breach."

"Is Bruce Wayne really that paranoid?" she asked.

Fox chuckled.

"I'm going to plead the Fifth on that one," he said.

The elevator came to a stop deep beneath the river. Marveling at the elaborate security, she stepped out of the "office," only to find Bruce Wayne waiting for them in a cavernous underground complex that was as large and impressive as the ugly junkyard was not. She noted that he was no longer using his cane.

"I thought you might like to see what your investment built," he said.

At the center of the hangar-sized complex was a black steel sphere, at least five feet in diameter, girded by segmented steel rings that she quickly identified as powerful electromagnets. Blinking green lights and gauges were embedded in the surface of the sphere. Diagonal steel trusses supported the core assembly, suspending it several feet above the floor. An instrument panel was located at the base of the left-hand buttress.

Drainage from the river flowed through wide concrete troughs in the floor.

At last, Miranda thought. She savored the sight of the revolutionary fusion reactor. "No radiation, no fossil fuels," she said. "Free, clean energy for an entire city."

"If it worked," Bruce said. "It doesn't." He flipped a switch on the control panel. The core hummed to life, glowing brightly from within. Lit gauges registered a sudden surge of energy.

Then the device went cold. The gauges dropped back to zero.

"Ignition, yes," he stated. "But no chain reaction."

She didn't believe him.

"You've built a lot of security around a damp squib."

He gazed at her stonily, but remained silent. She thought she understood his reticence.

"About three years ago, a Russian scientist published a paper on weaponized fusion reactions," she commented. "One week later, your reactor started developing problems." *You don't have to be a nuclear physicist to see a connection*, she mused. "I think your machine works."

Wayne peered at her intently.

"Miranda, if it were operational, the danger to Gotham would be too great."

"Would it make you feel any better," she asked, "to know that the Russian scientist died in a plane crash six months ago?"

This did not seem to reassure him.

"Someone else will work out what Dr. Pavel did," he argued. "Someone else will figure out how to turn this power source into a nuclear weapon."

"Then why show this to me?" she asked.

"I need you to take control of Wayne Enterprises... and this reactor."

She was aware of his current financial difficulties. How could she not be?

"And do *what* with it?"

"Nothing," he said firmly. "Until we can find a way to guarantee its safety."

"And if we can't?"

"Decommission it," he said. "Flood it."

She was dismayed by the very idea.

"Destroy the world's best chance for a sustainable future?"

"If the world's not ready, yes," he replied.

She stepped closer to him. He caught a whiff of an exotic perfume.

"Bruce, if you want to save the world, you have to start trusting it."

"I'm trusting you."

"Doesn't count," she said. "You have no choice."

But he wouldn't let it lie.

"I could have flooded this chamber any time over the last three years," he said. "I'm choosing to trust you, Miranda, and that's not the easiest thing for me." Intense eyes implored her. "Please."

She nodded.

Fox cleared his throat, politely intruding on the moment.

"Excuse me," he said, "but we have a board meeting to get to."

* * *

The board of directors had convened an emergency meeting. Lucius Fox, as CEO, sat at the head of the long oak table, while Bruce Wayne occupied the other end for the first time in years—and possibly for the very last time.

John Daggett rose to address the board. He appeared even more arrogant than usual.

"I'd like to point out that we have a non-member here," he protested. "Highly irregular, even if it is his family name above the door."

All eyes turned toward the last surviving Wayne. Douglas Fredericks, one of the board's senior members, spoke up. He was a dignified older gentleman with a mane of snowy white hair, who had seldom been afraid to speak his mind. Bruce had always respected his honesty.

"Bruce Wayne's family built this company," Fredericks protested, "and he himself has run it—"

"—into the ground, sir," Daggett interrupted. He glanced around the table. "Anyone disagree? Check the value of your stock this morning. Gambling on crazy futures didn't just lose Mr. Wayne his seat on this board, it's lost us all a lot of money.

"He needs to leave."

"I'm afraid he has a point, Mr. Wayne," Fox said.

"I understand." Bruce rose from the table. "Ladies and gentlemen." He exchanged a look with Miranda as he slipped out the door.

* * *

A hush fell over the board room as the latch clicked behind him.

"All right," Daggett said, breaking the silence. He puffed out his chest. "Let's get down to business."

"Right away," Fox agreed.

He winked at Miranda.

A crowd had gathered outside Wayne Tower. Angry shareholders and hungry reporters shouted at Bruce as he exited the building. Cameras clicked away at a rapid-fire pace. TV crews captured the chaos on film.

"Mr. Wayne!" a reporter from the *Gotham Gazette* hollered. "How does it feel to be one of the little people?"

Bruce ignored him, and all of the questions. He looked around for his car.

"I'm sorry, sir," a company valet said sheepishly. "They had the paperwork—" Then Bruce saw his new sports car being towed away.

First the Lamborghini, he thought, *and now this. I wonder if I still have cash enough for a cab.*

A police cruiser was parked at the bottom of the steps. The young police officer—Blake—emerged from the car. He called out to Bruce.

"Looks like you could use a lift."

CHAPTER EIGHTEEN

Daggett stormed into his penthouse, slamming the door behind him. His face was purple with anger as he stomped across the floor.

"How the *hell* did Miranda Tate get the inside track on the Wayne Board?" he demanded to no one in particular. "Was she meeting with Wayne? Was she *sleeping* with Wayne?"

Stryver tried to calm his boss.

"Not that we know of—"

"Clearly you don't '*know of*' everything, do you?" Daggett wanted answers and he wanted them immediately. "Where's Bane?"

"We told him it was urgent," Stryver said.

Daggett looked at his watch.

"Then where is that masked—?"

A deep voice interrupted him.

"Speak of the devil..." it said.

Daggett spun around to find Bane standing behind him, his meaty arms crossed atop his chest. Air hissed from the hulking mercenary's mask.

"...and he shall appear."

Daggett clutched his chest, startled by Bane's sudden appearance. Where had the ugly merc come from, and how had he gotten past the penthouse's supposedly first-class security? Between Catwoman and Bane, Daggett was starting to think *anybody* could get past his guards.

Nearly scared me out of a year's growth, he thought. *Who does he think he is? The Batman?* But he tried to regain control of the situation.

"What the hell's going on?" he demanded.

"The plan is proceeding as expected," Bane stated flatly.

Hardly, Daggett thought. "You see me running Wayne Enterprises?" Regaining his composure, he got in the mercenary's face. "Your stock exchange hit didn't work, friend. And now you've got my construction crews working all hours around the city? How *exactly* is that supposed to help my company absorb Wayne's?"

Bane turned toward Stryver.

"Leave us."

"You stay right there!" Daggett ordered. "I'm in charge."

Bane placed his hand lightly on Daggett's shoulder.

A hint of amusement showed in his dark eyes.

"Do you feel in charge?" he asked.

A chill ran down Daggett's spine. He gulped as Stryver crept out of the room, leaving him alone with Bane. His mouth went dry, and suddenly his palms were sweaty.

"I've paid you a small fortune—"

"And that gives you power over me?" Bane asked.

It sure didn't feel like it at the moment. Bane's hand weighed heavily on Daggett's shoulder. The frightened millionaire was starting to wish he was still in the Catwoman's clutches. He tugged on his collar.

"What is this?" he asked nervously.

"Your money and infrastructure have been important," Bane explained. "Till now."

Daggett stared in horror at Bane's grotesque countenance. He had thought that the infamous mercenary was merely another hired gun—somewhat more expensive than most, yet nothing more. But as he peered into the masked man's pitiless orbs, he finally realized that Bane was working for no one but himself. And he was no mere soldier of fortune.

"What *are* you?"

"Gotham's reckoning," Bane answered. "Come to end the borrowed time you've all been living on..."

He gently took Daggett's head in his hands. A primordial dread washed over the tycoon. He looked into the face of his destroyer as he grasped what Bane actually was.

"You are true evil..."

"I am *necessary* evil—"

A sharp crack ended the discussion.

The patrol car cruised through Gotham. Bruce sat in the passenger seat, staring glumly out the window. He and Blake had the car to themselves—apparently, Blake's partner had taken a day off after chasing Batman all night.

It had been a long night for all of them.

"When you began," Blake asked, "why the mask?"

Bruce didn't see any point in denying it any longer. Blake had obviously sussed out the truth. And with Jim Gordon laid-up, he needed a reliable ally inside the police force. The young cop seemed a likely candidate.

"To protect the people closest to me," he explained. But Blake didn't buy it.

"You were a loner with no family."

Not entirely, Bruce thought. He remembered Rachel—and Alfred.

"There are always people you care about," he said. "You just don't realize how much until a bad man points a gun at them. Or until they leave..." His throat tightened and he needed a moment to collect himself. "The idea was to be a symbol. Batman could be anybody—that was the point." It felt odd to be discussing this openly with anyone besides Alfred, but who else was he supposed to talk with these days? Miranda Tate?

Selina?

Blake nodded.

"It was damn good to see him back."

"Not everybody agrees."

Blake shrugged.

"They'll figure it out in the end."

Bruce appreciated the young cop's faith in Batman. Maybe Blake was someone he could count on after all.

"Got anything on Bane's whereabouts?" he asked.

"Yeah, I got five *hundred* pages of tunnel records and a flashlight. I could use some help."

So could I, Bruce thought. He wondered who else might be able to give them a lead. A thought occurred to him, along with a memory of a certain glamorous cat burglar. And a kiss that still lingered in his memory.

"You know what?" he said. "Drop me off in Old Town..."

A short drive later, Blake pulled up to the curb across from a shabby-looking townhouse that had clearly seen better days. As a cop, he had answered more than a few calls in this notably dicey neighborhood. Mostly drugs, drive-bys, and domestic disturbances. He wondered what business Wayne had here.

"Don't wait," Wayne said. "I'll get a cab."

"You got money?"

A sheepish look came over Wayne's face.

"Actually, no."

Figured as much, Blake thought. He handed Wayne some bills and watched as the former billionaire crossed the street and disappeared inside the grimy townhouse. He was tempted to wait anyway, but then his radio squawked at him, announcing a nearby fender-bender. He frowned and pulled away from the curb. He felt bad about leaving Wayne in such a scuzzy district, but then he remembered how the one-time playboy really spent his nights.

If Bruce Wayne couldn't take care of himself, who could?

Selina was busy packing when she heard a familiar uproar out in the hall.

"I told you," Jen said loudly. "Money first."

"I don't think so," a man replied.

Selina froze, recognizing the voice. She rushed out into hall, where, sure enough, she found Bruce Wayne by the stairwell, talking with Jen. The younger girl grinned in wicked anticipation, waiting for her friend to pounce on the unsuspecting visitor, only to look puzzled when Selina merely scowled at Wayne instead.

"He's not a mark," Selina explained. "And he doesn't have a cent to his name, anyway."

Not for a moment did she think this was a coincidence. Regarding Wayne suspiciously, she let him into the crummy two-bedroom walkup she shared with her protégé. The peeling wallpaper, leaky faucet, and thrift store furniture were a far cry from stately Wayne Manor. The radiator hissed and wheezed asthmatically. Selina was briefly embarrassed by her low-rent digs, then mad at herself for caring what Wayne thought.

"Yeah, it's not much," she admitted with a smirk. "But it's more than you've got right now."

"Actually, they're letting me keep the house," he said.

Selina shook her head in disbelief.

"The rich don't even *go broke* same as the rest of us, huh?"

He didn't deny it.

Instead he spotted the open suitcase spread out atop a ratty couch.

"Vacation?" he asked.

I wish, she thought. "Let's just say that I've incurred the wrath of some people less susceptible to my charms than you."

"My powerful friend hopes to change your mind about leaving," he said.

She remembered ditching Batman on the roof.

"And how would he do that?"

"By giving you what you want."

If only, she thought. "It doesn't exist," she replied.

"He says it does," Wayne said, and he sounded certain. "He wants to meet. Tonight."

For a moment, she wondered how Batman knew about the Clean Slate anyway. Then she realized that he must have been eavesdropping on her rooftop confrontation with Daggett.

"Why?" she asked.

"He needs to find Bane. He thinks you'd know how."

She repressed a shudder at the mention. She'd had dealings with a lot of bad people in her time, but the masked mercenary was one of the few individuals who had ever truly scared her. Bane was the reason she had been packing.

"Tell him I'll think about it."

Wayne nodded and started to leave. She called out to him before he left.

"Mr. Wayne? I'm sorry they took all your money."

He glanced back, seeing right through her.

"No, you're not."

CHAPTER NINETEEN

Blake rushed through the hospital, searching for the right room. A pair of uniformed cops, posted outside a closed door, indicated that he had reached his destination.

The cops recognized him and waved him through.

He found Gordon sitting up in bed, talking to Foley. The injured commissioner was still pale, and uncomfortably gaunt, but he looked much better than he had when Blake had dragged him from the sewers. A new pair of glasses rested on his nose. An oxygen mask lay to the side.

Apparently it took more than a few bullets to take Gotham's top cop out of the game.

"Can we help you, officer?" Foley asked, scowling. He didn't look pleased to see the young cop.

"John Daggett's body was found in a dumpster an

hour ago," Blake reported. "I thought you might like to know."

Gordon eyed him curiously.

"Why?"

"Because Daggett's name is all over the permits I pulled to map the tunnels under Gotham." He handed Gordon a stack of files, the relevant documents flagged with Post-Its. Foley gave Blake the evil eye, but the young officer ignored him and spoke directly to Gordon instead.

"MTA maintenance, sewer construction..."

Gordon looked at Foley.

"Where did you get to with the tunnel searches?"

"Remind me to tell the detail to keep the hotheads out," Foley muttered, glaring at Blake. Then he turned back to Gordon. "We've had teams down there, but it's a huge network."

"Get more men," Gordon ordered. "Work a grid. I want him found—"

"Yeah, yeah. The masked man," Foley said. But he made it sound as if it was low on his list of priorities, especially now that Batman was back. "We're on it," he added.

Gordon leafed through the files, flipping through the pages and eyeing them hungrily.

"This is good work," he told Blake, looking up from the files. "Lose the uniform. You're working for me now." He cast a sideways glance at Foley. "We could use some hotter heads around here."

Foley purpled with suppressed anger, but kept his mouth shut.

"This could just be a coincidence," Blake hedged. Although thrilled by the promotion, he was acutely aware of the responsibility Gordon had just placed on him. He didn't want to inadvertently steer the commissioner in the wrong direction. *What if I'm wrong about this?*

"You're a detective now, son," Gordon said. "You're not allowed to believe in coincidence anymore."

Blake tried not to grin in front of Foley.

The sun was going down by the time the cab dropped Bruce off in front of the manor. A pounding rain drenched him as he splashed up the driveway, holding Lucius's newspaper over his head. The soggy tabloid provided meager protection from the downpour, quickly collapsing under the weight of the deluge. Soaked to the skin, he reached the relative shelter of the portico, where he rang the bell impatiently.

"Nobody's answering."

Miranda Tate stepped out from behind a marble column, looking similarly sodden. He wondered how long she had been waiting there.

"No," he replied ruefully. "I'm on my own, now."

"Do you have keys?" she asked.

He looked at her helplessly.

"I never needed them…" Alfred had always let him in before.

She took his hand.

"Let's find a window," she suggested

Breaking and entering proved distressingly easy. Bruce guessed that the servants had neglected to activate the household security system before departing in search of steadier paychecks. Shivering, he and Miranda forced open the French windows and took refuge in the great room. Water dripped off them onto the carpet.

He turned on the lights.

"Fox worked the board like you've never seen," she reported, shaking the rain from her dark hair. "Daggett's out of the picture, and he's not happy."

He set the wet newspaper down on a table. Ink bled from the headline on page one of the business section.

FROM BILLIONAIRE TO BUM

"I'll take care of your parents' legacy," Miranda promised.

He believed her.

"Hope you didn't just like me for my money," he said.

She kicked off her wet shoes and came in closer. Her striking blue–gray eyes looked deeply into his. He caught another whiff of her perfume.

"Suffering builds character," she whispered, and then she kissed him—passionately. Surprised by the heat of her ardor, he took her in his arms and kissed her back, feeling her soft curves through their soggy garments. He couldn't help comparing her kiss to the one Selina Kyle had planted on him at the masquerade.

Miranda's kiss felt less like a challenge and much more intimate. It was just what he needed right now.

Without warning, the lights went out.

Their lips came apart. They clung to each other in the darkness.

"What's that?" she asked.

Bruce looked at her sheepishly.

"I think my power's been shut off."

A short time later, they nestled together in front of a crackling fire. Wet clothes lay discarded upon the floor. Heaps of fluffy cushions and comforters formed a cozy love nest in front of the hearth. Miranda extricated herself from Bruce's arms long enough to tend the blaze.

"You're pretty good at that," he commented.

She stirred the burning logs, the glow of the fire burnishing her bare skin.

"When I was a child we had almost nothing," she said, and her voice sounded distant. "But on the nights when we had a fire, we felt very rich, indeed."

She returned and snuggled beside him once more,

drawing the covers over them. It warmed him more than any fire, he thought. It had been a long time since he had rested in the arms of a beautiful woman, let alone one as remarkable as Miranda Tate.

She might be worth losing a fortune for.

"I assumed your family was wealthy," he said. It dawned on him how little he had cared to learn about her—and what a mistake that may have been.

"Not always. Not when I was young."

A pale scar marred the otherwise flawless perfection of her shoulder. He gently traced it with his finger.

"An old mistake," she said.

"I've made a few of those," he confessed.

His own chest bore a complicated tapestry of such marks, left over from the years of arduous physical training, and his career as the Batman. A burn from the fire that had engulfed Rā's al Ghūl's temple. An old scar where the Joker had once stabbed him.

She explored them by the firelight.

"More than a few." Then she treated him to an enticing smile. "We could leave. Tonight. Take my plane. Go anywhere we wanted."

It was tempting, he mused, especially after eight lonely years. But then he remembered Gordon in that hospital bed—and Officer Blake counting on him for help against Bane.

"Someday, perhaps. Not tonight."

She pulled him close, inviting his kisses. They folded into each other, forming a warm, beating heart at the center of the cold, empty house. Bruce lost himself in the moment—and in her.

For the first time in years, he didn't think about Rachel.

CHAPTER TWENTY

She slept like an angel, wrapped up in a blanket near the dying fire. Bruce studied her sleeping form, grateful for the warmth she had brought back into his life.

Then he silently slipped away.

Sorry, Miranda, he said silently. *It can't be helped.*

Part of him—a part that had been dormant for eight long years—wanted to stay with her. But that wasn't possible. A grandfather clock tolled midnight out in the hall, reminding him that he had an appointment to keep—with another woman. He crept quietly into the study and took the hidden elevator down to the Batcave. His working clothes waited for him in their locked closet. He took the cowl from the shelf.

If all went well, he might get back before Miranda woke up. If not…well, he would have some explaining to do. It wouldn't be the first time.

Minutes later, the Bat was roaring toward downtown Gotham. The lights of the city were spread out beneath the aircraft like glittering jewels just waiting to be stolen by the thieves and murderers who were his quarry. Late-night traffic cruised the streets hundreds of feet below.

Nearing the rendezvous spot, Batman killed the headlights and main engines. The Bat went into stealth mode as it quietly auto-rotated down into the city's sleeping concrete canyons. He checked the digital chronometer.

It was a quarter past midnight.

Right on time, he thought.

As arranged, Catwoman was waiting in a subway tunnel, just beyond the lit passenger platform. She paced impatiently along a service walkway, watching the trains go by. Her sleek black costume allowed her to blend in with the shadows. Night-vision goggles let her scan the tunnel in both directions.

All at once, she stopped pacing.

"Don't be shy," she said playfully.

He was impressed. There weren't many people he couldn't sneak up on when he wanted to do so. He didn't know what sort of training she might have received, but his own had been extensive.

Batman emerged from the darkness, joining her in the tunnel.

"Wayne says you can get me the 'Clean Slate,'" she said without preamble.

"That depends," he said gruffly. She eyed him warily.

"On what?"

"On what you want it for," he replied. "I acquired it to keep it out of the wrong hands."

Or claws, he thought.

"Still don't trust me, huh?" She didn't sound particularly surprised. "How can we change that?"

"Start by taking me to Bane."

Selina had stolen the fingerprints Bane had used to wipe out Bruce Wayne's fortune. With Daggett dead, she was now Batman's only link to the master terrorist. He hoped she could lead him to Bane's underground lair—the one Gordon had stumbled onto nights ago. He was certain the cops hadn't found it yet.

For a second, she looked as if she might try to talk him out of it, then she shrugged.

"You asked," she said, and without a warning she sprang down onto the tracks, making not a sound. Batman followed closely behind her as she led him into a murky service tunnel.

They descended deeper beneath the city, leaving the subway system behind as they treaded through a labyrinth of forgotten utility tunnels. Cobwebs hung from the ceiling. Rats scurried away. Water dripped down the walls. The noisome tunnels made the Batcave seem like a luxury resort.

Catwoman seemed to know where she was going. She stopped, peered around, and spoke, her voice low.

Even so, there were hints of echoes.

"From here, Bane's men patrol the tunnels," she said, "and they are not your average brawlers."

"Neither am I," he replied.

Footsteps echoed up ahead. She signaled Batman before grabbing onto a hanging pipe and swinging up and out of sight. Following her lead, he blended into the darkness.

Moments later, a squad of mercenaries came through, patrolling the tunnel. Leather jackets, military fatigues, and automatic weapons made it clear that these weren't maintenance workers, nor were they ordinary thugs. They methodically scanned the dimly-lit tunnel, but he could tell they didn't expect to find anything. Their guns were slung toward the floor.

Catwoman dropped nimbly behind them.

"He's behind you," she warned.

The lead mercenary spun around in surprise. His eyes widened at the sight of the feline intruder. Confusion was written over his face.

"Who?" he demanded.

Batman dropped from the ceiling, hanging upside-down like the creature that was his namesake.

"Me," he growled.

The startled soldier of fortune didn't even have time to raise his weapon before the hanging wraith slammed into him like a wave of darkness, and then vanished back into the shadows. Caught by surprise, the other gunmen opened fire. Muzzle flares lit up the murky tunnel, and bullets blasted away at the ceiling.

The echoes were deafening now.

Catwoman darted around a corner, pursued by a shouting mercenary. He tried to keep the elusive female figure in his sights, only to feel powerful hands grab onto his shoulders and yank him up into the dark. His terrified scream was cut off abruptly and his weapon clattered to the floor.

Two down, Batman thought.

He picked off the rest of the patrol, one by one. A grappling line yanked one man off his feet, so that his head smacked against the hard stone floor. Skulls were slammed together by hands that struck silently from the shadows. An expert jab to a crucial nerve center dropped another man to the floor. The guns went silent, replaced by echoing shouts and bone-crunching thuds.

Disposing of the last of the men, Batman caught up with Catwoman. He followed her down a dark tunnel and onto a long metal catwalk. The shadows were too deep for him to find details in his surroundings, but he heard run-off water rushing beneath them like an underground river. The lack of odor indicated that the water had been purified.

"Just a little further," she promised.

A heavy steel grate slammed down between them, like a portcullis in a medieval fortress. Bright halogen lights flared overhead, exposing a lair hidden deep within the sewers. A small army of mercenaries glared down from various elevated gantries and platforms.

The catwalk led between twin waterfalls that poured into a foaming channel one level below. There was some kind of headquarters located beyond the waterfalls—much like in the Batcave.

"Sorry," Catwoman said from the other side of the grate. "I had to find a way to stop them trying to kill me."

Batman realized then that she had deliberately lured him into a trap. He was disappointed by her betrayal.

"You've made a serious mistake," he growled.

"Not as serious as yours, I fear," a deep voice interjected.

Batman turned to see a masked figure emerge from behind the falling curtains of water. He recognized the man's elaborate mask and powerful physique from the grisly security footage Alfred had shown him before. Muscles rippled upon the killer's bare chest.

"Bane."

The infamous mercenary approached him.

"Let's not stand on ceremony here, Mr. Wayne."

Batman wasn't surprised that Bane knew his true identity. The man was connected to the League of Shadows, after all—he likely had heard of Bruce Wayne's tangled history with Rā's al Ghūl.

Catwoman, on the other hand, was visibly taken aback by the revelation. A look of regret came over her face, as though she was having second thoughts about betraying him.

Too late now, he thought. Selina Kyle was the least

of his concerns at the moment. Bane was the real threat to Gotham. *He murdered those people at the stock exchange—and nearly killed Jim Gordon.*

I can't let him hurt anyone else.

Without hesitation he launched himself toward his enemy. His cloak spreading out behind him, he swooped at Bane, drawing back his fist to deliver a knockout blow. His clenched knuckles flew at Bane, who caught it easily with his bare hand, squeezing it until the bones ground together.

Grunting, Batman attempted a gut punch with his other fist, but the mercenary effortlessly blocked the blow. He had, indeed, been trained by Rā's al Ghūl and the League of Shadows.

"Peace has cost you your strength," Bane declared. "Victory has defeated you."

Stronger and faster than anyone Batman had ever fought before—even in his prime—Bane slammed into Batman, knocking him backward. A roundhouse kick swept his legs out from under him, sending him tumbling off the catwalk toward the raging sewers below. Batman hastily extended his cape, using it to glide down on to a concrete ledge located near the base of the waterfalls. He winced in pain, bruised even beneath his protective armor.

This wasn't going well...

Bane clambered after him, swinging down on a chain, while his men watched in disciplined silence, enjoying the duel. Hoping to buy some time, Batman plucked a handful of miniature flash-bangs from his Utility Belt and flung them at his pursuer. The charges went off like firecrackers, producing a disorienting barrage of sparks, noise, and smoke.

Yet Bane didn't even flinch.

"Theatricality and deception are powerful agents," he acknowledged, quoting the timeless wisdom of Rā's al Ghūl. "To the uninitiated."

Alfred was right, Batman realized. This man was not to be underestimated. *It's going to take everything I have to beat him—if it's even possible.*

Determined to put Bane on the defensive, Batman lunged at him again, striking out with his fists and boots. Bane effortlessly countered his moves. It was like fighting Rā's again, except that Bane was younger and stronger than their shared mentor. He targeted the weak spots in Batman's body armor, inflicting the maximum pain possible, while seeming to possess no weaknesses of his own.

They broke apart, facing off between the flowing channels. Bane looked like he was just warming up.

"But we are the initiated, aren't we, Bruce? The League of Shadows." He glared at Batman over the bizarre mask that hid the bottom half of his face. Scorn dripped from his voice. Air hissed from the mask. "And you betrayed us..."

"Us?" Batman echoed. "You were excommunicated—from a gang of psychopaths."

Bane rejected the accusation.

"Now I *am* the League of Shadows," he said, "here to fulfill Rā's al Ghūl's destiny..."

By destroying Gotham?

Never, Batman thought. Too many good people— including Rachel and his parents—had worked too hard to make the city a decent place to live. This masked lunatic needed to be stopped—just like the Joker and Rā's al Ghūl.

He hurled himself at his opponent, knocking him onto his back beneath the foaming waterfall, where Batman hammered his masked face again and again. Clear water cascaded over them, making the Dark Knight's black armor gleam slickly. Any normal thug would already be out cold, but Bane just absorbed the blows until Batman took a moment to catch his breath.

He let up, just for a moment, and Bane's brawny arms shot out like rockets, smashing Batman aside.

The mercenary rose to his feet.

"You fight like a younger man," he said, his voice betraying no hint of the punishment he had received. "Nothing held back. No reserves." He flexed his own muscles as he advanced. "Admirable. But mistaken."

Batman was breathing hard. He realized Bane was right. Eight years of retirement had taken its toll on his endurance and reflexes. He wasn't the same man who had defeated Rā's al Ghūl nearly a decade ago. *That* Batman had just begun his career.

A smarter strategy was needed. He flipped a switch

on his belt, triggering an EMP that knocked out all the lights, throwing them all into total darkness. Then he retreated into the sheltering blackness. Night-vision lenses in his cowl allowed him to keep an eye on his adversary, who seemed to take the blackout in his stride.

Bane turned slowly, addressing the all-encompassing shadows. He didn't seem worried.

"You think darkness is your ally," Bane said. "But you merely adopted the dark. I was *born* in it. Formed by it…"

Moving as silently as a ghost, Batman circled, looking for an opening. There had to be some way to bring the other man down. He just needed to strike when and where Bane least expected. And he needed to make it count.

This could be my last chance.

"I didn't see light until I was already a man. And by then it was nothing to me but *blinding*."

Without warning, Bane lunged backward into the darkness and caught Batman's throat in his grasp. Only the reinforced neckpiece kept his windpipe from being crushed in an instant.

"The shadows betray you, because they belong to *me*…"

He slammed Batman into the concrete floor, hard enough to dash any other man's brains out. His bare fists pounded on Batman's cowl with unbelievable force, blow after blow smashing down like a jackhammer.

Concussed and breathless, Batman couldn't fight back as Bane hammered on the cowl until finally, incredibly, the hard graphite shell *cracked*.

No, Batman thought. *That's not possible.*

One final blow put him down for the count. Bane rose, towering above his battered foe. He gestured upward at the vaulted ceiling high above the vast subterranean chamber. Through blood-streaked eyes, Batman saw that a series of holes had been drilled into the ceiling. Explosive charges had been placed in each of them.

But why? he wondered through the pain. *To what purpose?*

"I will show you," Bane said, "where I've made my home while preparing to bring justice to Gotham. *Then*...I will break you."

A mercenary tossed a detonator to Bane. His men backed away, seeking shelter in side tunnels and alcoves. Catwoman watched anxiously from the other side of the grate. She covered her ears.

Bane pressed the button.

The charges went off, causing a controlled implosion high above their heads. Thunderous echoes rocked the chamber, hurting Batman's ears. The ceiling caved in and rubble rained down into the sewers, splashing water everywhere.

Artificial light poured down from above, revealing the lower levels of Applied Sciences.

It can't be, Batman thought in horror. Then

realization struck home. *We were under Wayne Tower all this time.*

The bottom had dropped out of Lucius Fox's secret weapons storehouse. Dangerous prototypes lay scattered about like treats from some deadly, high-tech piñata. A tumbler, its desert camouflage of little use in these dismal catacombs, landed atop a pile of rubble. Loose papers and bits of ash wafted down through the jagged gap in the ceiling.

"No," Batman murmured weakly.

"Your precious armory," Bane confirmed. "Gratefully accepted." He swept his gaze over the fallen spoils. "We will need it."

To wage war on Gotham?

Bane's men clambered up into the violated bunker. They moved efficiently, ransacking Applied Sciences even as security alarms blared stridently. The mercenaries set up a bucket brigade to hand the stolen goods from each man to the next, down into the tunnels. The other tumblers were hauled toward the gap.

I can't let this happen, Batman thought. *I can't...* He staggered to his feet, swaying unsteadily. His cracked cowl slipped, and he tasted blood in his mouth. His head was swimming. The entire chamber seemed be spinning around him, and he felt sick to his stomach. Through the fog, he recognized the symptoms of a serious concussion.

Nevertheless, he raised his fists.

Bane turned back toward him.

"I wondered which would break first—your spirit..."

Batman threw a punch, but didn't come close to connecting. Bane lunged forward and lifted his foe high above his head. Batman tried to twist free of the grasp, but could not get away.

He had nothing left.

"...or your body," Bane concluded.

Savagely, Bane brought Batman down onto his knee, forcibly bending the Dark Knight's spine backward. A horrific *crack* echoed throughout the lair.

Catwoman gasped out loud.

At that, Bane dumped Batman onto the ground, to lie helplessly in the puddles. He crouched and tugged the cracked cowl off his victim, exposing the battered and bloody face of Bruce Wayne. Then he beckoned to his men, who picked up the limp, unresisting body and carried it off into the tunnels. Bane held onto the cowl as a trophy.

Standing triumphant beneath Wayne Tower, he contemplated the hollow, empty eyes of the Dark Knight's cowl.

Forgotten for the moment, Catwoman slunk away into the shadows.

CHAPTER TWENTY-ONE

Blake knocked impatiently at the door of Wayne Manor. It was the middle of the afternoon, but no one answered, not even the butler. Worried, he nosed around the windows, yet couldn't spot any signs of life inside the mansion.

A pair of French windows showed evidence of having been forced open.

Not a good sign, he thought. He considered calling it in, only to decide against it. Bruce Wayne had important secrets to protect. Blake didn't want to risk blowing them on a false alarm. *Maybe Wayne just forgot his keys.*

Troubled, he returned to an unmarked police cruiser that was parked out front. Despite repeated attempts to contact Wayne, he hadn't heard from the bankrupt billionaire since dropping him off in Old Town the day before. He was half-tempted to invest in a Bat-Signal.

Or perhaps there was someplace else he ought to check out first.

He drove straight to the same scuzzy street where he had last seen Wayne. Parking himself across from the dilapidated townhouse, he settled back and waited. It felt strange not to be wearing his uniform anymore. A new coat and suit marked his promotion to detective. He wondered what his old partner was up to now.

Ross had taken the news like a champ. No jealousy, no envy, just sincere congratulations. Blake already missed working with him.

Not that he wanted to go back...

He didn't have to wait long before an attractive woman—who seemed far too elegantly attired for this part of town—exited the building. A stylish wide-brimmed hat shaded her striking features. It was the same dark hue as her fashionable black dress and matching gloves. A small collection of luggage suggested that she was going on a trip.

Something about her struck him as familiar, but it took him a moment to place her. A memory—of a frightened young woman bumping into him on her way out of that sleazy underworld bar—flashed through his brain. That had been the night Gordon was shot.

He took a closer look at the woman on the sidewalk.

Holy crap, he thought. *It's her.*

It all fell into place. Congressman Gilly had claimed

he'd been abducted by a woman—a woman matching her description. The congressman had been a bit vague, no doubt to protect his own reputation—and marriage. But now it made sense.

What had Gordon said again? That he wasn't allowed to believe in coincidence anymore.

The woman hailed a cab, and climbed into the back seat. As it pulled into traffic, he followed suit, and got on the radio.

"Get Commissioner Gordon," he said. "Tell him I've got a line on the congressman's kidnapping."

Selina made it through airport security without a hitch. Her boarding pass in her purse, she walked briskly through the international terminal, trying not to attract the wrong kind of attention.

According to the departures monitor, her flight was on-time and leaving soon. With any luck, she would be an ocean away from Gotham before the day was over.

Or perhaps it wouldn't be that easy.

Heading toward her gate, she spotted a uniformed police officer checking her out. Judging from his expression, he wasn't just appreciating her figure. Was there an all-points bulletin out on her already?

Time to improvise, she thought.

Veering away from the main concourse, she ducked into a secluded service corridor, ignoring the signs that said it was for authorized personnel only. As she expected, the cop followed her. He rounded the corner, only to find her applying a fresh layer of ruby-red lipstick.

"Excuse me, miss," he said sternly. "I need to see your ticket and identification, please."

Acting surprised, she fumbled in her purse.

"Would you mind?" she asked, handing him her hat. He accepted it without thinking. *Big mistake*, she thought. Her fist punched right through the crown of the hat, delivering a sharp blow to his chin. She grabbed him before his limp body hit the floor.

A janitor's closet provided a convenient hiding spot. She crammed the unconscious cop into it and placed the mangled hat on his head. It didn't exactly go with his uniform, but she liked to think it made a statement.

Better you than me, she thought.

Her brown hair neatly tied up in a bun, she closed the closet door and slipped back onto the concourse. Her flight was already boarding by the time she reached her gate. She trotted confidently down the jetway—only to spot two scowling airport security guys waiting at the end, right before the entrance to the plane.

Changing her mind, she turned around and started to head back the way she'd come. But a clean-cut young man in a cheap suit stood waiting at the other end of the jetway, blocking her exit. She quickly recognized him as the helpful cop she had ditched during the police raid on the bar.

He smiled and held up his badge. It looked brand-new.

So much for the French Riviera.

She looked up as Blake entered the interrogation room, carrying a thick file. A pair of cuffs had replaced the elbow-length black gloves she had been wearing earlier.

Harsh fluorescent lights illuminated a stark white chamber. Soundproof ceramic tiles cut the room off from the outside world, isolating the suspect. One-way mirrors, mounted on the wall, captured their reflections. A closed-circuit camera monitored the proceedings.

He sat down at the steel table across from her and started the tape recorder. This was his first formal interrogation as a detective, and he wanted to do it by the book.

"I showed your picture to the congressman," he told her. "And guess what?"

"Don't tell me," she guessed. "Still in love?"

"Head over heels," he acknowledged. "Pressing charges, though." He smacked the file down onto the table. "You've made some mistakes, Ms. Kyle."

She shrugged.

"Girl's gotta eat."

"You have an appetite," he observed, flipping through the file's contents. He glanced up from a list of her greatest hits to look her directly in the eyes. "Why run? You can't hide from us with this record."

She met his gaze without evasion.

"Maybe it's not you I'm running from."

"Who then?" He took a shot. "Bane? What do you know about him?"

Her cocky attitude went away.

"That you should be as afraid of him as I am."

She means it, Blake realized, hearing genuine fear in her hushed tone. "We can offer you protection…"

She shot him an incredulous look, like they both knew it was a joke. Then she looked away from him, idly checking her reflection in one of the mirrors. Blake got the distinct impression that she'd given him as much as he was going to get for the time being—at least on the record.

He switched off the tape and stood up from the table.

"When I spotted you," he said, "I was looking for a friend. Bruce Wayne."

The name got her attention. She didn't say anything, but he could tell she was hiding something, and it seemed to bother her. He stepped between her and the mirror. His eyes entreated her.

"Did they kill him?"

For the first time since he'd entered the room, she couldn't meet his gaze.

"I'm not sure," she confessed.

Blake's heart sank.

CHAPTER TWENTY-TWO

Feverish images dragged him up from the dark. Screams, sobs, and maniacal laughter surrounded him. Broken bodies crashed to earth. He was falling down a long dark shaft. A black, skull-like visage gazed down on him, coming closer and closer...

Bruce opened his eyes, drifting back to consciousness.

Disoriented, he found himself lying on his back on a rough wooden cot. He stared upward at a sooty stone roof that looked as though it had been carved from solid rock. He glimpsed prison bars out of the corner of his eye. His Batsuit was gone, replaced by coarse, filthy rags. His head throbbed and his throat was parched.

Whiskers carpeted his pale, clammy face. He tried to sit up, only to experience an excruciating jolt of pain. He sank back onto the cot, gasping in agony.

It all came back to him.

Bane. Wayne Tower. His back bent backwards until...

Someone stirred to his right, and he realized that he wasn't alone in the cell. He tried to roll over to see who it was, but even the attempt was torture.

Heavy footsteps approached the cot. A massive figure squatted beside him. Densely muscled shoulders curved upward into a thick neck supporting a familiar masked face. The dark skull from his fever dreams seemed to gaze down on him.

Bane.

"Why didn't you just kill me?" Bruce rasped, his throat sore from disuse.

"You don't fear death," Bane answered. "You welcome it." He shook his head. "Your punishment is to be more severe."

Bruce understood now. He glared furiously at his captor.

"You're a torturer..."

"Yes," Bane agreed. "But not of your body. Of your soul."

Bruce tried to hold onto his anger, but the pain was too great. He let out a sharp gasp. Bane blurred before his eyes as he felt the darkness encroaching on his vision. He fought to stay conscious.

"Where am I?" he asked.

"Home," Bane replied. "Where I learned the truth about despair. As will you."

Bruce forced himself to look around, turning his head as little as possible. Through the rusty iron bars of his cell, he glimpsed what appeared to be an enormous underground complex carved into the sides of a gigantic pit. Metal stairs and catwalks connected rows of terraces that led into deep, cavernous cell blocks. The entire structure resembled a huge inverted pyramid or ziggurat that was almost Escheresque in appearance.

Wretched figures clad in frayed peasant garb populated the place, trudging wearily about their labors. There appeared to be no guards—only prisoners. Angry shouts and screams came from the other cells. The early morning sunlight filtered down from a vast circular shaft rising hundreds of feet above the bottom of the pit. Higher up, crumbling ledges and outcroppings jutted from the weathered stone sides.

It was like being at the bottom of a colossal well.

Bane rose from Bruce's bedside and crossed the cell to the bars.

"There is a reason that this prison is the worst hell on earth." He lifted his masked countenance toward the distant sunlight. "Hope. Every man who has rotted here over the centuries has looked up to the light, and imagined climbing to freedom. So simple, so easy. And, like shipwrecked men turning to seawater from uncontrollable thirst, many have died trying.

"I learned here that there can be no true despair without hope." He looked away from the light, fixing his pitiless gaze on Bruce.

"So as I terrorize Gotham, I will feed its people hope to poison their souls. I will let them believe they can survive, so that you can watch them clamber over each other to stay in the sun." He pointed to an ancient-looking television set up just outside the bars of Bruce's cell. A cable ran from the television into the crude, rough-hewn masonry.

"You will watch," Bane continued, "as I torture an entire city to bring you pain you thought you could never truly feel again. Then, when you have truly understood the depths of your failure, we will fulfill Rā's al Ghūl's destiny. We will destroy Gotham. And when it is done—when Gotham is ashes—*then* you have my permission to die."

Bane turned to depart, leaving Bruce alone in the dismal cell. A barred door swung shut, its rusty hinges squeaking in protest. He wanted to shout at Bane, say something defiant, but it would have been nothing but an empty gesture. He couldn't even move without agony.

The pain overwhelmed him again and the darkness swept over him. His eyes drooped and fell shut.

He could still hear the screams, even in his sleep.

Blackgate Prison was a maximum-security penitentiary located on one of the smaller islands in Gotham Harbor. Now that the Dent Act had made it all but possible for the city's criminals to cop an insanity plea, it had replaced Arkham Asylum as the preferred location for imprisoning both convicted and suspected felons. The worst of the worst were sent here, except for the Joker, who, rumor had it, was locked away as Arkham's sole remaining inmate.

Or perhaps he had escaped. Nobody was really sure.

Not even Selina.

She gazed up at Blackgate's forbidding gray walls and watchtowers as she was escorted into the facility, wearing an absolutely hideous orange jumpsuit. Her long brown hair was tied back behind her head. A pair of steel handcuffs accessorized her convict garb. She would have preferred a pair of diamond bracelets.

After being processed, she was led down the middle of a multi-level cell block. Rows of inmates, locked in their cells, hooted and hollered at her as though they had never seen a woman before. Obscene jeers, whistles, and catcalls followed her down the length of the long, dreary corridor. They rattled their cages like monkeys in a zoo.

She had always liked the big cats better.

The guard in charge of the block looked askance at his new prisoner.

"We're locking her up in here?"

Selina was the only female prisoner in sight. This part of Blackgate wasn't exactly co-ed.

"The Dent Act allows non-segregation based on extraordinary need," the warden explained. He kept a close eye on her. "First time she broke out of a women's correctional, she was sixteen."

Fifteen, she thought, *but I looked mature for my age*.

A hulking convict—who was as ugly as he was muscle-bound—groped for her through the bars of his cage. Pudgy fingers strained to reach to her. He licked his lips, practically drooling like a dog in heat.

"Little closer, baby," he said coarsely.

"Why, honey," she purred, "you wanna hold my hand?"

Making it easy for him, she slipped his greedy hands between her own handcuffed ones, and then executed a flawless cartwheel, snapping both of his arms.

Bone splintered noisily and the steroid case shrieked in agony even as the guards rushed to separate them.

She landed on her feet and kept on walking, not missing a step.

The hoots and whistles died away.

"She'll be just fine," the warden predicted.

The elevator let Fox and Miranda off on the top floor of Wayne Tower. They strolled toward the executive boardroom.

"I don't see the need for a board meeting on the energy project," he protested. He didn't have time for a meeting right now, not when he was still dealing with the raid on Applied Sciences. Even a *partial* inventory

THE DARK KNIGHT RISES

of all the prototypes that had gone missing was enough to keep him up at night. He didn't like to think about those inventions falling into the wrong hands.

"Bruce got a lot of things right," Miranda said. "Keeping the board in the dark wasn't one of them."

Lucius wasn't sure he agreed with that, but Miranda was president of Wayne Enterprises now, so he needed to respect her opinion. Bracing himself for a contentious exchange, he politely opened the door to the boardroom and escorted her inside.

Where he found a different kind of meeting already in progress.

The board members sat around the conference table, ashen and trembling. Armed intruders held them captive at gunpoint, while an intimidating masked figure occupied the head of the table. Lucius recognized him as the same ruthless killer who had staged the raid on the stock exchange, wiping out Bruce Wayne's fortune. Newspaper reports on the attack had identified him as a notorious mercenary known only as Bane.

"This meeting is called to order," the man said.

Fox and Miranda froze, staring aghast at the masked man and his gunmen. Lucius stepped protectively in front of Miranda.

"Chair and president," Bane said, addressing them. He was dressed for combat, wearing a khaki utility harness with plenty of pouches, and rugged gray trousers and boots. He crossed his beefy arms.

A pistol was stuck in his belt. He glanced around the conference table. "I also need one ordinary member. Mr. Fox, would you care to nominate?"

For what? Lucius wondered. Bane's mockery of business protocol left him speechless and confused.

"No," Douglas Fredericks said, speaking up. The dignified older man rose to his feet. "I volunteer."

Fox was impressed by his colleague's courage. He hoped it wouldn't cost him too dearly as the mercenaries rounded up the three of them. Helpless against the armed soldiers, he couldn't help wishing that Wayne was still a member of the board. Bruce would know how to handle a situation like this.

But no one had seen Bruce Wayne in days.

Or his nocturnal alter ego.

"Where are you taking us?" Fox asked cautiously.

"Where you buried your resources," Bane answered. "The bowels of Gotham."

Fox shivered involuntarily at the killer's words.

CHAPTER TWENTY-THREE

A nurse helped Gordon pull himself up to a sitting position. It hurt, but maybe not as much as before. A dog-eared copy of *A Tale of Two Cities* sat on a bedside table. Detective Blake stood by the hospital bed, waiting patiently for the nurse to depart.

He closed the door behind her when she left.

"So you think our friend is gone again?" Gordon asked him.

The young detective nodded gravely.

"This time he might not be coming back."

Gordon's face fell. The whole time he'd been stuck in this damn bed, the one thing that had kept him going was the knowledge that Gotham's Dark Knight had returned. But it seemed as if that hope had been short-lived.

Where is he? Gordon wondered. *What's happened to him?*

The door swung open again, and Foley barged into the room, visibly agitated. He was short of breath, as though he had run all the way up the stairs. Beads of perspiration dotted his brow.

"Okay, Commissioner," he said, gasping, "you were right!"

Gordon sat up straight, his pains forgotten.

"What's happened?"

"Your masked man kidnapped the Wayne Enterprises board," Foley reported. "He let most of them go, but took three down into the sewers."

Gordon winced at the thought. Memories of the tunnels, of his own blood spilling into the chilling waters, sent a chill through his entire body.

This is it, he realized. *Bane is making his move.*

"No more patrols," he ordered. "No more hide and seek. Send every available cop down there to smoke him out."

Foley hesitated.

"The mayor won't want panic—"

"So it's a training exercise," Blake suggested.

For once, Foley seemed to welcome the younger man's input. He looked guiltily at Gordon.

"I'm sorry I didn't take you seriously—"

Gordon cut him some slack. Foley was a good cop. He had just taken for granted that the bad days were gone. Gordon had known better.

"Don't apologize for believing the world is in better shape than it is," the commissioner told him. "Just fight to make it true."

Foley nodded, seeming to understand at last. He left to carry out Gordon's orders. Blake moved to follow him, but Gordon called him back.

"Not you," the commissioner said. "You're telling me the Batman's gone. So you chase up the Daggett leads, any way you can."

They needed to do more than just find Bane. They had to find out what he was up to, before it was too late. Daggett's name had been all over the excavations in the tunnels, and now he was dead. There had to be a connection. And *somebody* had to find it.

If not Batman, then maybe Blake.

Water dripped onto on Bruce's dry, cracked lips. An old man with shaggy white hair leaned over him, squeezing the liquid from a dirty rag. One cell over, separated from them by sturdy iron bars, a blind Middle Eastern man squatted against a rough stone wall. He appeared to be in his seventies. Milky cataracts clouded his eyes.

He muttered something in a tongue Bruce couldn't place. An obscure dialect of Persian, perhaps, or Arabic.

"He asks if you would pay us to let you die," White Hair translated. An Eastern European accent suggested that he had been born somewhere far beyond this hellish pit. A ragged wool vest hung over his scrawny frame. He was dressed like a peasant, but had an air of ravaged gentility. "I told him you have nothing."

Bruce grimaced. He lay miserably atop the cot, from which he hadn't stirred for who knew how long. Feverish and weak, he'd lost all track of time, drifting in and out of awareness. His head pounded, and the searing pain in his back was a constant companion, even in his sleep. Existence had become an endless ordeal he could never escape. He could not even clean himself.

"Do it for the pleasure," he said bitterly. But the nameless European placed a stale piece of bread to Bruce's lip. He shrugged apologetically.

"They pay me more than that to keep you alive."

Chanting, coming from outside the cell, caught Bruce's attention. Slowly, painfully, he rolled his head to see what was going on. Daylight, its presence just as tantalizing as Bane had promised, provided barely enough light to see.

A crowd of prisoners had gathered around a stocky, well-built inmate who could have had a career as a carnival strong man. He stood on one of the upper levels, just below the mammoth shaft that led to the surface.

Another prisoner, whose face was liberally covered in tattoos, handed the strong man a rope, which he tied around his brawny chest. More prisoners crowded the various terraces and stairways. They joined in the chanting, which sounded more dirge-like than encouraging.

"He will try the climb," the European said.

The other end of the rope ran through a pulley system that had been hammered into a ledge about a third of the way up the shaft, hundreds of feet from the top. It served as a safety measure, Bruce realized, as the strong man began to scale the crumbling stone wall. Rugged outcroppings and narrow crevices were scattered irregularly along the rocky face, offering occasional purchase for the climber's bare hands and feet.

He made his way slowly up the shaft, the chanting growing louder and louder as he climbed toward the light. At one point he slipped, and almost lost his grip on the wall, but managed to recover. The safety rope trailed behind him as he rose.

Secure handholds and footholds grew scarcer and further apart the higher he went. He paused on a narrow ledge, gazing up at the challenge ahead. The next available shelf was at least a twelve-foot jump away. Bruce would have been hesitant to make such a leap even as Batman. It was a daunting prospect.

The strong man perched upon the foothold, searching in vain for some other way to proceed. Far below him, the chanting egged him on, growing in intensity. The man gazed up at the distant sunlight and made up his mind. As the chanting peaked, he jumped for the higher purchase—and missed.

Screaming, he plummeted toward the bottom of the pit. The safety rope snapped taut partway down and he swung into the unforgiving stone wall, hitting it with bone-crushing force. The chanting fell silent as the battered prisoner was slowly lowered down on the rope. His head drooped limply. Blood dripped from his smashed face and torso.

The spectators retreated back to their cells.

"Has anyone ever made it?" Bruce asked.

His caretaker shook his head.

"Of course not."

One cell over, the blind man barked in protest.

"What does he say?" Bruce asked.

"He says there is one who did," the European admitted. "A child..." He shuddered. "A child who had been born in this hell."

Bruce knew whom he meant.

"Bane."

The other man flinched at the name. He seemed anxious to change the subject.

"An old legend. Nothing more."

Shoving the last of the bread between Bruce's lips, he hurried to leave the cell. Once outside, he paused to switch on the TV.

"Don't," Bruce pleaded. He had no desire to witness whatever horror show Bane had in store. But his caretaker left the TV on. He shrugged apologetically.

"Whatever they want you to see," he said, "it's happening soon."

CHAPTER TWENTY-FOUR

Where are they taking us? Fox wondered.

Bane's men led their hostages out of Wayne Tower through the jagged hole in the floor of Applied Sciences. They made their way across the debris into a confusing maze of tunnels somewhere beneath the city. The dismal catacombs were dank and dark, but showed evidence of recent modifications, and even new excavations.

The engineer in Fox tried to figure out the purpose of the construction. Somebody had clearly put a lot of time and labor into retrofitting the underground.

But why?

As he tried to assist Miranda and Fredericks, Lucius was dismayed to see the mercenaries brandishing his own inventions—weapons and equipment he had designed for the US military…and the Batman.

Incendiary mini-mines the size of jacks, magnetic steel grapples, smoke and gas capsules, high-tech eavesdropping equipment, even a trio of stolen tumblers.

Thank God Bruce took the Bat, he thought, *before we were raided.*

They came at last to a large, damp tunnel lit by flickering fluorescent lights. It looked as if it had been newly excavated, perhaps as recently as the last few days. Fox had no idea where beneath Gotham they were, although it felt as if they had been walking for miles.

We could be anywhere, he realized.

Bane's men planted explosive charges on a freshly hewn wall at the far end of the tunnel. Standing off to one side, looking distinctly ill at ease, was an older man about Fox's age. He didn't look at all like a mercenary. He paced nervously, his face drenched with sweat. He ran his hand through disorderly white hair. Armed escorts kept a close eye on him

Miranda stared at the stranger in surprise.

"Dr. Pavel?"

Fox recognized the name of a renegade Russian scientist who was believed to have perished in a plane crash some months ago. It was Leonid Pavel's work, he recalled, that had persuaded Bruce to mothball the fusion project indefinitely.

What's he doing here? Fox wondered. *Another of Bane's prisoners?*

The mercs finished placing the charges. They stepped away from the wall and signaled Bane.

He nodded at them.

An explosion rocked the tunnel.

Police and SWAT teams prepared to invade the underground. Foley glanced up at the sky as he coordinated the massive raid, operating from the 49th Street subway station. The sun was going down, but that hardly mattered where his teams were going.

Assault teams reported in from all around the city, massing in the thousands outside every subway station, manhole, and drainage pipe. As soon as he gave the go-ahead, pretty much the entire GCPD was going to descend and begin scouring every tunnel and rat hole until they rooted out Bane and his hostages.

The deputy commissioner just wished he'd done this earlier.

"Go," he ordered.

A SWAT team, its members equipped with faceless black helmets, body armor, and assault rifles, converged on the mouth of a large drainage tunnel. Before they got too far, however, a low, echoing boom sounded from somewhere deeper within the sewers.

The men exchanged tense looks, but headed in anyway, following orders that had been given to thousands of other officers throughout the city. Flashlights swept the slimy walls of the tunnels. Weapons were locked and loaded. Radios kept them in touch with all the other teams.

One way or another, they were going to find Bane.

Bane led the way into the reactor chamber. Dust and smoke filled the air as Fox and the others stumbled over the rubble and into the top-secret energy project beneath the river. Water from the drainage channels spilled over onto the wreckage. Fox felt sick to his stomach as they approached the reactor.

All at once, Dr. Pavel's presence made horrible sense.

Bane shoved Fox toward the control panel.

"Turn it on," he ordered.

No. Fox shook his head. This was exactly what Bruce had sacrificed so much to prevent. *I can't allow this, no matter what.*

Bane drew a gun from his belt and held it to Fredericks' head.

"I only need one other board member," he said. "Shall I have my men fetch another?"

Fox remembered the other hostages they had left behind at Wayne Tower. Was it possible they were still in danger? He prayed that the man was bluffing.

"I won't do it," he said.

Fredericks maintained his dignity, but still trembled

as Bane cocked his weapon. An old friend of Thomas Wayne, he had always been a staunch defender of the Wayne legacy. Would a gun now take his life as well?

"All right, stop." Miranda hurried forward and, before Fox could even try to stop her, placed her palm down on a biometric scanner. The control panel beeped, confirming her identity. Buttons and gauges lit up. She turned and pleaded with Fox, her dark eyes moist.

"Lucius, you'll kill this man and yourself, and barely slow them down."

As much as he hated to admit it, she had a point. Bane held all the cards. Defying him at the expense of their lives would be nothing but an empty gesture, and leave him unable to fight back later on.

I'm sorry, Bruce, he thought. *I have no choice.*

He reluctantly placed his own hand on the scanner. Bane lowered his gun and motioned for Fredericks to do the same. A final beep activated the reactor core, which began to glow brighter and brighter as a fusion reaction ignited inside the suspended metal sphere, generating vast amounts of energy. Gauges on the core recorded the steady increase in power production.

Unlike the rigged demonstration Bruce had staged for Miranda before, the reaction did not peter out after a few minutes. It continued to grow in intensity as— deep within—atomic nuclei combined with increasing frequency, releasing vast amounts of power in the form of high-energy neutrons. It was the same process, Fox knew, that powered the sun.

And hydrogen bombs.

Dr. Pavel stared at the reactor, transfixed by the sight. Bane turned toward the scientist.

"Do your work," he commanded.

Roused from his scientific reverie, Pavel scurried to obey. Bane turned back to his men and gestured toward the hostages.

"Take them to the surface," he instructed, effectively dismissing Fox and the others. "People of their status need to experience the next era of western civilization."

Fox didn't like the sound of that.

What does he mean to do with that reactor?

But Bane did not bother to elaborate. He merely stood by silently as his men dragged Fox and the others back into the tunnels.

CHAPTER TWENTY-FIVE

Gotham Stadium was home to the big game between the Gotham Rogues and the Rapid City Monuments. The new $300 million arena was the jewel of Mayor Garcia's urban renewal program, built on top of a formerly blighted stretch of riverfront property. The huge open-air venue was built of stone, steel, and glass.

Flanked by security, the mayor greeted reporters outside the VIP entrance. Cameras captured his photogenic visage. Reporters hurled questions, all about the game.

"Mr. Mayor!" a busybody from the *Gotham Post* called out. "We're seeing literally *thousands* of police heading into the sewers—"

"A training exercise, that's all." The mayor's winning smile grew slightly forced. He planted a

Rogues cap on his head. "Now, if you'll excuse me, I've got tickets to watch our boys thrash Rapid City."

Ducking the press, he was escorted to his private luxury box overlooking the horseshoe-shaped arena. More than sixty thousand eager sports fans—many sporting Gotham black-and-yellow—crowded the bleachers. An electronic scoreboard advertised major brands and products. More than two acres of natural grass covered the playing field, just waiting to be torn up by the competing teams.

This was the kick-off game of a brand new season and hopes were high that the Rogues would go all the way this year. The mayor hoped so; a Super Bowl victory wouldn't hurt his poll numbers.

He waved to the crowd as he took his seat.

Now if Foley and his officers could just take care of their little problem downstairs.

The GCPD had been searching the underground all night without success. There seemed no end to the branching tunnels and sewers, which were practically a city in themselves. Weary cops and SWAT teams waded through the fetid water, sweeping their flashlights back and forth. Boots pounded on old brickwork or concrete, or else splashed through the disgusting drains.

A grid search based on outdated Gotham blueprints had them converging on the center of midtown, albeit well beneath the city streets. With any luck, they were closing in on the terrorists.

Ross hoped so. He trudged down yet another dirty tunnel behind the rest of his squad. A yawn escaped his lips. He'd been at this for hours, and all he'd found was way too many rats and spiders and bugs. The sewers stank like, well, sewers, and he figured he was going to need a new uniform when this was over. No way was he getting *this* smell out of his clothes.

Sorry, Yolanda, he apologized in advance to his wife. Given a choice, he would have much rather been home with her and their daughter. Little Tara was turning five next week, he reminded himself. He still needed to pick up her present. *Maybe after I get out of these stinking rat holes.*

A lizard scurried over his boot and he kicked it away in disgust. Garbage floated past him on a greasy river of muck. A cobweb brushed across his face. He felt as if he was hiking through the world's biggest latrine. His feet were wet and cold and he wanted a hot shower more than he had ever wanted anything in his life.

This sucked, big time.

Blake got promoted just in time, he decided, more than a little envious of his old partner. *Wonder what they've got him doing now?*

John Blake cruised through an ugly industrial district, checking in with Gordon via his cell phone. His butt was sore and he would have killed for a cup of coffee—or maybe a few hours' sleep.

"I've been to half of Daggett's cement plants," he reported. "Logged locations they've poured for underground construction."

"*Anything strange about the pourings?*" Gordon asked from his hospital room. Static added to the hoarseness of his voice.

Blake pulled the car over to consult his notes. A crumpled map was spread out across the passenger seat next to him. Red dots, scribbled on the map, indicated all the pouring sites his research had identified. He tried—and failed—to find any clues on the map.

"Honestly, commissioner, I don't know anything about civil engineering—"

"But you know about patterns," Gordon insisted. "Keep looking."

If you say so, Blake thought, signing off. He checked the address of the next cement plant on his list. *I just hope this isn't a wild goose chase.*

He couldn't help wishing that he was underground, taking part in the manhunt for Bane instead. That was where the real action was.

He hoped that Ross and the others were okay.

Sweating, Dr. Pavel stepped away from the reactor. His sleeves were rolled up and he was breathing hard. Much of his task had involved reprogramming the reactor's safety parameters and neutron flux allowances, but he had also needed to tinker with the magnetic coils and plasma containment units.

A case of sophisticated tools lay at his feet, along with discarded bits of shielding. Essential baffles and dampeners had been replaced with more volatile materials. The sphere's access panels were once again closed.

"It is done," he announced dolefully. "This is now a four megaton nuclear bomb." That was roughly two hundred times more powerful than the bombs that had devastated Hiroshima and Nagasaki during World War Two.

Bane nodded in approval. He called to his men.

"Pull the core out of the reactor."

"You can't!" Pavel blurted, his face draining of color. "This is the only power source capable of sustaining it. If you move it, the core will decay in a matter of months—"

"Five, by my calculations," Bane replied calmly.

Pavel was confused. Did Bane not appreciate the danger? He tried desperately to explain.

"And then it will go off!"

"For the sake of your family, Dr. Pavel, I hope so."

Stunned, the scientist watched as the men began to disconnect the core. He wrung his hands anxiously. Not for the first time, he found himself wishing that he had died in that plane crash, after all.

God forgive me, he thought. *What have I done?*

* * *

Blake had been tempted to stop for lunch, but instead he drove straight to his next destination—a cement factory on the outskirts of town. A chain-link fence topped with razor wire surrounded the grounds. Hot gases jetted from the heating tower. Storage silos rose above the plant. Grinding mills churned noisily. He parked outside and approached the gate.

A guard scowled at his badge before letting him through the fence.

"Boss is about to leave," the man grumbled as he escorted Blake across the lot. Bags of powdered cement were piled high on wooden pallets, waiting to be shipped out. Metal bins and barrels sat upright amidst the pallets. A front loader was on hand to transport the bags and barrels onto trucks. Cement dust was everywhere.

An odd chemical odor nagged at Blake's memory.

Where do I know that from?

They walked past a parked cement mixer. Keeping his eyes open, Blake spotted a familiar face. He veered away from the guard to accost a driver who was standing outside the vehicle.

"Hey!" Blake called out, getting the man's attention. The driver turned toward him. "I know you. That was you outside the stock exchange, right?"

The man's stony face might as well as have been cast in cement. He crossed his arms belligerently.

"When?"

"*When?*" Blake echoed in disbelief. "When half the city's cops were trying to pull onto Castle Street, and your truck shut them out."

Hard to imagine the guy had forgotten that particular altercation.

"Oh, yeah," the driver said, as though only just recognizing Blake. "You're that cop—"

"Detective, now."

The driver snorted, unimpressed by his promotion. Blake heard the guard come up behind him. The approaching man must have reached for something in his pocket. Metal jingled against loose change. Blake felt the hairs rise on the back of his neck.

"And as a detective," he added, "I'm not allowed to believe in coincidence any more—"

He spun around, drawing his sidearm just in time to see the guard lunging at him with a knife. Reacting quickly, he swept the man's arm aside and fired in self-defense. The sharp report of the gun cut through the factory noises and the guard toppled backwards, clutching his chest. Blood spurted from his wound.

Oh my God, Blake thought. *I think I killed him.*

But he couldn't deal with that now. The driver grabbed him from behind, holding onto his arms. Blake tried to break free from the grip, but the man was strong and knew what he was doing.

Blake held on tightly to his gun, but couldn't get off a clean shot as along as the guy kept behind him. The driver twisted Blake's gun arm, trying to break it. The cop grunted in pain.

In desperation, he fired backward at the nearby front loader. The bullet ricocheted off the vehicle's heavy steel bucket, catching the driver in the back. He jerked violently, then hit the ground like a bag of cement.

Gasping, Blake knelt to check on the man, whose life already seemed to be slipping away. His body twitched spasmodically. Ragged breaths slowed to a stop. Blood trickled from the corner of his lip.

"What were you doing?" Blake shouted at him, furious that the information he needed might be slipping away. He wanted to pound the man's face in, just for making him pull the trigger. His voice was hoarse with emotion. "What?!"

The driver twitched one last time, then went still. His chest stopped moving, and his eyes glazed over. Blake checked for a pulse, but it was no use.

The man was dead.

Both men were dead.

Feeling sick to his stomach, Blake stared at the gun in his hand, which suddenly felt like it weighed a ton. He had never killed anyone before—not even in the line of duty. Bile rose at the back of his throat. He clenched his teeth to keep from throwing up.

Instinctively he hurled the gun to the ground. Shaking, he somehow managed to pull his phone out of his pocket. He dialed Gordon.

His boss's voice mail picked up.

"Commissioner," he said, trying to keep his voice as steady as possible. "I'm at the 14th Street plant with two dead witnesses and a lot of questions. Call me—"

He glanced around to make sure nobody else was coming after him, but the gunshots seemed to have scared all the other workers off. He stooped to retrieve his firearm, just in case, when that odd odor caused his brow to furrow. He sniffed the air suspiciously, tracing the smell to a collection of unmarked steel barrels resting alongside the wooden pallets.

His jaw dropped as he finally identified the odor.

"Commissioner," he reported urgently. "They've got Polyisobutylene here—" He surveyed the scene, taking in the plant's inventory. "And motor oil." The pieces came together to form an alarming picture. "They weren't making cement—they were making *explosives*—"

An awful possibility hit him with the force of revelation. He ran to his vehicle and grabbed his charts. His eyes frantically scanned the map, hoping he was wrong, but the telltale pattern of dots only confirmed his worst fears.

"Oh, God."

He dived behind the steering wheel and peeled out of the factory parking lot, spraying gravel behind him. He drove furiously back toward headquarters, pressing the gas pedal to the floor, while shouting into his radio.

"Patch me into Foley!"

A maddeningly calm voice responded. "Deputy Commissioner Foley is overseeing the operation—"

"They're heading into a trap!"

Foley followed his men into the subway tunnel, putting the lights of the platform behind him. He was tired of waiting. He needed to check on the search with his own eyes. He owed Gordon that much.

He owed Gotham that much.

"Sir!" a lieutenant came running after him. He thrust a radio into Foley's hand. "It's Blake. He says it's urgent."

Foley took the radio. As much as he hated to admit it, the hotheaded young detective had been on the ball so far.

"Foley," he said.

"*It's a trap!*" Blake's voice shouted. "*Pull everyone out! Bane's been pouring concrete laced with explosives—*"

Foley froze in his tracks.

"Where?"

"*There's a ring around the tunnels*, Blake answered. "*They're gonna blow it and trap the cops underground!*"

Foley spun around and stared back at the mouth of the tunnel, which suddenly seemed dangerously far away. His mouth went dry.

"Pull out!" he shouted. "Pull 'em out!"

He raced toward the light.

The boiler room was in a sub-basement of the stadium, far below the cheering crowds. With all eyes on the field, no one was watching as Bane's men broke through the basement floor. Drills and explosive charges had carved out a path from the tunnels below. The mercenaries climbed up into the stadium.

Bane emerged from the underground. His utility harness was strapped to his chest.

The National Anthem could be heard wafting down from above. He imagined thousands of sports fans, standing at attention as they paid tribute to bombs bursting in the air. No doubt the mayor had his hand over his heart.

The mercenaries advanced to the empty locker room tunnels. They took out their detonators. Bane cocked his head at the sound of the kickoff, like a hunting dog scenting the wind.

Now, he decided.

"Let the games begin."

The men hit the detonators.

Foley scrambled for the light. Along with his men, he raced out of the subway tunnel only heartbeats before explosions rocked the underground. The tunnel roof collapsed behind him, and enormous slabs of concrete crashing down onto the tracks. Sparks flared from the electrified third rail.

A billowing cloud of dust and debris filled the station. Booming echoes were amplified by the tunnel walls, forcing him to throw his hands over his ears. Cops and SWAT team members dived for cover. An injured officer screamed.

Somehow Foley managed to stay on his feet. Panting, he made it all the way back to the passenger platform before turning around to inspect the damage. Pulverized stone and concrete caked his sweaty face. He coughed hoarsely, choking on the dust. His eyes bulged from their sockets.

Oh my God...

Tons of fallen concrete blocked the mouth to the tunnel. Frantic radio reports, coming from all around the city, confirmed Blake's dire prediction. Explosions and cave-ins had closed off every entrance to the underground, trapping thousands of cops beneath the city. Foley gazed in horror at the heap of rubble. He may have gotten out just in time, but what about the rest of his people?

He already knew the answer.

Practically the entire GCPD had been buried alive.

CHAPTER TWENTY-SIX

The football spiraled through the air.

Come to daddy, the Gotham receiver thought as he caught the ball and made a break for the end zone. The hometown crowd went wild, screaming their lungs out as he started his run, pursued by the visiting linebackers. He ran past the mayor's box, guessing that His Honor was cheering, as well, and ducked past a Rapid City cornerback who was trying to block him.

The looming goal posts called out to him. He could practically taste his victory.

Touchdown, here I come!

The mayor's box exploded, raining blood and debris onto the field. The cheers turned into screams. People panicked and leapt from their seats. Smoke blew over the field.

What the—?

Confused, the receiver glanced behind him— and saw the grassy field drop away into the earth, swallowing players. Rogues and Monuments alike tumbled into a smoking chasm that seemed to be chasing after the receiver as eagerly as any opposing linebacker. The pigskin slipped from his fingers as he sprinted even faster than before, desperate to stay ahead of the collapsing field.

An earth-shaking rumble competed with the shrieks of more than sixty thousand spectators, many of whom were already stampeding for the exits. The terrified player stumbled past the end zone, abandoning all thought of scoring.

Get me outta here!

The street erupted all around Blake's cruiser, throwing chunks of asphalt into the air. Thick black smoke billowed up from below. Manhole covers shot upward. Water gushed from broken fire hydrants. Street lamps toppled over, crashing onto streets and sidewalks.

Snapped electrical wires sparked and hissed. Pedestrians ran in terror. Horns honked frantically, adding to the tumult. Brakes squealed. Sirens blared. Vehicles collided.

Struggling to keep control of his car, Blake swerved wildly to avoid the bright orange flames shooting up from an open manhole. His notes and maps went flying around the cabin. An empty coffee cup toppled over.

Blake swore out loud, gripping the steering wheel with white knuckles.

The Granton Bridge collapsed behind him. The massive towers, deck, and cables crashed into the river in what appeared to be a controlled demolition. Dozens of cars, trucks, and taxis plunged down into the icy water.

Further ahead and off to the right, he saw the Sallow Bridge come crashing down as well, severing the east side of midtown from the mainland. He guessed that the other bridges had been sabotaged, as well.

Bane is cutting Gotham off from the world, he realized. *But why?*

Another eruption went off directly beneath the cruiser, tossing the car over and onto its roof. It skidded across the exploding asphalt. Sparks and the screeching of metal against asphalt created yet more chaos. Blake's seatbelt and shoulder strap dug into him, holding him to his seat.

The windshield shattered. Metal crumpled around him. Geysers of smoke and flame spewed around the careening vehicle.

His world turned upside-down.

The once-green football field was now a smoking wasteland except for one narrow strip of turf that had survived the disaster. Rubble and dead bodies littered what was left. The pigskin itself had vanished into the chasm.

No one noticed.

Bane's men poured out of the locker room tunnel and onto the ruined field, forming a protective gauntlet for his entrance. More soldiers, he knew, were posted at all the exits, preventing his audience from leaving before the show was over. He had no intention of performing to an empty house.

He strode into view like a gladiator entering the coliseum. Everywhere members of the panicked crowd sobbed and shouted as they realized there was no escape. He observed with satisfaction that the television cameras were swinging in his direction. By now, he calculated, the live footage was airing on every channel all over the world.

He hoped Wayne was enjoying the broadcast.

A dead umpire, killed by a chunk of flying debris from the mayor's box, lay sprawled upon the turf. The man's headset appeared to have survived and Bane plucked it from the man's remains. It amused him to use the umpire's mike.

The panicked crowd grew hushed as Bane took command. He held out his arm for silence and raised the mike to the mouthpiece of his mask.

"Gotham!" he exhorted. "Take control of your city—"

* * *

Feeling as if he'd been shaken but not stirred, Blake squeezed out of his overturned cruiser and crawled onto the shattered asphalt. Flames and smoke still belched up from below. Groaning, he took a moment to assess his physical condition. As nearly as he could tell, he was scraped and bruised all over, but nothing seemed to be broken.

He spit a mouthful of blood onto the charred pavement. His teeth stayed where they were, thank God.

Enough about me, he thought. *I need to know what's happening.*

He crawled back toward his vehicle and reached inside the crumpled cabin. Straining, he managed to snag onto the radio. As he did so, a burst of static hurt his ears.

"Foley?" he asked anxiously.

"Jesus, Blake!" Foley answered, sounding hoarse and understandably distraught. *"Every cop in the city's down in those tunnels."*

Except me, Blake thought, *and...*

"Not every cop."

Racing against time, he pried his shotgun from inside the cruiser. A battered-looking sedan was cautiously making its way down the broken street. Scrambling to his feet, Blake ran to flag it down.

Gordon's heart-rate monitor started beeping rapidly. He awoke with a start, jolted from sleep by some sort of commotion outside his room. He had been having a nightmare about Bane and that shoot-out in the sewers.

Groggy and confused, it took him a moment to realize that something very bad was happening—for real. Screams, shouts, and the occasional burst of gunfire came from downstairs, as if the hospital lobby was under attack by persons unknown. The commissioner was gripped by an unsettling case of *déjà vu*, remembering the time the Joker had attacked this very same hospital to get to Harvey Dent, then blown up an entire wing afterward.

He shoved the disturbing memory aside to focus on the here and now. He had a pretty good idea he knew who was behind this disturbance—and who they were coming for.

Footsteps pounded up the stairs. He heard the invaders moving from room to room. Terrified patients screamed and shouted for help. Nurses and orderlies ran and hid. Occasionally there was the sound of a gunshot. Gordon realized that it was only a matter of moments before they found him.

He needed to check out of the hospital, and pronto.

Clenching his teeth to keep from crying out, he painfully dragged himself from the bed. His stitched wounds hated every movement, but held together—at least for the time being. He wheeled his IV tree across the floor. The needle in his arm hurt every time he jostled it. His bare feet shuffled over the cold tiles.

This was *not* what the doctor ordered.

* * *

The streets were full of confused and frightened people. Blake swerved the commandeered sedan around the shell-shocked pedestrians while dodging random gouts of flame and smoke. Smoke and soot blackened the faces of the stunned survivors. Rubble and smoking craters made for a bumpy ride that jarred Blake's spine all the way across town.

Toppled street lights and broken pavement turned the streets into an obstacle course. It was like driving through a war zone, which was apparently what Gotham had become. News reports coming over the car's radio claimed that terrorists had killed the mayor and taken control of the football stadium. More than sixty thousand people were being held hostage, while most of the police were still trapped underground.

I can't worry about that now, Blake thought. He knew who Bane's next target would be. *If I'm not already too late.*

The sedan squealed to a halt in front of the hospital. Blake bolted from the vehicle and raced up the steps into the lobby, which was worryingly deserted. Bullet holes perforated the walls and ceiling. Broken glass was strewn over the floor. The gift shop and reception desk had been shot up.

He heard gunshots upstairs.

Crap, he thought. *They've found Gordon.*

Taking the stairs two steps at a time, he dashed up

to the commissioner's floor. He burst into the corridor, gun high, only to freeze as he felt a warm steel gun muzzle at the base of his skull. The heat of the metal told him that the gun had been recently fired.

He swallowed hard. For a second, he thought it was all over for him.

"Clear the corners, rookie," Gordon scolded him.

Blake turned to see Gordon, wearing a rumpled hospital gown, lower his trusty Smith & Wesson. Four dead mercs lay in the hallway. Fearful patients peeked around the doors that led to their rooms.

"Get my coat, son," Gordon said.

CHAPTER TWENTY-SEVEN

Gotham Stadium had become the hottest spot on the planet, at least as far as the Pentagon was concerned. More than three hundred personnel were crammed into the National Military Command Center in Washington, DC, popularly known as the "War Room."

Rows of state-of-the-art computer and communications stations faced a huge array of illuminated maps and screens. Live footage from Gotham Stadium dominated the central screen as teams of analysts and military staff members, along with the rest of the world, attempted to assess the ongoing—and unprecedented—situation.

Air Force General Matthew Armstrong, five stars gleaming on his epaulets, watched with concern as the terrorists rolled an ominous-looking device onto what remained of the playing field. The glowing metal sphere was mounted atop a wheeled trolley. Its design did not match any weapon of mass destruction with which he was familiar.

"This is the instrument of your liberation," Bane declared. CIA analysts had already identified the masked madman as the same terrorist who had staged the attack on the Gotham Stock Exchange last week. Apparently, that had just been his opening number.

"Satellite shows a radiation spike," an analyst reported. "Whatever it is, it's nuclear."

The tension in the room shot up another notch. All eyes remained glued to the monitors, where the terrorists dragged a bedraggled, middle-aged man onto the field and thrust him to his knees before Bane.

"Identify yourself to the world," the terrorist leader ordered.

"Dr. Leonid Pavel," the man said, his voice shaking. "Nuclear physicist—"

Bane turned the scientist's face toward the cameras, even as intelligence experts scrambled to verify the man's identity.

"Pavel is confirmed dead," a CIA analyst reported, calling up the data from a computer. "Plane crash on an agency pull out of Uzbekistan." She compared the man on the monitor to a photo from their database. "But it certainly looks like him—"

The general had to agree. He rubbed his chin, pondering the situation. This was getting more serious by the moment. He stared up at an illuminated screen tracking their response.

A squadron of F-22 fighter jets was already streaking toward Gotham.

On the TV monitors, Bane placed a hand on Pavel's shoulder. The kneeling scientist shuddered visibly.

"Tell the world what this is," Bane instructed.

"A fully primed neutron bomb. With a blast radius of six miles."

Bane nodded.

"And who can disarm this device?"

"Only me."

"Thank you, doctor."

With the whole world watching, Bane effortlessly snapped the scientist's neck. Pavel's body dropped onto the grass. Screams erupted from the bleachers. People gasped in the war room.

"The bomb is armed," Bane said, ignoring the screams. "The bomb is mobile, the identity of the triggerman is a mystery. One of *you* holds the detonator. We come not as conquerors, but as liberators to return control of this city to the people. At the first sign of interference from the outside world, or of people attempting to flee, this anonymous Gothamite—this unsung hero—will trigger the bomb.

"For now, martial law is in effect. Return to your homes, hold your families close, and wait." He threw out his arms. "Tomorrow you claim what is rightfully yours."

Bane turned and left the field. His men rolled the

bomb after him, leaving Dr. Pavel's body behind on the desecrated turf.

A hush fell over the war room.

"Pull back the fighters," the general said finally, breaking the silence. "Start high-level reconnaissance flights. And get the President on the line."

God help us all, he thought.

Gotham Bridge was the only one left standing. By sunset, tanks and troops were already advancing on the city. Captain Willis Parker, in charge of the operation, just wished he had a clearer sense of their mission strategy. How did one recapture a city being held hostage?

A squad of mercenaries held the bridge. There was no sign of Bane, but one of his men stepped forward, holding a bullhorn. An amplified voice challenged the approaching army.

"Tanks and planes cannot stop us from detonating our device," he warned. "Send an emissary to discuss terms of access for supplies and communication."

Captain Parker figured that was his cue. After a hasty conference with his superiors, he marched toward the apex of the bridge, his hands held open in front of him. Washington was anxious to hear the terrorists' demands, so he walked until he was within spitting distance of the enemy. The lead terrorist had the shaggy, undisciplined look of a professional mercenary—and the dead eyes of a stone-cold killer.

"How many of you are there, son?" the captain asked, receiving only a sullen glare in response. Staring the man squarely in the eye, he attempted to give the terrorists a much-needed reality check. "You don't have enough men to stop twelve million people leaving that island."

"No. We don't," the mercenary conceded. "But you do."

The captain snorted.

"Why in hell would we help you keep your hostages?"

"Because if people start crossing the bridge, Gotham gets blown to hell." He didn't sound like he was bluffing.

Confronted with such a ghastly scenario, Parker tried to think of a compelling counter-argument, but failed. It was hard to argue with an armed nuclear weapon.

The President of the United States addressed the nation:

"*The people of our greatest city are resilient,*" he said. "*They have proven this before, and they will prove this again.*"

Lying helplessly upon his cot, untold miles away from Gotham, Bruce watched the broadcast. All day and night, images of the burning city had seared themselves into his anguished brain. Aerial photos revealed a ring of fire circling his city. Experts and commentators soberly weighed its chances of survival.

Bane's nightmarish invasion of the football stadium had been replayed constantly, until Bruce knew every moment by heart. He had recognized the reactor core, of course, and knew just what it was capable of doing.

"*We do not negotiate with terrorists,*" the President continued, "*but we do recognize realities...*"

Tears streamed down Bruce's face.

The darkened streets were all but deserted, as Gotham's cowed citizens took seriously Bane's admonition to stay indoors. Blake warily drove toward home, while Gordon slumped beside him in the passenger seat. The detective tried to avoid the craters, cracks, and rubble, but Gordon still flinched at every bump. The rough drive had to be hard on his wounds.

They listened grimly to the President's speech.

"*As the situation develops, one thing must be understood above all others. People of Gotham, we have not abandoned you.*"

Blake scowled at the radio. "What does that mean?"

"It means we're on our own," Gordon translated. "I have to get in front of a camera—"

"Sir, they'll kill you the second you show your face."

"The mayor's dead," Gordon said. "I'm the symbol

of law and order. Bane says he's giving Gotham back to the people. They need to know that I could lead."

Blake frowned.

"Bane's never going to let that happen."

"Then he'll show his true colors."

Maybe, Blake thought. "And you'll be dead," he replied.

Gordon stared silently out the window.

CHAPTER TWENTY-EIGHT

Light poured through the barred window of Selina's private cell. She stretched out on her cot, enjoying the sunshine, until a rumbling noise interrupted her nap.

Annoyed, she rose and went to the window. Then her eyes widened at the sight of three tank-like vehicles, painted in desert camouflage, rolling toward the prison. She couldn't help noticing that the vehicles bore a distinct resemblance to the Batmobile once used by a certain legendary Dark Knight.

Those can't be his, she realized. *They aren't black, or sexy enough.*

Excited shouts roused the entire cell block. Blackgate had been under lockdown ever since the day before, when all those explosions had made it feel as if they were having an earthquake. The guards all appeared distinctly jumpy—and more than a little scared. She couldn't be sure, but it looked as if several of them hadn't even shown up for work today.

She wondered what was up.

As she watched from the barred window, a crowd gathered outside the prison walls. News crews were on hand as the tanks came to a halt in front of the gates. Curious citizens braved the streets to see what was happening. Her heart sank as Bane emerged from the lead tank, wearing a fur-lined winter coat with a raised collar.

Guilt mixed with fear as she recalled how the vicious mercenary had broken Batman, right before her eyes. She suddenly wished she had made it out of Gotham in time.

The French Riviera was sounding better and better.

Bane stood atop the tank, his coat open despite the cold. He turned to address the media. A hand-held microphone carried his sinister voice all the way up to her cell. A hush fell over the entire cell block as everyone stopped to listen. Prisoners and guards alike strained to hear his words.

"Behind you stands a symbol of oppression," Bane declared. "Blackgate Prison. Where a thousand men have languished for years. Under the Dent Act. Under the name of this man."

He held up a photo of a handsome blond hero.

"Harvey Dent. Held up to you—and *over* you—as a shining example of justice and good."

* * *

Blake's bachelor apartment was small and spartan. He had never expected to entertain the police commissioner there, but life was full of surprises these days.

He rummaged through the kitchen cupboards, foraging for supplies, while Gordon rested on a lumpy couch Blake had once rescued from a crack house. Borrowed clothes had replaced Gordon's hospital gown. They fit, sort of.

"We're gonna keep moving you," Blake said, "till we can get you in front of a camera."

Gordon stared gravely at the TV set, where Bane could be seen delivering a speech in front of Blackgate Prison. The masked maniac set fire to Harvey Dent's photo. His voice boomed from the television.

"*But they supplied you a false idol,*" the lunatic said. "*A straw man to placate you. To stop you from tearing down this corrupt city...*"

Hardened criminals peered through the barred windows of the prison. They started cheering raucously in the background.

"*...and rebuilding it the way it should have been rebuilt, generations ago.*" Bane dropped the burning picture. The ashes fell to the pavement in front of his tank.

"*Let me tell you the truth about Harvey Dent. In the words of Gotham's police commissioner, James Gordon.*"

Blake turned away from the cupboards, wondering

what exactly Bane was trying to pull here. Gordon shifted uneasily upon the couch. Onscreen, the mercenary leader unfolded a sheath of crumpled papers. He began to read aloud.

"'*The truth about Harvey Dent is simple in only one regard—it has been hidden for too long. After his devastating injuries, Harvey's mind recovered no better than his mutilated face. He was a broken, dangerous man, not the crusader for justice that I, James Gordon, have portrayed him to be for the last eight years. Harvey's rage was indiscriminate. Psychopathic.*

"'*He held my family at gunpoint, then fell to his death in the struggle over my son's life. The Batman did not murder Harvey Dent—he saved my boy.*'"

Blake stared aghast at the screen. He couldn't believe what he was hearing.

"'*Then Batman took the blame for Harvey's appalling crimes, so that I could, to my shame, build a lie around this fallen idol.*'"

Gordon lowered his face to his hands.

"'*I praised the madman who tried to murder my own child.*'"

The crowd fell silent, stunned by what they were hearing, as Bane continued reading.

"'*The things we did in Harvey's name brought desperately needed security to our streets. But I can no longer live with my lie. It is time to trust the people of Gotham with the truth, and it is time for me to resign.*'"

Bane folded the papers and put them away. He

gazed out over the speechless crowd, which included reporters and neighborhood toughs. Guards and inmates watched intently from inside Blackgate's forbidding stone walls and towers.

Bane called out to the mob.

"*Do you accept this man's resignation?*"

At first no one responded, but then a few angry faces in the back started shouting.

"*Yes!*"

More voices took up the cry. Inside Blackgate, the prisoners started cheering even more boisterously than before. They whooped and pounded against the bars of their cells. A TV camera zoomed in briefly on an attractive female face in one of the windows. Her guarded expression offered little clue as to what she thought of all this.

"*Do you accept the resignation of all the liars?*" Bane demanded. "*All the corrupt?*"

"*Yes!*" A chorus of voices, both inside and outside the prison, gave Bane their answer. "*YES!*"

Blake looked away from the TV in disgust. He stared accusingly at Gordon, who sat mutely on the couch. His guilty expression was all the evidence the detective needed. His own face hardened.

"Those men, locked up in Blackgate for eight years, *denied parole* under the Dent Act," he said flatly. "Suspects held indefinitely without trial. Based on a lie."

"A lie to keep a city on fire from burning to the

ground." Gordon looked up at him. He sounded like he was trying to convince himself. "Gotham needed a hero, someone to believe in—"

"Not as much as it does now," Blake said harshly. "But you betrayed everything you stood for."

Gordon gave the younger man a rueful look.

"There's a point, far out there, when the structures fail you. When the rules aren't weapons any more, they're shackles, letting the bad get ahead." His voice was both sad and tired. "Maybe one day you'll have such a moment of crisis. And in that moment, I hope you have a friend like I did. To plunge their hands into the filth so you can keep yours clean."

Disillusioned, Blake was in no mood to grant Gordon absolution.

"Your hands look plenty filthy to me, commissioner."

He went back to packing.

The cell block was in an uproar. Nervous guards looked on apprehensively, clutching their weapons with sweaty palms as Selina's fellow prisoners reacted loudly to all the excitement outside. A few of the more cowardly turnkeys abandoned their posts, slipping away while they still could. She couldn't blame them. Judging from some of the rumors she'd heard, Bane had no great love for prisons—or their guards.

Standing atop his tank, Bane signaled to one of the other armored vehicles. A formidable-looking gun turret swiveled toward the prison gates. Selina could see where this was going—and she wasn't sure what she thought about it.

If Bane was in charge of Gotham now, she might be safer in her cell.

"We take Gotham from the corrupt," Bane ranted, shouting over the clamor of the mob. "The rich. The oppressors of generations who've kept you down with the myth of opportunity. And we give the city to you, the people. Gotham is yours—none shall interfere.

"Do as you please!"

Hellfire blasted from the cannon, blowing the heavy iron gates to pieces. Twisted metal fragments clattered down onto the sidewalk, leaving an open, smoldering cavity in the walls of the prison.

"But start by storming Blackgate and freeing the oppressed," he continued. "Step forward, those who would serve…"

Bane's men rushed the prison, surging through the burning gates. The mob chased after them, eagerly joining in the revolt. Pounding boots trampled over the blackened remains of Harvey Dent's photo. Alarms sounded, but the outnumbered guards offered little resistance.

The cell doors slid open and the prisoners poured out, trashing the place on their way out. Unlucky guards—the ones who hadn't fled or hidden in time—found themselves on the receiving end of eight years of pent-up grudges. It wasn't a good day to be wearing a uniform or a badge.

Taking advantage of the chaos, Selina quietly slipped away through the throng.

CHAPTER TWENTY-NINE

In the hours and days that followed, Bane's fiery oration was played constantly over the airwaves, as all that he prophesized came to pass.

"For an army will be raised..."

Mercenaries had handed out weapons to the prisoners escaping Blackgate. Shots were fired into the air in celebration, as the criminals rampaged through Gotham, encountering no resistance. Other men and women, eager to join in the looting, poured into the streets as well, swelling the ranks of the ad hoc army. They found the city ripe for the taking.

Looters invaded a tree-lined boulevard across from the park. What had once been one of Gotham's tonier neighborhoods was overrun by a lawless horde that stormed the luxury apartment buildings. Gun-wielding rioters shot off the locks or battered down the doors. Hopelessly outnumbered, cowed doormen and security guards either retreated from the mob or else joined the insurrection. Mercenaries, convicts, gang members, vandals, anarchists, and opportunists whooped uproariously as they helped themselves to the homes of the rich and famous.

"The powerful will be ripped from their decadent nests..."

On Park Boulevard, looters ransacked a palatial penthouse apartment. High-end televisions, computers, and other pricy electronics were seized and fought over before being hauled out the door. Drawers were yanked out and dumped onto the floor, the better to rifle through their contents. Antique desks and chairs were overturned, priceless vases and paintings trashed.

The one-time owners of the apartment, an investment banker and his much younger trophy wife, cowered in a corner as the rioters rooted through their closets, tossing designer dresses and tailored suits onto the floor. Thirstier looters raided the well-stocked liquor cabinet, passing around rare vintages of wine and bottles of fifty-year-old Scotch and bourbon. Empty bottles shattered against the walls. Costly spirits spilled onto an imported Persian carpet. Cuban cigars were smoked with abandon.

* * *

"*And cast into the cold world the rest of us have known and endured...*"

At first, the terrified apartment owners thought that they themselves might be spared, that the rioters were only after their possessions. But then men with guns descended upon them and herded them roughly out into the street, where they were rounded up along with the rest of their scared and affluent neighbors. Despite the cold fall weather, and not even given a chance to dress for the outdoors, they were marched at gunpoint away from their former homes.

Raucous laughter followed them down the block. Thrown rocks and garbage pelted them. An empty bottle hit the banker in the face.

"*Courts will be convened...*"

The stock exchange, site of Bane's first assault upon Gotham's wheelers and dealers, was converted into a mock courthouse attended by crowds of jeering spectators. An escaped convict who had traded his orange prison jumpsuit for an ill-fitting black robe presided over the trial of the banker and his wife. They found themselves accused of high crimes and treason against the people of Gotham. They clung to each other, shivering in the dock, as Jonathan Crane, a convicted killer who had once terrorized the city, pronounced sentence on them.

He pounded his gavel upon the trading floor's

elevated bell podium.

The mob roared in approval.

Bane watched silently from an upper gallery.

"The spoils will be enjoyed…"

A once-exclusive apartment became Party Central. Dozens of squatters occupied the penthouse, helping themselves to whatever the first wave of looters had left behind. Winos, addicts, prostitutes, and homeless runaways cracked opened bottles of champagne, spraying one another with the foam while trampling over broken furniture and heirlooms. Hookers and crackheads put on an impromptu fashion show, modeling liberated furs and jewelry. A drunk peed in a corner.

Selina kept to herself, frowning as she watched the revelry.

"Blood will be shed..."

Officer Ross peered up at the daylight, high above his head. The light penetrated a narrow storm drain partially clogged with shattered concrete. A basket full of supplies was lowered into the ruins of the tunnels, where he and hundreds of other cops found themselves buried alive.

At first, he had expected the city to launch a full-scale rescue, employing heavy machinery and teams of workers to dig their way down to the trapped personnel, but apparently that wasn't happening anytime soon. They remained stuck in the sewers.

He remained stuck in the sewers. Away from his wife and daughter.

Ross grabbed onto the basket, which contained stale bread, moldy fruit, and dented cans of lunch meat. His stomach growling, he handed them out to the other officers, hoping it would be enough, but knowing that it wasn't.

He shivered, trying to remember what it was like to be warm.

"But the police will live, until they are ready to serve true justice..."

The reactor core glowed brightly, and lit gauges crept toward the red zone, as the large metal sphere was loaded into the back of an unmarked black truck. Mercenaries made sure the bomb was secured within the vehicle.

"This great city will endure. Gotham will survive."

Inside the truck, a digital counter ticked toward zero.

Bruce couldn't bear to watch the news coverage any longer. Gritting his teeth against the pain, he rocked back and forth on his cot—until he rolled over the edge and landed on the hard stone floor. A harsh grunt escaped his lips as he placed his palms against the grimy floor and pressed against it.

His caretaker stared at him in confusion, as if fearing that his charge had fallen by accident. Not until Bruce managed to lift his face a few inches from the ground did it become obvious that—insanely—he was trying to do a pushup.

Just one rep, Bruce ordered himself. *You can do it!*

His screaming spine thought otherwise.

The blind man barked next door. Sightless eyes turned toward Bruce as the man strained his ears to hear the exertions. Despite his handicap, he seemed to grasp what was happening.

"He says you must first straighten your back," the European translated. He helped Bruce roll over onto his back. Every motion sent a bolt of searing pain up his spinal column. The rough stone floor felt like a bed of nails.

"How would he know?" Bruce asked.

"He was the prison doctor," the other prisoner revealed. "A morphine addict who incurred the displeasure of powerful people. Including your masked friend."

"How?"

The prisoner sighed, perhaps realizing that Bruce would only keep asking. Or maybe he simply hoped to distract Bruce with a story. In any event, the European spoke softly, his voice hushed and doleful.

"Many years ago, during a time of plague, Bane

was attacked by the other prisoners. The doctor's fumbling attempts to repair the damage left him in perpetual agony. The mask delivers a gas that holds his pain at bay."

Good to know, Bruce thought. "Is Bane the child you spoke of? Was he born here?"

The prisoner nodded.

"The legend is that there was a mercenary working for the local warlord, who fell in love with his daughter. They married in secret." He retrieved a rope from the hall and tied it under Bruce's arms. "When the warlord found out, he condemned the mercenary to this pit. But then exiled him instead, dropping him at the side of a barren road.

"The mercenary understood that the warlord's daughter had secured his release, but he couldn't know the true price of his freedom. She had taken his place in the pit."

Bruce shuddered at the thought of a woman in this awful place. So far all the prisoners he'd seen had been men. There did not appear to be any guards. Apparently, they weren't needed. The prisoners had been left to police themselves.

"And she was with child," the European continued. "The mercenary's child." He gestured toward the blind man in his cell. "The doctor delivered the child, back when his eyes were still young and could see the light. But one day, years later, he forgot to lock the cell behind him."

* * *

Years ago:

A Madonna in hell, the mother wore a native shawl over her slender shoulders. She backed against an unyielding stone wall as a crew of lustful prisoners, seizing the opportunity, barged into her cell. Muslin masks concealed the men's faces.

She reached for the child, wanting to protect her offspring.

But instead the child charged at the invaders, knife in hand. The blade slashed at the men, drawing blood...

"Innocence cannot flower underground," the European said. "It was to be stamped out. But the child had a friend. A protector."

A sinewy figure, his face also veiled by muslin, came to the child's rescue. Threadbare garments hung on his frame. Deflecting a knife blow with his arm, he pulled the furious child away from the invaders. A snarling inmate, his face sporting a bloody gash, grabbed for the child, but the protector intercepted the man's arm and, with a deft move, broke it at the elbow.

Bone snapped loudly. The man dropped to his knees, clutching his arm in agony.

The other prisoners lunged at the woman. Making a brutal choice, the masked man held onto the frantic child and dragged the youngster into the shadows, away from the attackers, who fell upon the woman like a pack of ravening wolves.

Her screams finally trailed off into silence.

"The child's guardian showed the others that this innocence was their redemption. To be prized." The European shook his head mournfully. "The mother was not so lucky."

The blind doctor shouted from his cell. Bruce's caretaker nodded in understanding.

"This is Bane's prison now," he said. "Bane would not want his story told."

He knotted the rope securely beneath Bruce's arms, and then hurled the end over the open door of the cell, running around to take hold of it. Tugging on the rope, he pulled Bruce upright against the bard.

Bruce screamed as if he was being tortured upon the rack.

Which—in a sense—he was.

The pain was like nothing he had ever known. Worse than the time the Scarecrow had set him on fire, or when the Joker had stabbed him in the side. Worse than the time he had hauled Ducard up over the edge of that cliff with just one arm.

He convulsed in torment, praying to pass out. He wasn't sure how much longer he could endure it, even after everything he had already been through. Oblivion would have been a mercy.

But there was no such luck.

The European tied the rope to the metals bars of the door. His fingers explored Bruce's spine, which only increased the torture. Razor-sharp spasms of pain rocketed up and down his brutalized body. He bit down on his lip as his caretaker located the source of the pain.

Bruce tasted blood.

"You have a protruding vertebra," the man said. "I'm going to force it back."

"How?" he asked, and he braced himself.

Without warning, the man punched him in the back, hard enough to rattle the door's rusty hinges. Bruce howled like a damned soul, suffering the most excruciating torment of hell, before finally sagging against the iron bars. Only the unforgiving rope, digging into his armpits, kept him from collapsing onto the floor. He hung limply.

"You stay like this," the other prisoner said. "Until you stand."

Bruce finally lost consciousness from the pain.

CHAPTER THIRTY

Days and nights blurred together as Bruce hung within the cell, drifting in and out of delirium. Noises came and went from the pit outside. The tantalizing light of hope retreated and returned, over and over again. Only the pain in his back was constant, giving him no relief.

The ghosts of his past tormented him.

"Did you not think I'd return, Bruce?"

He looked up to see Rā's al Ghūl standing before him. His long-dead mentor appeared just as he had the last time Bruce had seen him. He was a tall, bearded man wearing a stern expression and a severe black suit. Bruce had originally known him as "Henri Ducard," and had only later realized that Ducard was merely a convenient alias for the true master of the League of Shadows.

Icy blue eyes regarded Bruce with wry amusement.

"I told you I was immortal," he said.

No, this is impossible, Bruce thought. He vividly recalled a speeding monorail crashing to the street in a fiery explosion. "I watched you die," he gritted.

Rā's did not deny it.

"There are many forms of immortality."

A memory surfaced from the past, of the two of them sitting before a campfire beside a frozen lake. The older man had spoken tersely of his own tragic history.

"*Once I had a wife*," *he said.* "*My great love. She was taken from me.*"

The tapestry came together in Bruce's mind. Returning to the present, he stared at Rā's.

"You were the mercenary," he said. "Bane is your child. Your heir."

Rā's nodded.

"An heir to ensure that the League of Shadows fulfills its duty to restore balance to civilization."

Bruce knew what that meant.

"No…" But Rā's continued.

"You yourself fought the decadence of Gotham for years—with all your strength and resources, all your moral authority. And the only victory you could achieve was a lie. Finally, you understand. Gotham is beyond saving."

"No!" Bruce shouted. He strained against the rope holding him up. The pain in his back was nothing compared to the agony of knowing that his city was in peril—and there was nothing he could do about it.

Rā's passed sentence on Gotham, as he had so many years before.

"It must be allowed to die."

Winter came to Gotham.

Snow blanketed the deserted street as a tumbler patrolled the city, its thick tires carving deep tracks in the soggy white accumulation. Pools of dirty brown slush drowned the street corners. Icicles hung like stalactites from eaves and cornices. A bone-chilling wind howled through the concrete canyons. Feeble sunlight fought a losing battle against the cold.

Shivering, Blake crouched behind a parked SUV, holding his breath until the combat vehicle rounded the corner. Melting slush trickled down a storm drain. Blake hoped Ross and the other entombed cops were collecting the icy water. Nearly three months had passed since Bane had sprung his trap, and the buried officers had been living on scraps and captured vermin ever since. It was a wonder that the buried officers hadn't yet completely given up hope.

Hang in there, buddies, he thought.

He fed a kite string down through the grate until he felt a tug on the other end. *Ross*, he assumed, although his former partner was too far down to see. He could only imagine what it was like for the poor cops trapped in the underground all this time, away from their families and loved ones.

Three months in the dark.

Three months stuck in a hole while Bane and his followers ran roughshod over Gotham.

It must be getting damn cold down there.

Blake pulled up the string, and there was nothing there. The note he'd attached to it had been removed. It was a crude way to stay in contact, but it was something. At least Ross and the others knew they hadn't been forgotten.

If only there was something more we could do for them, he thought. *Someday.*

A breeze kicked up, and the biting air stung his face. His breath frosted in front of his lips. It was time to get out of the cold.

A red plastic gas container sat on the sidewalk beside him. He picked it up and hurried away, promising himself that he would deliver another message soon. He made a mental note to check in on Ross's family again—they were having a hard time of it, too.

Avoiding the major boulevards, he stuck to back alleys and secondary streets as he cautiously made his way across town. Even though it was broad daylight, the streets and sidewalks were largely deserted. Law-abiding folks were huddled in their homes, trying to ride out the occupation.

Bane's "army" of mercenaries and miscreants appeared to be staying indoors, as well. Blake found himself grateful for the harsh winter weather, which reduced the odds of running into any roving bands of troublemakers. He just needed to keep an eye out for the more dedicated enforcers. Otherwise, he'd end up on trial just for being a cop.

The subway would have been faster, but all lines had been shut down by the cave-ins. The monorail and buses had stopped running, too. Taxis were as scarce as law-abiding citizens—driving a cab was like asking to be carjacked. All of the schools, libraries, and post offices had been closed for months. Most had already been looted. Heaven help you if you needed a doctor or dentist.

The temperature continued to drop. By the time he made it to St. Swithin's, he could barely feel his toes anymore. His cheeks felt red and raw. He stamped the snow off his boots before slipping into the building via a back door. He locked it carefully behind him.

No longer just a home for orphans, the shelter was packed with homeless refugees, either driven from their homes or hiding from Gotham's new masters. Men, women, and children huddled in every corner, camping out even in the halls and stairwells. Many still had the shell-shocked look of disaster victims.

Blake spotted Father Reilly consoling a weeping family in the lobby. He took the priest aside and handed him the gasoline can.

"For the bus," he said, "in case there's a chance to evacuate. Keep it in here. People are siphoning parked cars."

The priest looked grateful, but exhausted.

"Really?"

Blake smirked.

"How do you think I got it?"

"Right." Reilly didn't scold Blake for the theft. They both knew that these were desperate times for the good people of Gotham. The elderly priest had more important issues on his mind. "Any news? Is the commissioner—?"

Blake cut him off.

"Less you know, Father." He glanced around to make sure no one had been listening. "How're the boys?"

"Power's been on more, so they get some TV."

Blake was glad to hear it. That probably made Reilly's job a little easier. He took a moment to warm up a bit, toasting his hands over a rusty radiator, before heading back toward the exit. He had another long, frigid hike in front of him.

The priest stopped him before he reached the door.

"Blake, be careful out there," Reilly warned. "They're hunting down cops like dogs."

Tell me about it, Blake thought.

He went back out into the cold.

* * *

Selina prowled through the trashed apartment, which looked more like a crack house than a penthouse. Empty bottles, cigarette butts, pizza crusts, discarded tins of caviar, and other garbage were strewn upon the hardwood floors, attracting mice and cockroaches. Hungover partygoers slept it off on the sofas, in comfy chairs, and on carpets. Someone vomited loudly in the master bathroom.

At least he made it to the toilet, she thought. *This time.*

She was half-tempted to go back to her cramped digs in Old Town, but, no, that was the first place Bane would come looking for her—if she was still on his hit list. Chances were that she was safe, now that Bane no longer needed to tidy up any loose ends. Still, there was no point in pushing her luck. Better to keep her head down and blend in with the other strays.

Besides, she reminded herself, *I always wanted a Park Boulevard address.*

A glint of broken glass caught her eye. She bent to pick up a shattered picture frame. A torn photo showed a happy family smiling for the camera. Selina wondered what had become of them.

A hand fell on her shoulder.

"What's that?" Jen asked.

A sparkly Versace gown—one size too large—hung on her petite frame. Tasteful jewelry glittered on her neck and fingers. Selina was surprised that nobody had taken the bling from her yet. Maybe it was because people knew the girl was under Selina's protection.

That would be helpful.

She had traded her own orange prison togs for a practical black sweater and slacks. The look had attracted a few squatters, but their new roommates had quickly learned not to mess with her.

Selina contemplated the photo.

"This was someone's home," she said. But Jen just shrugged.

"Now it's everyone's home."

A tumbler rolled by outside. Selina peered out the window at it. She frowned at what Gotham had become.

"'Storm's coming,' remember?" Jen said, looking confused at her friend's somber mood. She toyed with the jewels around her neck. "This is what you wanted."

"No," Selina realized. "It's what I thought I wanted."

CHAPTER THIRTY-ONE

The European cautiously untied the rope, ready to catch Bruce if he fell.

The delirium had passed, taking the ghosts with it, and Bruce could think clearly again. But that wasn't enough. He had to know if he was still broken.

Bracing himself for the pain, he took a deep breath and placed his weight upon his bare feet.

A wave of dizziness assailed him, and he tottered slightly, but the light-headedness was only momentary and he steadied himself. His legs felt weak and rubbery from disuse, but at least he was standing on his own power again. His bad knee still bothered him, but he wasn't going to let that stop him.

"That's enough for today," his caretaker said anxiously. He came forward to offer assistance. "You should rest."

Bruce shook his head. He had rested enough already. Gotham needed him.

He took a step forward.

And another.

Days passed as Bruce rebuilt his body. His caretaker watched in wonder as Bruce did pushups against the floor of his cell, working until sweat dripped from his pale, unshaven face. Breathing hard, he pushed himself to his limits—and beyond. His back still ached, but it was bearable now, and getting better over time. Or so he wanted to think.

He paused for a moment before trying for another fifty reps.

The European sat on a bench a few feet away. He watched Bruce with a puzzled expression. "Why build yourself?"

Bruce pushed himself up off the floor again.

"I'm not meant to die here."

The decrepit television set played in the background. A caption running beneath the latest news coverage read, "*SIEGE OF GOTHAM: DAY 84.*"

"Here? There?" The older prisoner indicated the TV screen. "What's the difference?"

Bruce ignored the man's fatalistic attitude. That was the pit talking. He couldn't afford to let his spirit weaken, even for a moment. He had work to do.

So he pushed himself ever harder.

One…two…three…

Finally, it was time to climb for the sun.

Bruce emerged from his cell and walked out to the base of the colossal shaft that led to the surface. Glancing down, he saw that a large pool of stagnant green water waited at the bottom of the pit. Greasy scum floated on top of the pool. Inmates waded through the water, which did not appear nearly deep enough to cushion a fall, at least not from a great height.

He lifted his gaze. He intended to go up, not down.

The tattooed prisoner wrapped the safety rope around Bruce's chest, as he had for that other climber, months earlier. A crowd of curious prisoners gathered to watch, the European among them. Money changed hands as the inmates wagered on how high Bruce might get. He stared up at the distant sunlight, hundreds of feet above his head. Then he approached the wall.

If Bane can do it, so can I.

He found the first handhold and began his ascent. Rock-climbing was nothing new to him, although he found himself wishing for high-quality crampons or even the sturdy bronze spikes on Batman's gauntlets. He climbed slowly, conserving his strength for the more arduous challenges he would encounter further up. Excited voices rose from below as the crowd observed his progress.

The chanting began anew.

I wonder how the betting is going.

The climb grew steadily more difficult as the bulges became less frequent and the gaps between the crumbling ledges grew wider. A throbbing pain pulsed along his spine, but Bruce pushed it aside. Pain he could deal with. All that mattered was getting out of this pit—and back to Gotham.

At last, he came to the precipice that had defeated the strong man. He stood on the brink of the ledge, gazing up at the next stone shelf, which was at least twelve feet away. Back in Gotham, he would have used his gas-powered grappling gun, but that was hardly an option here. He would have to make the jump the old-fashioned way, the way Bane had.

The chanting of the prisoners urged him on. He paused to make sure the safety rope was secure before backing up as far as he could in order to get some semblance of a running start. His bad knee felt like it was on fire, but he willed himself to ignore it.

He took a deep breath.

Here goes nothing.

He leapt for the upper ledge, stretching out his arms as far as they could reach. He arced upward, wishing for actual batwings that could carry him up and away from the pit. His outstretched fingers brushed against the rugged stone edge of the ledge...

Then slipped away.

Gravity seized him and he plunged toward the shallow pool below. He fell at least a hundred feet, accelerating every second, before the rope brutally broke his fall, jolting his already aching spine.

A scream died behind gritted teeth. He swung into the hard stone wall, barely turning his face away in time. The bone-jarring impact knocked the breath from his body. His ribs felt as if they'd been hit with a hammer.

The chanting fell away and the crowd dispersed now that the day's entertainment was over. Only a handful of inmates watched as the tattooed man gradually lowered his dangling body back down into the pit. Bruce collapsed onto a steel gantry.

The European sighed, unsurprised by the outcome of the climb. The blind doctor listened attentively, then turned away.

"I told you it could not be done," the European said. He helped Bruce to his feet.

Bruce winced with every step, and his ribs felt freshly bruised.

"You told me a child did it."

"No ordinary child."

Older now, the child approached the climbing wall even as the protector fought off the other prisoners— those who sought to halt the climb. Did the crazed inmates wish to prevent the child from escaping, or did they simply want to keep the youngster from dying in a foolhardy bid for freedom? The child didn't care. All

*that mattered was seeing what lay beyond the pit—
and wreaking his vengeance on the rest of the world.*

*Scrambling up the sides of the shaft, the child
reached the fatal precipice that had killed the hopes
of so many other climbers. Determined eyes glanced
down at the protector, who was losing ground against
the horde of maddened prisoners. They were swarming
over him. Knives drawn, they fell upon the protector
just as an equally bloodthirsty mob had attacked the
child's mother, years before.*

*For an instant, the child was tempted to turn back
and fight beside the outnumbered champion.*

*The child stared down at the masked warrior. Their
eyes made contact.*

Go, the man ordered silently. Now.

*The child jumped over the abyss. Desperate hands
grabbed onto solid rock. A small body swung up onto
the ledge.*

"A child born in hell," the white-haired prisoner said.
"A child forged by suffering. Hardened by pain."

He shook his head sadly at Bruce.

"Not a child of privilege."

Defeated, Bruce staggered back to his cell.

CHAPTER THIRTY-TWO

Supply trucks approached the checkpoint on the bridge. Armed mercenaries inspected the trailer of an idling eighteen-wheeler, finding only crates of emergency rations. A guard helped himself to an energy bar before giving the driver the go-ahead.

The truck drove through the snow-covered streets, which were badly in need of plowing, until it pulled up in front of a dimly lit supermarket. A long line of Gothamites—stretching all the way down the block—waited miserably along the sidewalk, braving the frigid winter weather for a chance to replenish their dwindling stores. Hungry children cried impatiently.

Inside the truck, hidden from view, the lid of a crate opened just a crack. Captain Mark Jones, US Special Forces, peered out to make sure all was clear. Finding the trailer compartment free of hostiles, he climbed out from beneath several bags of rice and rapped the sides of four other crates.

A quartet of Special Forces operatives, wearing nondescript civilian clothing, emerged from the boxes and checked their automatic weapons before concealing them once again.

We made it, Jones thought. *We're in Gotham.*

"Now for the hard part," he muttered aloud.

The back door of the truck rattled open and he and his men began to unload the supplies. A nervous-looking store manager met them at the door and guided them into the back of the store, then down a flight of stairs into a storeroom in the basement. There they were greeted by four plain-clothes cops.

"You have ID?" Deputy Commissioner Foley asked.

Jones recognized Foley from his briefing.

"Of course not."

Foley eyed the newcomers warily.

"How can we trust you?"

"We don't have any choice," James Gordon said. He and a younger man stepped out of the shadows at the rear of the room. They wore heavy coats to protect them against the chill of the basement. Both were carrying.

"Commissioner Gordon?" Jones was glad to see the wounded man up and about. There had been conflicting reports about his status. He held out his hand. "Captain Jones. Special Forces."

"Captain," Gordon replied. "Glad to have you here."

Jones glanced around the storeroom, anxious to assess the situation.

"How many of you are there?"

"Dozens," Gordon said cautiously. "I'd rather not say exactly. But the men trapped underground number almost three thousand."

Jones whistled softly. That matched with what he had heard.

"What kind of shape are they in?"

"They've been getting water, food," Gordon said.

"Could we break them out?"

"Yes, sir." The younger cop stepped forward. "Take out the mercenaries guarding the outflow pipe south of Ackerman Park, blow the rubble, you've got a hole big enough for ten at a time. I'm in contact with my partner—they're waiting for the day."

Jones was skeptical, but it was one of his men who voiced it.

"Men who haven't seen daylight for three months," the man said.

"Men with *automatic weapons*," the young cop stressed, "who haven't seen daylight for three months."

Good point, Jones acknowledged silently. *That has to count for something.*

"What about the bomb?" he asked. "The satellite can't see any radiation hot spots."

"They keep it on a truck," Gordon reported. "It must have a lead-lined roof. They move it constantly."

Jones nodded. The brass had suspected as much.

"But you know the truck?"

"They've got three of them," Gordon said. "The routes don't vary much."

A *shell game*, Jones realized.

"What about the trigger man?"

"No leads," Gordon said. He paused, then offered his own theory. "It's a bluff. Bane wouldn't give control of that bomb to someone else."

"We can't take that chance," Jones said. "Until we have the triggerman, we just track the device, smuggle men over—"

That clearly wasn't enough for the young cop, who spoke up.

"Meanwhile Gotham lives under a warlord," he said irritably, "like in some failed state."

"Dial it back, officer." Jones sympathized with the man's frustration, especially after nearly three months, but they needed to keep cool heads where that nuke was concerned. "This situation is unprecedented. We can't do anything that might risk millions of lives."

The young hothead turned to his boss.

"Aren't you going to tell him?"

"Captain," Gordon began, "things are more complicated than you think. There's somebody you need to meet." He addressed the young cop by name. "Blake?"

Blake nodded and gestured for Jones and his men to follow him. Puzzled, Jones trailed Blake back upstairs. Weapons in hand, they departed the supermarket via a rear exit and stealthily made their way down a series of back alleys and side streets.

Jones let Blake take point. They were on his turf now.

What's this all about? he wondered.

Several blocks later, they crept through the back door of what turned out to be an empty bank. The teller booths were deserted. The vault and safety deposit boxes had already been looted. Their footsteps echoed throughout the lifeless building as they crossed the lobby and rode the elevator to the top floor offices—which proved to be home to several displaced refugees.

Sleeping bags and makeshift cots lined the carpeted corridor. Homeless people camped out in the hall and offices. Trash cans were overflowing with empty food containers and wrappers.

"I was up here looking for a vantage point," Blake explained tersely. "Found the people who run the corporation that owns it living here."

Jones regarded the huddled survivors.

"Which corporation?"

"Wayne Enterprises," a distinguished-looking black man answered. He came forward to meet them, accompanied by an attractive brunette several years his junior. His collar was unbuttoned and his sleeves were rolled up. She wore a belted plum tunic and black leggings.

"Captain, meet Mr. Fox," Blake said. "Mr. Fox, I'd

like you to brief the captain."

"Hold on," Jones said. He cast a pointed look in the woman's direction.

"Miss Tate is fully aware of the situation," Fox assured him.

"And as CEO of Wayne Enterprises," she said, "I have to take responsibility for it."

Jones gave her a closer look.

"Why?" he asked.

"Because, captain, we built it."

"You built the bomb?" He didn't understand. This hadn't been in his briefing.

"It was built as a fusion reactor," Fox said, keeping his voice low. "The first of its kind. Bane turned the core into a bomb, then disconnected it from the reactor."

"And here's the important part," Blake prompted.

"As the device's fuel cells decay," Fox said, "it's becoming increasingly unstable, until the point of detonation."

Blake spelled it out.

"The bomb's a *time bomb*."

"And it *will* go off," Fox stated gravely. "In twenty-three days."

Jones couldn't believe his ears. An already hellish situation had just gotten infinitely worse. He reeled at the news.

"Bane's revolution's a sham," Blake explained. "He's watching Gotham rearrange its deck chairs while the whole ship's going down. Your appeasement plan might not be as practical as you thought."

Jones scowled at Blake. The young cop was right, but that didn't mean he had to like it. He looked again at Fox.

"Could you disarm it?" he asked.

"I don't know," Fox said. "But I could reconnect it to the reactor. Stabilize it."

That was something, at least. Jones considered his next move, adapting to this distressing new intel.

"We have to let the Pentagon know."

"They'll be monitoring our frequencies," one of his men cautioned.

"We have no choice," Jones said. Washington had to know that there was a ticking clock in this scenario. "Let's move away from this location, then call it in."

Blake didn't disagree. Taking leave of Fox and Miss Tate, he escorted Jones and his men back to the elevator. Jones wanted to put at least four or five blocks between them and the bank before he broke radio silence. He waited impatiently for the elevator to reach the ground floor. All of a sudden, every moment counted.

A chime sounded. The elevator door slid open and Jones led his team out into the vacant lobby. They were halfway across the floor when all hell broke loose.

Mercenaries sprang up from behind desks and counters, wielding machine guns, opening fire on the ambushed soldiers. Bullets tore apart the lobby's ornate walls and furnishings. Caught in a crossfire, the soldiers cried out and jerked like malfunctioning marionettes before dropping to the floor. Blood spilled across the polished tiles.

Dammit! Jones thought. *How'd they find us already?*

He swung his assault rifle toward their attackers, but the enemy already had the drop on them. Hot lead tore through his meat and bones. Pain exploded like miniature neutron bombs all over his body.

Crap!

Blake dived back into the elevator. Bullets blew through the door as it slid shut behind him, and he flattened himself against the wall. He waited a second to see if any of Jones's men had survived the ambush long enough to join him, then he hit the button for the top floor.

Gunfire, and the cries of dying soldiers, rang out from below.

Sorry, captain, Blake thought. *I wish your mission had ended differently. You and your men deserved better than this.* But he couldn't worry about the murdered soldiers now. Fox and the others were still in danger. They needed to get out of there, pronto!

The elevator hit the top floor. Blake rushed out into the corridor.

"Fox!" he hollered. "Somebody sold us out!"

* * *

Fox and Miranda were already in the hall, trying to herd everyone toward the fire exits. They had all heard the gunfire downstairs. Terrified refugees screamed and shouted. Pandemonium spread through the corridors and offices.

"Take Miranda," Fox urged Blake, putting her safety first. Blake grabbed the woman by the wrist and hurried toward the back stairs, even as the elevators chimed once more.

Mercenaries burst out, firing high. Overhead lights exploded. Sparks and broken glass rained down on the crowded hallway. More screams came from the cornered refugees. People scurried into the nearest offices or threw themselves flat.

Blake dragged Miranda down the stairs.

"Down on the floor!" a gunman shouted.

Fox froze in place. Realizing there was no escape, he raised his hands above his head and lowered himself to the floor.

Jones lay gasping upon the blood-stained floor of the lobby, surrounded by the bodies of his unlucky brothers-in-arms. A crimson pool spread beneath him, his shattered limbs twitched uselessly. An awful cold swept over him, chilling him to the bone. He felt his life slipping away.

No, he thought desperately. *Not yet. I need to warn Washington about that nuke.*

Heavy footsteps approached. He looked up to see a huge man crossing the lobby toward him. Bane. The terrorist leader nudged Jones with the toe of his boot, eliciting an agonized gasp. He bent to examine the dying soldier. His bizarre mask, which now figured prominently in the nightmares of the entire world, concealed his intentions. Yet cold black eyes held not a hint of sympathy or compassion.

Jones glared at him defiantly.

"I'll die before I talk."

Bane nodded. "I'm on your schedule, captain."

A powerful hand clasped itself over Jones's mouth and nose, cutting off his air. The soldier tried to breathe, fighting for even a few more minutes of life, but Bane's grip was too strong. He convulsed upon the floor, then stopped struggling...forever.

"There were people upstairs," a mercenary reported as Bane rose from the dead captain's body.

"Give them over for judgment." He gestured at the lifeless remains of the American soldiers. "Hang them where the world will see."

CHAPTER THIRTY-THREE

Barbaric images flickered upon the television screen. A headline crawled along the bottom of the report.

SPECIAL FORCES BODIES HANG IN THE CABLES OF GOTHAM BRIDGE

Bruce stared in horror at the corpses strung up on the bridge as a warning. Bloody flags were wrapped around their bodies, looking like shrouds. It was something out of the Dark Ages—not a modern American city. Not Gotham.

Furious, he hurled a rock at the screen. It exploded in an eruption of sparks and broken plastic.

What is Bane doing to my city?

The knowledge that such atrocities were transforming Gotham drove Bruce to accelerate his already-brutal exercise regime. Endless pushups, squats, and stretches filled his every waking hour until he barely remembered to eat or sleep. It was as if the League of Shadows was training him, all over again. One cell over, the blind doctor listened to Bruce's exertions. He spoke out in his obscure dialect.

"He says the leap to freedom is not about strength," the European translated.

Bruce disagreed. He shadow-boxed inside his cell, throwing punches and kicks at the empty air.

"My body makes the jump."

"Survival is the spirit," the blind man said, surprising Bruce by speaking in broken English. His accent was thick, but his meaning came through, more or less. "The soul."

"My soul's as ready to escape as my body," Bruce insisted. *Maybe more so.*

The blind man shook his head.

"Fear is why you fail."

"I'm not afraid," Bruce countered. "I'm angry." He punched the air, imagining Bane's ugly face before him. He visualized that grotesque black mask cracking beneath his knuckles, the same way Bane had cracked Batman's cowl. He couldn't wait to get even.

Soon, he promised himself.

Finally, he was ready to attempt the wall again.

The rope knotted around him once more, the thick

coils chafing against his bruised ribs, he began to climb. A much smaller crowd gathered this time. Most of the prisoners had already seen this show; they had little interest in an encore. Only a handful of inmates watched with vague interest.

That was fine with Bruce. He wasn't doing this for an audience.

Angrily, letting his fury drive him, he scaled the wall again, seeking out remembered handholds and crevices. Despite his familiarity with the cliff face, the climb wasn't any easier. Breathing hard, he *fought* the wall as if it was yet another enemy, keeping him away from Gotham. He thought about Gordon, lying in that hospital bed.

About the attack on the football stadium.

About those bodies, hanging from the bridge...

I'm coming for you, Bane.

A loose piece of rock came away in his hand. Losing his grip on the wall, he fell once more. The rope yanked taut, digging into his chest and armpits, and he swung into the wall again. If anything, the collision felt more brutal than before. The pain of yet another failure battered his soul even as the unforgiving stone punished his body. He dangled upside-down, high above the scummy green pool at the bottom of the pit.

A distant glimpse of sunlight taunted him.

Down below, the blind man shook his head, while the European played cards with a skinny, underfed inmate, who glanced up at Bruce hanging helplessly overhead. A drop of sweat fell onto the card table.

"Shouldn't you get him down?" the bony prisoner asked.

The European shrugged and played another card.

"He'll keep."

Only eight years old, Bruce lay at the bottom of the abandoned well. His arm throbbed as though broken. Frightened and in pain, the frenzied flapping of the bats still echoing in his mind, he watched anxiously as his father descended on a rope to rescue him. Thomas Wayne hurried to comfort his son.

"And why do we fall?" he asked.

Bruce knew the answer. Had known it his entire life.

"To learn to pick ourselves up."

Bruce awoke on his cot, no longer a child, but trapped once again at the bottom of a pit. This time his father would not be coming to rescue him. He would have to save himself.

But how?

The blind doctor sat beside the cot. He cleared his throat to get Bruce's attention.

"You do not fear death," he said. "You think this makes you strong. It makes you weak."

Bruce didn't understand. He had always fought to overcome his fear.

"Why?" he asked.

"How can you move faster than possible," the other man asked, "fight longer than possible, if not from the most powerful impulse of the spirit? The fear of death. The will to survive."

Self-preservation, Bruce realized. He got up on his elbow, ignoring the latest battery of aches and bruises.

"I do fear death," he said. "I fear dying in here while my city burns with no one there to save it."

"Then make the climb," the blind man said.

I've already tried that, Bruce thought. *Twice.*

"How?" he asked.

"As the child did. Without the rope." The blind man cackled. "Then fear will find you again."

Bruce pondered the doctor's words all night, weighing the risks, before finally reaching a decision. Early next morning, he prepared for what was bound to be his final ascent, one way or another. He tucked a few scraps of bread into a rough wool coat, which he then folded into a makeshift shoulder pack.

The European watched him pack.

"Supplies for your journey?" he asked derisively. Nearby prisoners laughed as Bruce marched toward the cliff face yet again, this time decked out as if he actually expected to reach the top. His caretaker followed after him, intrigued by Bruce's new demeanor. At the foot of the climb, the tattooed man offered Bruce the safety rope.

Bruce shook his head, and waved it off.

Not this time.

That did it. Word rapidly spread that the crazy American had refused the rope. A crowd gathered to watch the literally death-defying ascent. Carefully, methodically, relying less on raw fury than before, he climbed the treacherous rock face. He tested each bulge and crack, unwilling to throw away his life through carelessness or impatience.

The familiar chanting began anew.

He never wanted to hear it again.

For the last time, he approached the fatal jump. As he hoisted himself onto the ledge, he startled a nest of bats roosting beneath it. They exploded from the side of the cliff in a flurry of leathery wings that momentarily transported him back to that abandoned well, so many years ago. The bats screeched in his ears, buffeting his face and body, threatening to dislodge him. His heart pounded wildly.

A long-buried fear came flapping out of his past.

Good, Bruce thought.

The bats circled up to the opening, like an omen. Bruce caught his breath, walked to the edge of the precipice, and gazed down, reminding himself how far there was to fall this time. Wide-eyed prisoners stared up at him, waiting for him to plunge to his death. The chanting grew louder and more insistent. His mouth went dry.

This is it, Bruce thought. *All or nothing.*

Fearing for his life, but fearing for Gotham more, Bruce contemplated the awful drop a final time, then jumped for the sun.

A hush fell over the pit as the entire prison population watched in suspense. Time seemed to skip a beat. Blood rushed in Bruce's ears like the flight of the bats. He reached out with both hands...

And caught hold of the ledge above.

Wild cheers erupted from the pit as he pulled himself up onto the next ledge. The ancient stone was rough and weathered, but held fast beneath his weight. Hundreds of feet below, he heard the European laugh in disbelief. Looking down, he saw him hug the tattooed man in celebration.

The blind doctor nodded.

The morning sun beat down on Bruce as he climbed the last few feet to freedom. He peered warily over the edge of the pit and was greeted by a vast, desolate landscape. No guards were stationed at the mouth of the pit—it would have been considered a waste of manpower. With any luck, Bane wouldn't even hear that he had escaped.

A huge, forgotten stone fortress, its imposing walls and towers showing the ravages of time, loomed over the pit. Rocky hills beckoned in the distance. An arid desert stretched for miles in every direction.

He had a long hike before him.

But first he found a thick coil of rope that was attached to the base of an ancient stone wall. It was used to lower new prisoners—and the occasional supplies—into the pit, then drawn up afterwards. He unwound the rope and tossed its free end down into the hole.

Free yourselves, he thought. *I need to get moving.*

He shouldered his pack and started walking.

CHAPTER THIRTY-FOUR

The basement of the stock exchange was now a dungeon. Stockbrokers, lawyers, executives, industrialists, and other modern-day aristocrats huddled together in the crowded prison, which bore little resemblance to the luxury they had once enjoyed.

Lucius Fox, one-time CEO of Wayne Enterprises, tended to his fellow captives, offering a calming presence in these hellish circumstances, but many of the prisoners were beyond solace. They wept or cursed or retreated into their own minds, hugging themselves as they rocked catatonically in the corners. The dungeon reeked of fear and desperation.

I don't belong here, Philip Stryver thought. *There's been some mistake.* He paced impatiently, keeping apart from the other prisoners. His bespoke suit was

rumpled and dirty. He needed a shave and shower—
badly. His waxen features were drawn and haggard.
His breath was sour.

Bane double-crossed us, he fumed resentfully. *This
isn't what we planned!*

A door banged open and the mercenary's men
invaded the basement. Trembling prisoners backed
away, fearful that their time had come. Fox stepped
protectively in front of a party of Wayne Enterprise
executives. He faced the newcomers with dignity.

But the guards weren't here for Fox. Sullen eyes fell
on Stryver, who found himself grabbed by the men.
They held onto him roughly as he squirmed and tried
unsuccessfully to break free. He shouted frantically as
he was dragged from the dungeon.

"I want to see Bane!" he shouted. "There's been a
mistake! *Take me to Bane!*"

Ignoring his protests and demands, the men hauled
him upstairs to the main trading floor, which now
served as the occupation's kangaroo court. A jeering
crowd of lowlifes and ruffians hooted as he was
dragged before the exchange's famous bell podium.
Armed bailiffs—along with the vicious mob—quelled
any hope of making a break for it. He wouldn't get five
yards before being gunned down or torn apart.

"This is a mistake!" he kept insisting. "Where's
Bane?"

"There's been no mistake, Mr. Stryver," a cool,
sardonic voice corrected him from the podium.

Stryver looked up at what was now the judge's bench. His heart sank as he saw who was presiding over his trial.

Dr. Jonathan Crane had once been chief administrator of Arkham Asylum for the Criminally Insane, but his illicit experiments on human subjects—and involvement in a terrorist plot to flood Gotham with his trademark "fear gas"—had turned him into a wanted criminal. Thanks to the Batman, he had been remanded to Blackgate Prison, until Bane "liberated" its inmates. Clearly, he was thriving under the new regime.

A slender, ascetic gentleman with a cultured voice and pale blue eyes, Crane wasn't wearing his ragged burlap "Scarecrow" mask at the moment, but that was small consolation to the frightened prisoner in the dock. Crane was infamous for his obsession with instilling fear in others.

In what sort of world, Stryver wondered in despair, *does a sadistic nutcase like Crane end up as a judge?*

"You are Philip Stryver?" Crane asked. "Executive vice president of Daggett Industries?"

Stryver nodded cautiously.

"The same Philip Stryver who for years has lived like a prince off the blood and sweat of people less powerful?"

Stryver didn't like the way this was going.

"Call Bane!" he insisted. "I'm one of you—"

Then he spotted a masked figure watching silently

from the gallery. Bane showed no evidence of intending to intervene. Stryver's shoulders sagged in defeat as his last hope evaporated.

"Bane has no authority here," Crane declared. "And your guilt is self-evident. This is merely a sentencing hearing." He waved his gavel airily. "The choice is yours, death or exile."

"*Death!*" the mob shouted. Peering around, Stryver was confronted by a sea of bloodthirsty faces. People spat at him and hollered. "*DEATH!*"

Stryer gulped, choosing the lesser of two evils.

"Exile." Something told him it wouldn't be that easy, however.

"Sold!" Crane banged his gavel against the podium. "To the man in the cold sweat."

Mercenaries yanked Stryver from the dock, actually *protecting* him from the maddened crowd, who appeared all too inclined to tear him limb from limb with their grubby hands. He had only a few minutes to appreciate his escape from the "courthouse" before he was loaded, handcuffed, into the back of a van along with several other condemned executives and professionals.

Stryver recognized their faces from the society pages and business sections of the Gotham papers—if nothing else, he was still in the company of the A-list. Stone-faced guards watched over the men as they were driven away towards God-knew-where.

Exile, he thought. *That doesn't sound too bad.*

Who in their right mind would want to live in Gotham these days, anyway?

After a short drive, the van braked to a halt and the exiles were herded out into the cold. A biting wind blew steadily, making him wish he were better dressed for the weather, as they found themselves down by the docks overlooking the Gotham River, which appeared to have frozen over. A dirty white crust of ice and snow partially covered the flowing currents that could still be seen underneath.

The frosted ruins of a demolished bridge were piled along the shore. Stryver shivered and hugged himself in a futile attempt to stay warm. He gazed at the waterway with trepidation.

The guards, many of whom sported prison tattoos, prodded the exiles down slippery, ice-encrusted wooden steps to the edge of the river. A smirking mercenary unlocked Stryver's cuffs. He nodded at the winding frozen expanse.

"Follow the thick ice," he instructed. "Try to swim, you're dead in minutes."

Stryver looked at the man with dawning horror. He shuddered, and not just from the cold.

"Has anyone made it?"

The guard snorted and turned away. Stryver hesitated, backing away from the river, until he felt the muzzle of an automatic rifle poke him in the back. Peering over his shoulder, he found no pity or room for negotiation in the surly faces of Bane's men. It seemed he had no other options.

Maybe I can do this, he thought. *Perhaps the ice is strong enough after all.*

Working up his nerve, he stepped cautiously onto the frozen surface. He shuffled forward, trying to tread where it appeared thickest. His handmade Italian shoes offered no purchase, and he slipped. The ice creaked and groaned beneath him. The other side of the river seemed impossibly far away.

One step at a time, he thought. *Just a little further...*

He got all of a hundred yards before the ice shattered beneath him. He screeched loudly, throwing out his arms, as the river swallowed him whole.

The guards led the next "exile" onto the ice.

The empty office building had become a command center. A map of the city was spread out atop a desk. The shutters were drawn to keep in the light—and keep out prying eyes.

Gordon examined the map, surrounded by a handful of officers who had managed to avoid being trapped underground. Many had been retirees, green cadets, inactive, or assigned to desk duty. The commissioner valued their grit and loyalty, but wished there were more of them.

A whole lot more.

"Where the hell are they?" He glanced impatiently at his watch. "It's not like we have a lot of time here."

"How long?" Sergeant Richards asked. He was a ten-year veteran, and Gordon knew he had a wife and kids in the city.

"The bomb goes off tomorrow," Gordon said. We've got about eighteen hours to do something."

"To do what?" Richards pressed.

"We mark that truck, get a GPS on it," Gordon said. "*Then* we can start thinking about how to take it down." It wasn't much of a plan, he had to admit, but it was a start. If nothing else, it beat sitting around waiting for that damn bomb to go off.

He just wished to hell that Lucius Fox hadn't been seized by Bane. They needed his expertise where the nuke was concerned.

We have to get Fox back—before Bane gets rid of him.

There was a rap at the entrance. Everybody tensed up, and reached for their weapons, until a rookie peered through a peephole and gave the thumbs up. He unlocked the door and let the newcomers in. Blake entered the command center, followed by ten or so cops. Gordon counted them off as they came in.

Exactly ten. Disappointed, he edged over to the detective and lowered his voice.

"That's it?" he asked. Blake just shrugged. Gordon stepped back and scanned the faces of their reinforcements. It took him a second to realize that someone was missing.

"Foley," he said. "Where's Foley, dammit?"

He grabbed his coat and headed for the door. Blake moved to block him.

"You shouldn't be out on the streets."

Gordon shoved past him and stormed out. The temperature was still well below freezing, but he hardly noticed the cold. His growing fury kept him hot under the collar. Stamping through the snow, he marched several blocks to a modest brownstone that seemed to have survived the worst of the rioting. Obscene graffiti defaced the walls, but a sturdy wooden door was still in place.

He climbed the steps and stabbed the doorbell.

At first, no one answered, so he kept on pressing it. Only the need to avoid raising too much of a ruckus kept him from pounding on the door with his fists. Finally, he pressed down hard on the bell, and didn't let up.

Come on, Foley, he thought so intently he had to make certain he hadn't said it out loud. *I know you're in there!*

Stubborn persistence finally paid off. Multiple locks disengaged and the door opened by a crack, offering a partial glimpse of Foley's wife, Jennifer. She looked tense and uncomfortable.

"Jim. He's not here—"

He wasn't buying it, and he shouted past her at the hallway beyond.

"You're sending your wife to the door, when the city's under occupation?"

Foley appeared—disheveled and haggard—at the end of the corridor. No longer the dapper up-and-comer, he wore a rumpled bathrobe over a tee-shirt and sweatpants. He looked like he hadn't shaved in days. Guilt was written all over his face.

"Wait in the kitchen, honey," he said, and Jennifer nodded. She retreated from the foyer, leaving the two men alone. Gordon stared accusingly.

"What did you do, burn your uniform in the back yard?" he demanded.

Foley tried to explain.

"Jim, you saw what they did to those Special Forces."

"You forgotten all the years we went out on patrol, with every gangbanger wanting to plant one as soon as our backs were turned?"

"That's different, and you know it," Foley replied defensively. "These guys run the city. The government's done a deal with them."

"Deal? Bane's got their balls in a vice. That's not a deal!"

"You move against Bane, the trigger man's gonna hit the button—"

Gordon still didn't buy any of it—not Foley's excuses, and not that whole "trigger man" crap.

"You think he's given control of that bomb to one of 'the people'? You think this is part of some revolution?" Gordon scoffed at the notion. "There's one man with his finger on the trigger—Bane."

Foley still tried to justify his cowardice.

"We have to keep our heads down till they can fix this," he said. "If you still had family here maybe you'd—" He caught himself, perhaps fearing that he'd crossed a line.

But Gordon had bigger things on his mind than his own failed marriage. If anything, it was a mercy that Barbara and the kids were hundreds of miles away.

"This only gets fixed from *inside* the city, Foley." He softened his tone, trying to get through to the man. "Look, I'm not asking you to walk down Grand in your dress blues. But we've got to do something before this maniac blows us all to hell."

Foley stared at his slippers, unable to meet Gordon's eyes.

"I'm sorry, Jim. I gotta—"

"Keep your head down?" Gordon said after him. "What's that gonna do tomorrow, when that thing blows?"

"You don't *know* that's going to happen," Foley said. Then he closed the door in Gordon's face, ending the conversation. The commissioner stood alone upon the stoop, abandoned by his own second-in-command.

The wind suddenly felt a whole lot colder.

"I hear you're looking for men, commissioner."

Gordon turned around to find Miranda Tate standing behind him, wearing a winter coat over her tunic and leggings. Blake waited below on the sidewalk. He shrugged as if to say there was nothing he could do about the woman's presence.

"How about me, instead," she volunteered.

Gordon appreciated the offer, but he needed cops, not business executives.

"Miss Tate, I can't ask you—"

"My company built it," she insisted. Nevertheless, he tried to let her off the hook.

"Bruce Wayne built it."

"And he wanted to destroy it," she said. "It was me who wouldn't listen." She stared at him. "Please."

Gordon looked at Blake, then back at Miranda. Lord knows he was in no position to be picky about his allies. He could use all the help he could get, especially where that nuke was concerned.

So he nodded.

"Let's go."

CHAPTER THIRTY-FIVE

The kid ran like hell through the East End. A thin gray windbreaker provided scant protection from the cold, but that appeared to be least of his worries right now. Two snarling gangbangers, twice the kid's age and size, chased after him.

For a second, it looked as if the kid might get away, but then he slipped on a patch of icy sidewalk and tumbled to the ground. The hoods caught up with him and yanked him to his feet. Spittle sprayed from one punk's lips.

"You steal from us, you little bastard?"

The punk had bad skin and an ugly expression. His buddy wore a blue ski cap and a perpetual sneer. Tearing open the kid's backpack, Bad Skin pulled out a shiny red apple. He drew back his fist to wallop his prisoner, but before he could deliver the beat-down, a hand grabbed onto his arm and twisted it backward.

Bone cracked and the apple flew from his fingers.

Selina snatched it out of the air.

"You boys know you can't come in my neighborhood without asking politely."

Her hair hung loose above a black winter coat. A scarf was wrapped around her neck. Releasing the bully, she shoved him onto the slushy sidewalk, where he whimpered and clutched his broken arm.

His buddy still hadn't gotten the message, though. Drawing a knife, he lunged at her like a rank amateur. She easily grabbed his wrist, shoved his shoulder back with her other hand, and redirected his knife arm so that he stabbed himself in the backside. He yowled like a stuck pig as the blade sliced into his fat *gluteus maximus*.

That was enough for both of them. Cutting their losses, the injured hoods turned tail and ran, slipping and sliding in their haste to get away from her. She savored the sight before turning to check on the kid, who regarded her with a wide-eyed mixture of fear and awe. From the looks of him, he couldn't have been more than ten years old. Eleven, tops.

"Never steal anything from someone you can't outrun, kid," she advised him. That was something she'd learned a long time ago.

He stared longingly at the apple.

"Now *you're* gonna take it," he said, resentment in his voice.

It was a tempting prize, she had to admit. Fresh fruit was hard to come by in Gotham these days. She lifted it to her mouth and took a single perfect bite.

"Just tax," she explained.

Licking her lips, she lobbed the rest of the apple back to the kid, who wasted no time absconding with it, just in case she changed her mind.

A thank-you would have been nice, she thought, but she couldn't really blame the little guy for getting away while the getting was good. She knew what it was like to be hungry and on your own.

"Pretty generous for a thief."

It was a voice she had never expected to hear again. Spinning around, she found Bruce Wayne standing on the sidewalk behind her. He was dressed like a common laborer, with a scruffy beard and work clothes, but there was no mistaking the former prince of Gotham. His face was lean and weathered, but, much to her surprise, he was standing straight and tall—despite what Bane had done to his back.

The sound of that awful *crack* had haunted her dreams for months now.

"You came back," she said. "I thought they'd killed you."

"Not yet," he said.

She got her guard up.

"If you're expecting an apology—" But he shook his head, cutting her off.

"It wouldn't suit you," he said. "I just need your help."

"And why would I help you?" she asked warily.

He pulled a USB drive from the pocket of his jacket.

"For this. The clean slate."

"You're gonna trust me with that?" she responded. "After what I did to you?"

Truth to tell, she still felt bad about luring him into Bane's ambush. He hadn't deserved that, especially after he had helped her get away from those mercs. So *what* if he was a wealthy do-gooder looking for trouble? At least he wasn't a monster like Bane.

"I'll admit I felt a little let down," he said. "But I still think there's more to you. In fact, I think for you"—he held up the flash drive—"this isn't a tool, it's an escape route. You want to disappear. Start fresh."

Steal a brand new life, she thought. Tantalized by the possibility of reinventing herself completely, she greedily plucked the drive from his fingers. She looked it over, almost afraid to believe that it might be real. Then reality set in.

"Start fresh?" she said. "I can't even get off this island."

"I can give you a way off," he promised. "Once you've gotten me to Lucius Fox. I need you to find out where they're holding him. Then take me in."

Easier said than done, she thought. "Why do you need Fox?"

"To save this city."

"Who says it needs saving?" she challenged him.

"Maybe I *like* it this way."

"Maybe you do. But tomorrow that bomb's going off."

She felt the blood drain from her face—there was no reason to doubt him. If anyone was capable of nuking an entire city for his own twisted purposes, it was Bane. Suddenly, she saw her future going up in flames, but she tried not to let on how spooked she was.

"So? Get your 'powerful friend' on the case." Saving Gotham was Batman's job, not hers. She was just a thief, out to survive any way she could.

"I'm trying," he said. "But I need Fox."

First we ID the truck, Gordon reminded himself. *Then we figure out what to do next.*

He and Miranda strolled down a snowy street. Nobody seemed to be watching them, but he kept his head down and his coat collar up. Glancing around just to be safe, he discreetly slipped her the Geiger counter. Getting hold of the device had been a challenge in itself. He just hoped it paid off.

"Stay further up the block." He nodded at a pair of undercover cops loitering at a street corner up ahead. "They're gonna cross the street and try and slow the truck down. As it approaches, hit this button. If the needle hits two hundred, give me the signal and I mark the truck. Okay?"

She nodded and tucked the Geiger counter under her coat.

"*Head's up*," Blake's voice squawked from Gordon's radio. The rookie detective was playing lookout from atop a nearby building. The commissioner hoped he had good eyes.

"Copy that." He moved to take his position at the other end of the block, leaving Miranda partway between him and the men on the corner. Moments later, an ominous black truck rumbled into view, right on schedule. It honked its horn angrily, barely slowing down, as the two cops stepped out in front of the truck as if they were crossing the street.

Gordon held his breath as Miranda covertly scanned the vehicle with the Geiger counter. Then she gave him a thumbs-up.

Bingo, he thought. *Now we just need to keep track of that truck.*

He flung a magnetic GPS locator at the vehicle as it lumbered past him, throwing up a spray of wet snow. The locator flew through the air before sticking to the bottom of the truck, where, with any luck, it would go unobserved by Bane or his accomplices.

The truck disappeared around a corner, taking the bomb with it. Gordon regrouped with Miranda and his two men at the corner. He removed a GPS tracking device from his pocket and checked to make sure they still had the locator's signal. A flashing red dot tracked the truck—and the bomb—along its route.

"Got it," he said with a touch of elation. *Mission accomplished*, he thought. They knew where the bomb was now. The tricky part was going to be getting it away from Bane—and neutralizing it in time. Gordon wished he had a better idea of how exactly they were going to pull that off, especially since Lucius Fox had been captured by the enemy.

I hope nobody expects me to know how to stabilize a fusion reactor.

He was still worrying when they rounded the corner, and found themselves confronted by a squad of armed mercenaries. Dozens of Bane's soldiers emerged from doorways and alleys, training their weapons on Gordon and the others. Miranda gasped in shock.

The cops didn't even have a chance to draw their side arms.

"Commissioner James Gordon," a gunman barked. "You're under arrest."

Gordon bristled.

"On whose authority?"

"The people of Gotham," the terrorist said smugly. He gestured to his men and they surrounded Gordon and the others, stripping them of their weapons, then leading them away toward the stock exchange.

The commissioner resisted the temptation to glance up at the rooftop where he knew Blake had to be watching. He hoped the hotheaded young detective would be smart enough to keep his head down and not try something stupid.

Watch yourself, son, he thought. *It might be all up to you now.*

CHAPTER THIRTY-SIX

A hooded prisoner was shoved down the stairs that led into the dungeon beneath the stock exchange. Laughing, the guards kicked him down the last few steps, so that he landed in a heap upon the basement floor. A groan escaped the hood.

Someone moved to help him, and the guards mocked the Good Samaritan from the top of the stairs.

"Find this one a spot," one of them said. "He's got a big day tomorrow."

"We all do," his crony added. "It's not every day you bag Bruce Wayne."

The Good Samaritan gasped at the name. He hastily tugged the bag off the prisoner's head, exposing the scruffy, unshaven face of Gotham's most famous son, not seen by anyone in Gotham since before Bane took the city hostage.

Hello, Lucius, Bruce thought, gazing up at Fox. He exchanged a silent look with the older man before spotting Miranda in a corner, where she appeared to be comforting a worried mother and children. She waited until the guards had departed before rising and coming over to him. Despite her captivity, she looked just as beautiful as she had that night they lay in front of the fire.

"You picked a hell of time to go on vacation, Mr. Wayne," Fox said.

Not exactly my idea, Bruce thought, but he didn't have time for pleasantries. "How long till the core ignites?"

"The bomb goes off in twelve hours," Fox said.

Just as Bane had planned all along, Bruce knew.

"Unless we can reconnect it to the reactor," he said.

"If you can get it there," Fox promised, "I'll find a way to plug it back in."

Miranda sat beside them, listening thoughtfully to the discussion. After so many months, Bruce had no idea what to say to her. As far as she knew, he had just disappeared that night months ago, right after they made love.

"Can you get Miranda out?" Fox asked.

I wish I could, Bruce thought. "Not tonight," he replied. Then he turned toward her at last, unable to explain all that had happened to him—and all that he still needed to do. "I'm sorry," he told her. She nodded solemnly.

"Do what's necessary," she said, her voice steady.

Bruce appreciated her understanding. There would be time enough to sort things out between them, if and when Gotham survived. For now, he needed to focus on the bomb—and on Lucius.

"Tonight I need you," he told Fox.

"What for?"

"To get back in the game."

As if on cue, the door slammed open again. Catwoman sauntered down the stairs in her skintight black outfit and goggles, escorted by a pair of guards. The men treated her with overt respect. Apparently betraying Batman carried some weight under the new regime.

"Sorry to spoil things, boys, but Bane wants these guys himself," she announced, and she indicated Bruce and Fox. The guards complied by yanking the two men to their feet, cuffing them, and dragging them toward the exit. Bruce looked back at Miranda.

"I won't forget about you," he promised.

Their eyes met across the grimy basement. She smiled sadly.

"I know."

Catwoman rolled her eyes before gesturing to have her prisoners marched from the dungeon. Rifles in hand, the guards prodded the two captives along. Selina fell back between the thugs.

She waited until they were beneath the shadows of the towering marble colonnade before turning on the two soldiers in an almost balletic display of violence. A spiked heeled disarmed one man, only a split second before she slammed his head into the side of a column while simultaneously laying out the other guard with an open-handed jab to the throat. She moved with the speed and agility of her feline namesake.

A slender pick withdrawn from her belt quickly unlocked Fox's handcuffs, then Bruce's. He smiled and rubbed his wrists.

"I like your girlfriend, Mr. Wayne."

"He should be so lucky," she said before slipping away into the shadows between the columns. Within seconds, it was as if she was never there.

Fox arched an eyebrow at Bruce, who just shrugged in response.

They were free, and they had work to do.

Bright fluorescent lights flickered on, exposing a stark rectangular chamber hidden deep beneath a shipping yard owned by Wayne Enterprises. The bunker had served as an auxiliary base of operations during the restorations to the mansion, several years back. A bank of computer monitors occupied one wall, while the rest of Batman's equipment was stored away in hidden compartments.

It had been kept intact for those times when it simply wasn't convenient to rush all the way back to the manor. That it remained so made it clear that Bane was unfamiliar with this particular storehouse.

Bruce considered his options.

"Any move I make against Bane or the bomb, the trigger man sets it off."

"They can't be using radio or cell," Fox theorized. "Too much interference. Infrared doesn't have the range. It could only be micro-burst long wave."

Bruce concurred with Fox's assessment.

"Could you block it?"

"Yes, but I need the EMP cannon guidance mount from the Bat." He gave Bruce a wry look. "You remember where you parked?"

Bruce nodded. He opened a concealed panel in the wall, exposing a well-stocked armory. He took out explosive mini-mines, Batarangs, the grapple gun, his Utility Belt—all his old tools and weapons.

"Mr. Wayne?" Fox interjected. "Might be time for a shave."

Bruce raised a hand to his chin, feeling the bristling growth there, and conceded that Fox probably had a point. It wouldn't do for the Dark Knight to go into battle looking like Robinson Crusoe.

Doesn't really go with the image.

He pressed a button and a wire mesh cage rose from the floor. Inside the cage were a familiar black suit, cowl, and cape. He smiled grimly. Alfred had always encouraged him to buy in bulk. And he couldn't fault the logic.

It never hurt to have a spare.

* * *

This is a travesty, Gordon thought grimly. *A joke.*

He, Miranda, and the other cops were on "trial" before Jonathan Crane of all people. A mob of hoods, mercs, and escaped prisoners—many of whom Gordon was personally responsible for putting behind bars—crowded the former stock exchange, hooting and hollering at the disgusting spectacle. Bane himself watched from the upper gallery.

Gordon repressed a shudder at the sight of the masked madman who was close to destroying Gotham. The scars from his bullet wounds throbbed at the memory of his first encounter with Bane in the tunnels months ago.

If only we had stopped him then…

"The charges are espionage and attempted sabotage," Crane declared with an undisguised smirk. He was clearly enjoying this obscene role-reversal. "Do you have anything to say in your defense?"

Gordon thought Crane belonged in straitjacket, not a judge's robes. He refused to play along.

"No lawyer, no witnesses? What sort of due process is this?"

"More than you gave Harvey's prisoners, commissioner. Your guilt is determined. This is merely a sentencing hearing." He peered down from the podium. "What's it to be—death or exile?"

By now, word of the sadistic ritual down at the docks

had made its way across Gotham. As far as Gordon knew, nobody had ever made it across the frozen river before plunging beneath the ice. Bane and his people hadn't even bothered to dredge for the bodies.

"Crane, if you think we're going willingly out onto that ice, you've got another think coming."

The criminal psychiatrist waved away Gordon's insolence.

"Death, then?"

Gordon wasn't about to plead for his life. He spoke for his men, as well, but hoped that Miranda might be spared.

"Looks that way."

"Very well," Crane said, smiling. "Death...by exile." His gavel banged against the podium as the crowd cheered his verdict. Then Bane stepped forward and a hush fell over the "courtroom." He leaned toward one of his men and pointed toward Miranda.

"Bring her to me."

The stairwell was thick with dust and dimly lit. A flickering light bulb needed replacing. The top floor of the building had once housed Bruce Wayne's downtown penthouse apartment, but had been caught up in bankruptcy proceedings right before Bane took control of the city. From the looks of things, it had sat empty ever since.

Assuming we don't run into any squatters, Fox mused.

Bruce bounded up the stairs, while Fox huffed and puffed behind him. After sneaking around Gotham all day, he was definitely feeling his age, unlike Bruce, who looked as if he had been working out like an Olympic athlete. A fresh leg brace, recovered from the bunker, meant he didn't need to worry about his bum knee anymore, either.

Lucius paused to catch his breath.

"I think it's time to talk about my year-end bonus..." he said. *Assuming any of us are still alive by New Year's.*

Bypassing the top-floor apartments, they went straight to the roof of the skyscraper. Bruce keyed in a combination code that granted them access. A freezing wind hit them as they stepped out. The sun was setting to the west, lending the frozen river a lurid incarnadine sheen. Fox gazed soberly at the fallen bridges, and the mainland beyond. He wondered if he would ever set foot off the island again.

It's been a good life, he thought. *All in all.*

But he wasn't ready for it to end yet.

A frosted white tarp was draped over a large object parked inconspicuously on the helipad. A no-fly zone was in force above Gotham, as part of the terrorists' demands. All aircraft, private and otherwise, had been grounded.

Until now.

Bruce grabbed the edge of the tarp, shook loose the snow, and yanked it away, revealing the Bat, just as

Fox remembered it. The formidable aircraft looked none the worse for wear since its maiden flight. He couldn't wait to see it take to the night sky once again.

But first he needed to "borrow" that EMP cannon.

Doing his best to ignore the cold, he hurried forward and started taking apart the forward gun mount. The sleek black metal was freezing to the touch, but it couldn't be helped. Better a touch of frostbite, Fox reasoned, than death by atomic blast.

"She fly pretty well?" he asked.

Bruce nodded, coming over to assist him. Freshly shaved, he looked much more like his old self.

"Even without the autopilot."

"Autopilot?" Fox gave Bruce a puzzled look. "That's what *you're* there for."

Bruce smiled cryptically.

CHAPTER THIRTY-SEVEN

Darkness shrouded the frozen surface of the river, making it all-but-invisible. Pitch-black shadows lurked beneath the decapitated pylons of the bridge. Empty skyscrapers loomed on the other shore, long since evacuated by the US Armed Forces that were surrounding the island.

Standing at the Gotham edge of the river with his men, Gordon tried to calculate the distance across. Half a mile? Three-quarters? How wide *was* the Gotham River anyway?

Too wide, probably.

"Get going," a mercenary snarled. He fired his gun into the air for emphasis. At least a half-dozen mercs and escaped prisoners clustered on the docks and riverfront, waiting to see how far the prisoners got. Somebody tried to get a wager going, but nobody was willing to bet on the cops. The only question was who fell through the ice first.

The heavy betting was on Gordon.

Might as well get this over with, he thought.

Giving his men an encouraging look, he led them out onto the ice, which creaked and groaned alarmingly beneath their feet. He was grateful that Miranda Tate hadn't been forced to undergo this ordeal, as well, although he wasn't sure she was much better off in Bane's hands. Gordon hadn't known her long, but she had struck him as a smart, courageous woman.

He hoped she came out of this okay.

They made their way cautiously across the ice, fanning out to avoid placing too much weight on any one section. For the first time, Gordon was thankful for the weight he'd lost during his hospital stay and the lean times afterwards. A few extra pounds might be the difference between life and death.

If we have any chance at all.

When they were less than a hundred feet from their starting point, a peculiar odor caught Gordon's attention. He stopped and sniffed the air.

Was that…gasoline?

Glancing down, he spotted a pool of liquid atop the ice, reflected in the ambient light from the night sky. An emergency flare lay beside the puddle. Puzzled, he bent to pick it up.

"Light it up," a raspy voice growled in his ear.

Hope sparked inside Gordon, brighter than any

flare. He knew that voice. It was the same one that had spoken to him in his hospital room, months ago, the voice that had first asked him to help clean up Gotham all those *years* ago.

He's back, Gordon realized, overcome with relief. *Finally.*

As requested, he lit the flare by twisting off its cap and scratching the ignition button. A brilliant red flame shot from the business end and, trusting Batman with his life, Gordon thrust it into the puddle of gasoline.

The pool burst into flame, and a trail of fire raced across the ice until it reached one of the darkened buildings on the far side of the river. The bright orange flames spread up and across the face of the building, forming the silhouette of an enormous, flaming bat.

Gordon's heart surged at the sight. Now everybody in Gotham would know the truth:

The Dark Knight had risen.

"Dad! Check it out!"

Deputy Commissioner Foley's kids called him to the back window, the one that looked out over the river. Jennifer was already there, staring out in wonder.

"Honey, take a look!" she said. The excitement in their voices jolted him from his guilty torpor. He stumbled across the brownstone to the window. His jaw dropped at the sight of the flaming sign.

His conscience stirred.

Maybe there was still hope after all.

Bane strode the streets of Gotham, heading back from the courtroom to his headquarters in City Hall. This was the last time he ever expected to walk this route. Everything was in readiness.

After so many months, the culmination of his plans was less than a day away. Soon Gotham would see its last dawn—and the legacy of Rā's al Ghūl would be fulfilled at last. He hoped that Wayne was enjoying the show.

"Sir?"

Barsad approached from behind. Bane detected nervousness in the mercenary's tone. He turned to see what the matter was, and beheld the sign of the Bat burning brightly on the other side of the river.

"You think it's really him?" the lieutenant asked.

Bane's mask concealed his surprise. He had broken the Batman, and left him in the pit to languish in despair. There was no way Wayne could have arisen from that hell.

"Impossible…"

The burning symbol sparked a fire inside Foley, as well. Racing to the bedroom, he yanked up the floorboards to expose a hidden cubbyhole. His dress blues, neatly folded and ironed, were tucked inside the hole. Despite everything, he had never been able to bring himself to dispose of them.

He took the uniform out of hiding.

Distracted by the blazing sign, the guards at the river's edge were easy prey. Batman quickly neutralized them before they even realized what was happening.

Gordon and his men gratefully fled the melting ice, returning to the shore, which by that time was littered with unconscious mercs and hoodlums. Batman stood among them, his cape flapping in the wind. Gordon had never been so glad to see someone in his entire life.

The Dark Knight handed Gordon a compact metal box.

"This blocks the remote detonator signal to the bomb," Batman said. "Get it onto the truck by sunrise. They might hit the button when it starts."

Gordon didn't bother asking how Batman knew about the truck. He accepted the box gratefully.

"When what starts?"

Batman growled his answer.

"War."

CHAPTER THIRTY-EIGHT

The fiery bat could even be seen from the outskirts of Ackerman Park, where a large concrete outflow pipe drained into a shallow stream. A metal grate covered the mouth of the pipe, which emerged from a rocky hillside.

Skyscrapers rose on all sides of the park, enclosing the unlit woods and meadows. A pair of mercenaries was posted in front of the pipe, which was one of the few entrances to the underground that wasn't entirely sealed off. Ice coated the metal grate. Snow covered the ground.

The guards gasped at the sight of the bat-symbol. One of them stepped away from his post to get a better look. He marched toward an open clearing, out of view of his comrade, only to be waylaid by a dark figure that lunged out from behind a tree. A sharp blow dropped the guard to the ground with a minimum of fuss.

The attacker quietly dragged the unconscious merc into the shadows.

One down, Blake thought. *Let's hope his buddy didn't hear me.*

He crept around quietly, sneaking up on the second guard, who was peering into the darkness, searching for his compatriot. The man called out uncertainly.

Blake jumped him from behind, slamming his head into the ground. The guard went limp, but the detective kicked the man's rifle away just to be safe. He checked to make sure the merc was really out cold. The last thing he needed was to get suckered by a terrorist who was playing possum.

Was that all of them? Blake glanced around, but didn't see any other guards. Moving quickly—before any unwanted company could show up—he rushed to the tunnel entrance and shot apart the lock on the grate, allowing it to swing open.

"Ross?" he asked anxiously.

"Right here, pal," his old partner answered, squeezing up through the pipe exactly as planned. His gaunt, bearded face was that of a man who had been trapped underground, living on scraps, for months. His blue uniform was tattered and filthy. He reeked like someone who hadn't had a shower since those explosions back in the fall, but his gun looked clean and well cared-for.

Blake was glad to see that his partner had kept his priorities straight. He heard more men climbing up from the sewers. He hoped there were plenty of them.

We need all the help we can get—whether the Batman is back or not.

Extending his hand, he helped his friend out of the pipe. The bedraggled cop reached the surface and paused to take a deep breath of fresh air. His breath frosted. Blake could only imagine what that felt like, after being forced to inhale the noxious atmosphere of the sewers for weeks on end. No doubt he was looking forward to seeing Yolanda and little Tara again, too.

A shot rang out from the trees, and Ross staggered backwards, a crimson stain spreading across this chest. He fell lifelessly to the ground. His breath stopped misting.

No! Blake screamed inwardly, even as he dove for cover. *It's not fair! He was finally free...*

A small group of killers charged onto the scene, surrounding Blake. He tried to scramble away, only to feel the muzzle of an automatic rifle against the back of his skull. One mercenary kept Blake pinned to the ground while his comrades fired into the open mouth of the pipe, driving back the cops who were climbing out of the depths. Muzzles flared in the night. Screams echoed from deep within the tunnel.

The trapped cops fired back, trying to blast their way to freedom. Bullets ricocheted off the rubble clogging the pipe.

Blake glared furiously from the ground, wanting to avenge his partner, but the goddamn merc had the drop on him. He watched helplessly as another terrorist took out a hand-held detonator and called his men away from the pipe entrance.

They've planted charges!

The terrorist triggered the detonator and a deafening explosion shook the rocky ground, burying the pipe beneath a heap of rubble. Dust and smoke invaded his lungs, and he choked on the fumes.

Ross's dead body lay forgotten on the ground nearby. Was he better off than the cops who had seen a glimpse of freedom, only to be buried alive once more?

It was hard to say. But Blake had never felt so angry—or so helpless.

The merc cocked his gun, preparing to execute him on the spot, when without warning the gunman went flying to one side.

A menacing apparition, cloaked in midnight and shadows, dropped into the midst of the terrorists, tossing them around like crash dummies. Batarangs winged through the air, disarming gunmen and spearing arms and shoulders. Batman fought like a demon. Arms were twisted, legs knocked out from beneath their owners, broken teeth sent flying. One after another, battered bodies hit the dirt.

Blake scrambled to his feet, hoping to join in the fight, but it was already over. Silence descended. Batman stood over his fallen enemies.

One of them stirred slightly, groping for his gun.

"You missed a spot," Blake said.

Batman booted the stubborn merc in the head. Then he stalked toward Blake, his cape fluttering behind him. The pointed ears of his cowl cast an ominous shadow. Even knowing whose face lay beneath the cowl, Blake had to suppress a shudder. It was easy to forget that Batman was still human underneath.

"If you're working alone," Batman advised, "wear a mask."

Blake didn't see the point. It wasn't like he was Bruce Wayne or something.

"No one cares who I am."

"The mask's not for you. It's to protect the people you care about."

"Huh." Blake was impressed, and slightly confused, by how Batman had shown up just in time to save him. "And you always seem to know where those people are. How is that?"

"I lost someone once," Batman said. A hint of sorrow infiltrated his raspy growl. "Since then I break into their homes when they're sleeping and implant a tracking device on the back of their neck."

Right, Blake thought, chuckling. Then he reached back and felt the nape of his own neck. Was it just his imagination or was there a tiny lump of scar tissue there?

He stopped laughing.

Batman extracted a pair of mini-mines from his

Utility Belt. Flashing green indicators signaled that the compact black spheres were armed. He lobbed one over to Blake, while keeping the other for himself. He turned to face the mountain of rubble sealing off the pipe.

"On three," he said, drawing his arm back to throw the mine. Blake did the same. "One, two, three!" Together, they hurled the mines at the rubble.

Twin explosions rocked the hillside, causing loose gravel to tumble into the icy stream, but when the smoke cleared the tunnel was still blocked. The miniature mines had barely made a dent in the heap of shattered stone and concrete. Blake scowled in disappointment.

"No offense," he said, "but you got anything bigger in the belt?"

"That was to warn the men on the other side," Batman said. He gestured for Black to stay put, before vanishing into the woods that surrounded the demolished pipe. The young detective found himself standing alone with the unconscious terrorists, and the body of his dead partner.

He scratched his head.

"But how do we—?"

Barooom!

Cannons belched flame as a large bat-winged aircraft dropped into view in front of the cave-in. Blake scrambled backward, getting further out of the way, as the flare of the explosions lit up the night, blowing away the tons of debris blocking the tunnel.

He ducked his head and put his hands over his ears.

Thunder shook the park.

"Okay," he said, mostly to himself.

Moments later, there was nothing left of the barrier. Dozens of cops emerged from the pipe, staggering out into the cold night air. They were all skinny and ragged, half-starved from their ordeal, but they looked fit enough to fight—and mad as hell.

They clutched their weapons eagerly.

Blake gazed at Ross's body, bleeding out onto the snow. He knew just how the other cops felt.

"What now?" he asked grimly.

Batman appeared beside him without warning. He did that, Gordon had said. According to the commissioner, it took some getting used to.

"All-out assault on Bane," the Dark Knight said. "But you need to get the people you care about across the bridge."

Blake wanted to fight, not herd civilians.

"Why?" he asked.

"In case we fail," Batman said, speaking the unthinkable. "Lead an exodus across the bridge. Save as many lives as you can."

He understood the reasoning, but he didn't like it.

"Don't you need me here?"

"You've given me an army," Batman said. He watched the liberated cops as they climbed up from the sewers, first by the dozens, then by the hundreds.

There seemed to be no end to the tattered flood pouring out of the shadows and into the park. None of them appeared particularly interested in apprehending Batman. They knew who their true enemy was.

"Now go," the masked man said.

Blake nodded. He had been accused of being a hothead before, and maybe there was some truth to that, but he knew when he had to put his own anger aside. Avenging Ross would have to wait. He had a more important duty.

Sorry, partner, he thought. *I wish you could see Bane go down.*

He turned to leave, then paused to look back.

"Thank you," he said.

"Don't thank me yet," Batman said.

"I may not get a chance later."

Batman nodded. They both knew the odds were against them. They still had to defeat Bane and his army, *and* keep the bomb from going off.

At least now we have a fighting chance, Blake thought. *And the Batman on our side.*

He hurried back into the city.

CHAPTER THIRTY-NINE

Gordon checked on the metal box one last time before tucking it under his coat. Dawn would be arriving soon, but the sky was still dark for now. He and his men lurked in shadowy doorways, staying as far from the streetlights as humanly possible. The last thing they wanted was to be picked up by Bane's men again. Especially now that they had a chance to save Gotham—and take the city back.

He watched the deserted street, keeping one eye on his tracking device. He nodded at his men.

The truck was coming.

A rusty metal dumpster, its paint peeling, stood in a murky alley. Fresh snow covered its lid. Dented trash cans, piled nearby, were overflowing with refuse.

Garbage collection had been non-existent during the occupation. Rats scurried amidst the trash, emboldened by the chaos in the city.

The place smelled like a toilet. Catwoman wrinkled her nose. She was unimpressed—until Batman undid a latch and opened one side of the container, which hit the ground like a ramp. A thick layer of snow muffled the sound.

Hidden inside the rusty metal shell was the coolest-looking motorcycle in the world: the Bat-Pod.

Her eyes lit up.

"Oh, you shouldn't have..." Without waiting for an invitation, she hopped onto the cycle. She stretched out atop it, feeling its sleek contours beneath her. Eager hands explored the controls.

"The midtown tunnel's blocked by debris," Batman said gruffly. "But the cannons give you enough firepower to make a path for people."

She marveled at all the firepower it placed at her command. Machine guns, missile launchers, grappling hooks and cables—what more could a girl want?

"To start it, you—" Before he could finish, she hit the throttle, firing up the engines inside the wheels. The Bat-Pod growled beneath her, like a panther ready to spring. She liked the feeling.

"I got it," she said.

He took her word for it.

"We've got forty-five minutes to save this city."

"No," she corrected him. "I've got forty-five

minutes to get clear of the blast radius...because you don't stand a chance against these guys."

"With your help I might," he suggested.

She shook her head. He was fooling himself if he thought she was the sort to sign up for a suicide mission.

"I'll open the tunnel," she promised, "then I'm gone."

His dark eyes regarded her from behind his mask.

"There's more to you than that," he insisted.

She stared back at him, wondering what exactly he thought he saw in her. Was he deluded, or desperate, or what? A flicker of regret ran through her.

"Sorry to keep letting you down," she said. And she meant it.

He just stood there silently, as if waiting for her to change her mind. She found herself wishing that their paths had crossed under different circumstances. But perhaps it wasn't too late...

"Come with me," she implored. "Save yourself. You don't owe these people any more. You've given them *everything*."

"Not everything," he said. "Not yet."

Giving up on her at last, he turned and vanished into the night. She gazed after him for a moment, then settled back down onto the Bat-Pod. Her shoulders nestled into the steering shields.

She gunned the engines.

The Bat-Pod sped out of the alley and onto the

city streets. She raced across town, trying to outrun the doubts Batman had planted in her brain. The icy wind rushing past her face, and the speed and power with which the cycle handled, did little to soothe her turbulent thoughts. The roar of the engines failed to drown out the voices arguing at the back of her mind.

How dare he put her on the spot like that? Who did he think he was?

Who did he think *she* was?

Zooming through the icy avenues at breakneck speed, she reached the midtown tunnel in no time at all. Dozens of junked cars, including taxis, ambulances, and police cruisers, were piled in the entrance, blocking her way. The cars were heaped on top of one another, at least four layers high and who knew how deep. The barricade looked like an auto junkyard.

No way was anyone getting past it, unless...

Where exactly were those cannons again?

Dawn rose on Gotham City. A heavy snow fell from the sky as an army of cops, over a thousand strong, marched on City Hall, ready to take back their city or die trying. They stomped through the snow, past abandoned store windows and newsstands. SWAT teams in black helmets and combat armor marched shoulder to shoulder with beat cops and detectives. They weren't trapped or hiding any longer.

They wanted Bane to know they were coming.

But the mercenary had his own army. Hundreds of armed men poured out of City Hall and the surrounding buildings, forming an opposing line. They brandished their weapons and taunted the approaching cops. The clamor and echoes of thousands of angry shouts drowned out the howling wind. Shots were fired in the air. Bane had claimed City Hall as his headquarters. His army wasn't going to surrender it without a fight.

Foley marched at the head of the police forces, decked out in his full dress blues. A gold braid shone brightly on his shoulder. His chin was neatly shaved, his badge freshly polished. He held his head up, feeling like a cop for the first time in months. One way or another, he intended to do Gordon proud.

Forget promotions and politics, he thought. *This is what the job is all about.*

The armies faced off on Grand Street. Their numbers appeared evenly matched—until all three tumblers pulled onto Grand in front of the cops. They turned their gun turrets toward the advancing blue army. A loudspeaker blared at the police:

"DISPERSE. DISPERSE OR BE FIRED UPON."

Rows of cops regarded the tumblers apprehensively. Faces that hadn't felt the touch of sunlight for months went paler still. Foley realized they were seriously outgunned, but he did not back down. Still marching, glancing back at his troops, he saw that they were scared but determined. Brave men and women, veterans and rookies, held their ground. There would be no retreat, no matter what.

He had never been so proud to wear the uniform.

"There's only one police in this city," he called out, and he kept on going.

A great blue tide surged after him.

Bane emerged from City Hall. He watched the police approach from the atop the building's wide stone steps. He wore his brown utility harness over the rugged garb of a common soldier. He breathed deeply, inhaling the gas that kept his endless pain at bay. His hairless brow furrowed.

It seemed that the city's defenders were not going to let Gotham perish without one last, futile attempt at resistance.

So be it, he thought. Then he gave the order. "Open fire."

His order was communicated to the tumblers, which unleashed their cannons on the blue army. Unlucky officers were blasted into the air. Screaming cops crashed onto the street, turning the fresh snow red with their spilled blood. Maimed bodies writhed upon the ground, while others just lay still—or in parts. The line began to fall apart, as the survivors began to rethink their foolishness. Bane expected them to break ranks and run at any moment.

Then, out of the sky, the Bat came swooping over the street. Its own cannons targeted the tumblers, blasting away at them. The armored vehicles flipped over onto their sides, smashing down on the sidewalks. Smoke and flames rose from the mangled metal. Their wheels spun uselessly in the air.

Bane frowned behind his mask. This was not part of his plan.

The Bat rose above the army of cops, providing air support and encouragement. Cheering, the police rallied and charged the enemy. Gunfire erupted as the armies opened fire on each other, while opposing lines rushed toward their inevitable collision.

Bullets bounced off the Bat's armor plating as the armies met head-on in the middle of Grand Street like clashing tidal waves. Bodies hit the snow. Gunfire gave way to hand-to-hand combat as thousands of cops and criminals mixed and fought in close quarters. A multitude of shouts and grunts and curses added to the deafening tumult. Knives flashed, drawing blood, and fists collided with flesh and bone. Rifle butts were turned into bludgeons. Cops swung their batons.

Grand Street turned into a wide, snowy melee as the battle for Gotham spilled over onto the steps and sidewalks. No quarter was asked, nor was any given. Both sides wanted to prove who really ran Gotham—once and for all.

No longer needed against the tumblers, the Bat fell back and descended to the street behind the ranks of the cops. From his vantage point atop the steps, Bane glimpsed a caped figure emerging from the cockpit.

In his black armor and nocturnal disguise, Batman looked distinctly out of place by day, especially against the fresh white snow. The Dark Knight had finally come into the light.

No matter, Bane thought. *I broke you once. I can do it again.*

He strode down the steps toward his foe.

CHAPTER FORTY

Despite the distance, Catwoman heard the fighting. It sounded like an all-out war was being fought down by the City Hall, which was surely the case. And a certain caped vigilante was bound to be right in the middle of it.

Better you than me, she thought.

Sitting astride the Bat-Pod, she fired its cannons at the wall of junked automobiles. The missiles blew apart the barricade, sending mangled cars and car parts flying. She ducked to avoid being tagged by shrapnel, even as billowing clouds of smoke and dust obscured her view. Flaming chunks of metal rained down on either side of the tunnel. Blowing snow added to the chaos.

She wiped the wet flakes away from her goggles.

Did that do it? she wondered. Her finger hovered

again over the firing controls, in case she needed to unleash another salvo. *I haven't got all day here.*

But when the smoke cleared and dust settled, she saw that the mouth of the tunnel was open. She had a straight shot out of Gotham.

Now she just needed to take it.

Bane waded through the battle, searching for his true enemy. Thousands of men and women grappled around him, fighting for control of a city that would soon be nothing but a radioactive crater. Random bodies got in his way, and he brutally knocked them aside, using his fists, elbows, knees, and boots to clear a path through the overwhelming melee. Finesse wasn't an issue—he cared only about results, and removing any obstacles as quickly possible.

A uniformed officer, exchanging blows with an escaped murderer, had the misfortune to block Bane's path. The masked giant snapped the cop's neck with a single blow, then casually tossed him out of the way. He trampled over fallen bodies, both alive and otherwise. His eyes scanned the battlefield, looking for the only foe who mattered.

Where is he? Bane thought impatiently. *Where is Batman?*

He spotted a swirling black figure moving toward him, cutting a swath through raging mercenaries and rebels. Battered bodies fell by the wayside, thrown about by an armored figure whose own fists and boots never stopped moving, striking out with ruthless speed and precision. Bane recognized the modified fighting techniques of the League of Shadows. It angered him to see Rā's al Ghūl's lessons corrupted so.

But that is why Wayne can never win, he thought grimly. *He lacks the will to do what is truly necessary.*

Batman tossed a nameless hoodlum over his shoulder. He elbowed another attacker in the gut, while kicking a third opponent in the jaw with a steel-toed boot. A space cleared between him and Bane so that they came to face to face once again. They confronted each other across the blood-stained snow.

"You came back," Bane said. "To die with your city."

"No," Batman said. "I came back to stop you."

Unlikely, Bane thought. He had intended for Wayne to watch helplessly from afar as Gotham met its doom, but it seemed Batman was destined to perish on the same day as his city—at the hands of Rā's al Ghūl's true heir.

Perhaps it is better this way.

Seeing no point in further banter, he lunged, throwing powerful blows at the Dark Knight's cowl. He had smashed that ridiculous disguise before, and this time he would not stop until Wayne's unworthy skull was shattered, as well. He would soon claim another broken cowl as a trophy.

Batman fought back smartly, less recklessly than he

had in the sewers. He ducked and weaved, evading the worst of Bane's blows, while throwing surgical jabs and strikes at Bane's sides. A rabbit punch to his solar plexus was followed almost instantly by an elbow to his ribs. Bane absorbed the blows stoically. He was no stranger to pain.

His mask filled his lungs with anesthetic gas.

It would take more than a few hits to keep him from his destiny.

They fought in the middle of the street, surrounded on all sides by the sprawling conflict. Bane found himself impressed by Batman's skill and stamina, especially considering all that Bane had already done to him. No ordinary foe could have escaped the pit—as Wayne must have done. He saw now what Rā's al Ghūl had seen in this man so many years ago.

But Bane had come too far to be cheated of his ultimate victory. Both Batman and Gotham would die today.

He parried Batman's attack, then drove the caped hero back with a rapid-fire series of kicks and punches. The Dark Knight retreated onto the steps, deflecting the mercenary's attacks with his gauntlets and armor. Bane's steel-toed boots and bare knuckles smacked against his opponent's body armor, aiming for the joints and weak spots.

He managed to get his hands around Batman's neck, trying to snap it, but Wayne broke his hold by clasping his own hands together and delivering an upward thrust that drove Bane's arms apart and away. Even so, Batman staggered backward—he was on the defensive now, losing ground.

Bane clenched his fists, tensed, and threw another kick.

It was only a matter of time.

He lifted his eyes to the building he had claimed. High above them, framed in a top-floor window at City Hall, a dark-haired woman gazed down on the battle with a concerned expression on her lovely face.

Good, Bane thought. *Let her watch the Dark Knight fall once more.*

Gordon heard the fighting, too. He silently wished good luck to his brothers and sisters in blue. They were going to need it. Now he had to do his part to make sure there would still be a Gotham after the fight.

He reached beneath his coat to make sure he still had the box. He was no techie, so he took it on faith that it would jam any signals sent to the bomb, just as Batman had said it would. This wasn't the first time Batman had trusted him with the right tool at the right time. Like that antidote to Crane's fear gas. That had worked as advertised, so Gordon assumed the jammer would, too—if he could just get it to the truck in time.

He glanced at his watch. By his calculations, they had less than thirty minutes left.

He scanned the street impatiently.

"Come on, come on…"

Minutes dragged on endlessly until, *finally*, a large black truck rounded the corner. Gordon checked his GPS device to confirm that, yes, this was the same truck they'd identified earlier. He stared at it with a mixture of awe and horror. Even after everything that had happened, it was still hard to accept that the truck's lethal cargo was capable destroying all of Gotham City in a thermonuclear flash.

What if Bane—or someone else—triggered the bomb prematurely?

That's not going to happen, Gordon resolved. *Not on my watch*.

He signaled his men to put their plan into operation. All at once, a Greyhound bus, empty of passengers and commandeered from a downtown lot, pulled out in front of the truck, which slammed on its brakes a minute too late. The truck barreled into the side of the bus.

The din of crashing metal shook snow from nearby roofs and window sills as the truck came to an abrupt stop, its cab driven halfway through other vehicle. The driver smacked into his windshield, cracking the glass. Gordon hoped he was down for the count.

"Now!" he shouted.

He and his men burst from hiding, swarming the truck. They couldn't fire blindly for fear of setting off the bomb. A handful of guards, still dazed from the crash, stumbled from the cabin, trying to put up a fight, but some quality GCPD sharpshooting put them down in a hurry.

Gordon shot the lock off the rear door. He yanked it open and—gun in hand—rushed into the trailer.

It was empty.

He stared in shock at the vacant space. There was no sign of the bomb.

I don't understand, he thought, remembering how Miranda had confirmed the truck with the Geiger counter. He double-checked his GPS. This was the right truck all right...but it wasn't.

"That's impossible."

The bomb was still out there. Somewhere. His mind raced to remember the routes of the other trucks. Clutching the signal jammer to his chest, he jumped out of the truck and sprinted for the next parallel avenue.

"Come on!" he shouted. "Cut over to Fifth!"

He was afraid to look at his watch.

He didn't want to know how little time they had left.

CHAPTER FORTY-ONE

The snow was easing up a bit, but the day was still cold and raw as Blake hustled the boys out of St. Swithin's. Older ones assisted the younger orphans, all of whom were bundled up against the winter. A dilapidated yellow school bus idled at the curb. Blake raised his voice in order to be heard over the anxious babble of the children.

"Knock on doors, spread the word," he said, gesturing down the deserted city street. "The bomb's going to blow! Get out by South Street Tunnel or over the bridge!" Gotham's citizens cowered behind closed doors, unaware that time was running out for all of them. At least the kids could spread the message to folks who lived nearby—if any would listen.

As far as he knew, those were the only ways out of the endangered city. Blake wished there was time to warn more people, but that wasn't an option. He'd be lucky to save even these orphans—unless Batman and Gordon got to the bomb in time.

"Do two blocks," he ordered the boys. "Then get back to the bus!"

The battle raged on in the streets. Cops fought with cons and mercs, vying for control of Gotham, while Batman and Bane remained locked in combat on the steps of City Hall. Both men were intent on victory.

Defeat was unthinkable.

Batman hurled rapid-fire punches and kicks at Bane, delivering them with every ounce of strength and skill he could muster. He didn't bother with threats or tricks or theatrics. Bane knew all the secrets of the League of Shadows. He wouldn't be intimidated by the ominous guise of the Batman, either—and he would not stop until he had broken his foe again. One way or another, this would be their final contest.

But I'm fighting for Gotham, Batman thought. *I'm fighting for life.*

That would have to be enough.

A blinding-fast volley of strikes drove Bane back. Batman lunged to press his advantage, only to have a camo-colored tumbler roar between them, momentarily cutting him off. Snarling, Batman dodged around the armored vehicle and launched himself at Bane, who stood before City Hall's wide front doors, looking as though he owned the place.

Not in my town, Batman thought. *Not any more.*

He slammed into his foe, smashing him backward through the doors and into the building's elegant lobby. He landed on top as they crashed to the floor. Without letting up for a minute, he pounded Bane against the marble tiles, all the while remaining aware of his surroundings.

Batman spotted Miranda standing a few yards away, surrounded by a small cadre of mercenaries. She appeared unharmed, at least for the moment. But no one would be safe until Bane was put down—and the bomb was disabled.

Miranda's captors surged forward, coming to Bane's aid. There were too many of them, all heavily armed.

"Stay back," Bane ordered. "He is mine—"

Gathering himself, he threw his opponent off and sprang to his feet. Closing in, he hammered away at Batman's head with his fists, as though determined to shatter the cowl once more. Given time, he might even have succeeded, but Batman went after Bane's own mask first. The blades on his forearm ripped across the breathing tubes that connected it to the tanks. The medicinal odor of the anesthetic spilled into the air.

The effect was immediate. Without the gas to keep his pain at bay, Bane bellowed in agony. He reached for the mask, but Batman dropped him to the floor, where the anguished terrorist thrashed violently, unable to defend himself against the excruciating torment. Batman clamped a hand around his throat, holding him down, while using his free hand to search Bane's vest and pockets.

"Give me the trigger!" Batman growled. He knew it had to be on Bane's person somewhere. "You'd never give it to an ordinary citizen—"

Bane stared up at him through pain-soaked eyes. His wild convulsions calmed as he seemed to surrender to the pain. He gasped through his broken mask.

"I broke you," he said. "How have you come back?"

Batman remembered the pit.

"You thought you were the only one who could learn the strength to escape?"

"I never escaped," Bane rasped. "Rā's al Ghūl rescued me. That is why I must fulfill his plan. That is why I must avenge his murder."

Batman blinked in surprise. He didn't understand.

"The child of Rā's al Ghūl made the climb—" he began.

"But he is not the child of Rā's al Ghūl," a familiar voice whispered in his ear. Batman flinched, then froze in shock as Miranda leaned in closer. Her exotic accent colored her words. "*I am.*"

A knife expertly penetrated a joint in his suit, slicing into his ribs. It hurt, but not as much as the mocking humor in her voice.

"And though I am not 'ordinary,' I *am* a citizen...."

Her free hand removed the trigger from beneath her tunic.

Let's try this again, Gordon thought.

Another unmarked black truck rolled down the street, several blocks from where he and his officers had waylaid the empty decoy. Gordon still wasn't sure what had gone wrong there—that had definitely been the truck Miranda had tagged as carrying the bomb—

But there wasn't time to figure it out now. He could only pray that they had the right one this time.

Escorted by a solitary tumbler, the truck proceeded without stopping—until a pickup full of plain-clothes cops pulled out onto Fifth and opened fire on both vehicles. Watching from an alley, Gordon nodded in approval. He had been expecting this; his men had commandeered the pickup from a couple of mercs on their way here.

The cops shouted defiantly as they let loose with their weapons. Bullets pinged off the tumbler's armored shell.

That's it, Gordon thought. *Give 'em hell.*

The cops were hopelessly outgunned, though. They jumped from the pickup and scrambled for cover as the tumbler aimed its cannons and blew apart the hijacked vehicle. Within minutes, all that remained was a flaming pile of wreckage, and the fleeing cops were wisely making themselves scarce. They hadn't stopped the convoy—only slowed it down for a minute or two.

But that was enough. Taking advantage of the distraction created by his men, Gordon dashed from the alley and jumped onto the moving truck. He wedged himself into the narrow gap between the cab and the trailer, until a metal hatch blocked his progress. With any luck, the decaying core was inside the lead-lined trailer.

And it was only minutes away from detonating.

Not if I can help it. A sudden burst of acceleration almost threw him to the street, but he held onto the hatch for dear life and fumbled beneath his coat for the jamming device Batman had given him. It was hard to manipulate the compact metal box while hanging on to a speeding vehicle, but he struggled to turn it on.

A blinking light rewarded his efforts.

Please let this be the right truck, he prayed. *We're not going to get another chance.*

CHAPTER FORTY-TWO

The knife—which had once belonged to her martyred father—jabbed between Batman's ribs. Although he still had Bane by the throat, the Dark Knight could not move to defend himself. Just an instant's pressure and the blade would slice into a vital organ. She had Batman exactly where she wanted him.

At last.

"My mother named me Talia, before she was killed," she said, claiming her true identity now that the need for "Miranda Tate" had passed. Her voice echoed in the spacious lobby. "The way I would have been killed, if not for my protector...Bane."

For a moment her gaze turned inward as her memories raced back through the years, to the fateful hour she first saw the light.

* * *

The child, Talia, perched upon the stony ledge, nearing the top of her impossible climb. Only one daring leap, and freedom would be hers.

But the ugly sounds of violence, rising up from below, tugged at her. She glanced back down into the pit, where her faithful protector fought valiantly against a mob of crazed prisoners. The men swarmed over him, fighting tooth and nail. An angry hand clawed at his face, tearing the muslin mask away.

Bane gazed up at Talia, his youthful features exposed to the distant light. Their eyes met across the gap. He mouthed a single word:

"Goodbye."

Then the mob dragged him down. He disappeared beneath a tide of vicious kicks and blows.

Talia leapt for the sun.

"I climbed out of the pit," she said, remembering the desolate landscape that had greeted her so many years ago. "I found my father and brought him back to exact terrible vengeance, but by that time the prisoners and the doctor had done their work to my friend, my protector…"

She reached out and tenderly touched Bane's damaged mask, which bore testament to the suffering he had endured for her sake. He had paid the price for her escape—and was paying it still. Memories of blood and fury cascaded behind her eyes.

* * *

Led by Rā's al Ghūl, the League of Shadows descended upon the prison. An army of assassins rappelled down the sides of the pit before unleashing havoc upon the prisoners.

The Demon's Head himself was in the forefront of the slaughter, avenging the murder of his lost love and the captivity of his daughter.

The tempered bronze blades on his wrist-guards turned aside crude knives and spears. His sword tasted the blood of the prisoners. The butchery continued until Rā's found a badly injured youth lying on a filthy cot. Dirty bandages veiled Bane's face, but did nothing to relieve his endless pain…

"The League took us in," she recalled. "Trained us…"

Bane balanced atop upright wooden poles as the League's brutal instructors battered him with hard oak staffs, trying to knock him off his perch. Bare-chested, the scars on his back a visible reminder of his past, Bane dodged and deflected the blows, refusing to fall.

A crude mask—an early prototype—hid his face.

With pride, Talia observed Bane's indomitable spirit, yet Rā's turned away.

* * *

"But my father could not accept Bane," she said. "He saw only a monster who could never be tamed. Whose very existence was a reminder of the hell he'd left his wife to die in. He excommunicated him from the League of Shadows." An old anger crept into her voice as she contemplated the man lying on the floor.

"His only crime was that he loved me. I could not truly forgive my father..." She shifted her gaze to Batman. Her voice turned cold as ice. "Until you murdered him."

Then Batman spoke.

"He was trying to kill millions of innocent people—"

She cut him off.

"*Innocent* is a strong word to throw around Gotham, Bruce." She scoffed at the notion. "I honor my father by finishing his work. Vengeance against the man who killed him is reward for my patience." She twisted the knife—in more ways than one—and was rewarded by a grunt of pain. Blood trickled down the side of the Dark Knight's armor.

"You see, it's the slow knife...the knife that takes its time, the knife that waits years without forgetting, then slips between the bones. That's the knife—" With her other hand, she armed the trigger device. "—that cuts *deepest*."

She saw no point in waiting any longer. Batman

knew the truth now. He knew who had truly beaten him—and why. It was time to let Gotham burn, just as her father had intended long ago.

She pressed the firing button.

Nothing happened.

The truck rumbled down Fifth Street, jolting Gordon at every pothole.

He clung to the front of the trailer while watching the jammer intently. A blinking light indicated that it was doing its work, and promised at least a few more minutes of life for the city he had sworn to protect. Not for the first time, he thanked God for Batman and the amazing tools at his disposal.

Maybe Gotham still had a chance after all.

Talia stared in fury at the useless device in her hand.

"Your knife may have been *too* slow," Batman said, his voice taunting.

Static squawked from a guard's walkie-talkie. Scowling, he listened to an urgent message, then stepped forward.

"The truck's under attack," he reported.

Her mind racing, she put the pieces together. She knew who had been tracking the trucks.

"Gordon." She glared at Batman. "You gave him a way to block my signal." Then she shrugged and glanced at her watch. "No matter. He's bought Gotham *eleven* minutes." She called out to the guard. "Prepare a convoy. We must secure the bomb until it detonates."

The core was already well-guarded, but why take chances? She wasn't about to give Gordon and Fox an opportunity to pull off any last-minute feat of technical wizardry. The bomb was needed to fulfill her destiny.

Giving the blade one last twist, she sprang to her feet. Bane scrambled out from beneath. Gasping through his mask, he snatched a shotgun from the nearest mercenary and took aim at Batman.

But Talia stopped him.

"Not yet," she said. "I want him to feel the heat." Venom dripped from her voice as she faced the Dark Knight one last time. She wanted to savor this moment. "Feel the fire of twelve million souls you failed."

Suddenly a groan escaped Bane's damaged mask. What could be seen of his face was drawn with pain. No matter how stoic he strove to appear, she knew how much he was suffering. So she took a moment to carefully reconnect the tubes as best she could. He steadied himself as the soothing gas began to flow once again. That would relieve his torment to some degree, here at the end. It was the least she could do, after all he had endured for her.

"Goodbye, my friend," she said softly.

Bane nodded back at her. They both knew that they would never see each other again—not in this life. Soon the fire would devour them all—just as they had planned. Vengeance was all they had lived for.

She spun and, flanked by her guards, exited the lobby, stepping out into the cold. Three tumblers awaited her. She climbed into the lead one, taking a seat beside the driver. The vehicles pulled out in a convoy.

Fighting still filled the streets, but that was merely a sideshow now. The only combat that mattered was the battle for the bomb. The tumblers' cannons cleared a path through the tumult, blasting away cops and convicts alike. Explosions rocked the street. Frantic men and women scrambled for cover.

Except for one man.

Bloodied but still standing, his dress blues distinctly the worse for wear, Foley held the line. Talia recognized Gordon's second-in-command as he raised his sidearm and fired at the oncoming tumblers. It was a futile effort, but a courageous one. His devotion to duty was to be commended.

Very well, she thought. *Let him die fighting.* The armored vehicle smashed into Foley without even slowing down.

Batman watched as Miranda—no, Talia—left City Hall. Suddenly a flash of pain blocked his vision.

Having recovered his composure, Bane knocked Batman to the floor with the butt of the shotgun, then cracked open the breach to make certain there was a round in both barrels. Only the two of them remained in the lobby.

"You'll have to imagine the fire," he said as he snapped the action shut and leveled the weapon at Batman's face. "We both know...I have to kill you *now*."

Batman stared down the barrels of a gun, just as his parents had done decades ago. Bane's finger tightened on the trigger. An ear-splitting *boom* shook the building—

And Bane was blasted across the room. His smoking body slammed into a wall before sliding lifelessly to the floor. His wheezing breaths fell silent...forever.

Batman rose to his feet and turned toward Catwoman, who sat astride the Bat-Pod in the entrance to the lobby. Smoke rose from the bike's cannons.

"That whole 'no guns' thing?" she said. "I don't feel as strongly about it as you do."

CHAPTER FORTY-THREE

Uniformed cops guarded Gotham Bridge—as they had for months now. Armed sentries manned a barricade on the Gotham side, preventing any refugees from fleeing the city. Signs warned that anyone crossing the line would be shot.

Blake pulled the school bus up to the foot of the bridge anyway. Not wanting to provoke the troops, he parked it safely back from the barricade, and hurriedly unloaded the boys. He led them up the bridge toward the barricade, with Father Reilly bringing up the rear.

Barbed wire and roadblocks barred their way. A rifle-toting trooper, standing on the other side of the barbed wire, raised a bullhorn to his lips.

"*Stay there!*" the trooper shouted. "What are you doing?"

Blake held up his badge.

"Blake, MCU. I'm getting these kids to safety."

"Safety?" The trooper stared at Blake as if the young detective had lost his mind. "You're going to get us all *killed*. Anyone crosses this bridge, they blow up the city!"

"It's going to blow anyway," Blake insisted. "We need this bridge open right now."

"No one leaves the island," the trooper repeated. "Orders."

Blake fought to control his temper. He knew the trooper was just doing his job, but he didn't have time to explain about the decaying core. Hell, he barely understood the concept himself. All he knew for sure was that time was running out, and these kids were in his care.

"Whose orders?" he demanded. "Bane's?"

The trooper didn't budge.

"Police department's," he said stubbornly.

"Haven't you heard the shooting?" Blake replied. "The Batman's battling it out with Bane—"

"The Batman's dead," the trooper said. "Look, officer—"

"It's detective."

"Well, *detective*, you take one more step, we have to shoot you. Two more steps, we have to blow the bridge."

At that moment all Blake wanted to do was throttle the man. He heard the boys whimpering in fear behind him. Some of them were crying already. They didn't need to hear this.

He turned toward them.

"Wait for me back at the bus." The terror in their faces tore at his heart. They'd suffered enough in their short lives. They didn't deserve to have their futures cut short by a mushroom cloud.

If only he could get this stupid trooper to listen!

The tumblers caught up with the convoy on Fifth Street.

Talia let out a sigh of relief as they surrounded the truck that was carrying the bomb. Time was on her side. As long as the core remained undisturbed, no power on Earth could stop it from detonating in just a matter of minutes.

Gotham's time was almost up.

With that thought, she made a decision. She gestured to the driver, who pulled her tumbler up alongside the cab of the truck, matching its speed. The roof-access canopy retracted and she climbed out on to the angled hood of the tumbler. A biting wind blew against her face, threatening to dislodge her, but she had braved fiercer storms in her time.

She would ride with the bomb until Gotham met its doom.

Talia rose cautiously to her feet atop the hood and gestured. The truck's passenger-side door swung open.

Only a narrow gap separated the vehicles. The jump wasn't without risk, but it was nothing compared to that final leap from the pit, so many years ago. This was child's play by comparison.

Without hesitation, she jumped.

Batman and Catwoman had City Hall to themselves. Bane's smoldering corpse lay crumpled in a corner, but Batman knew that the greatest threats still remained. The bomb...and Talia.

"I need you on the ground, me in the air," he said. "We have to force that convoy east to the entrance to the reactor."

She nodded. There was no time for banter now, only action. She spun the Bat-Pod around and went racing down the front steps of City Hall.

Batman hurried after her.

Gordon squeezed through the hatch and into the trailer. He wasn't sure if the tumblers in the convoy had spotted him yet, but the sooner he got out of the open, the better. He held on tightly to the blinking jammer.

I'm not getting off this truck, he thought. *Not while I still have a job to do.*

A harsh white glow lit the interior of the trailer. The sudden heat came as a shock after the frigid cold outside. Gordon swallowed hard as he spotted the source of both the light and heat. The core. He recognized the large metal sphere from TV footage of Bane's grisly invasion at the football stadium, but he didn't remember it glowing this brightly before. Whatever chain reaction was going on inside the device, it was obviously ramping up in a big way.

Perspiration drenched his face. The glow was bright enough to hurt his eyes.

Guess this is the right truck after all, he thought. A digital timer was attached to the bomb.

Nine minutes.

"Your orders are out of date!" Blake argued. "The situation's changed."

"Listen, I'm a cop like you," he continued. "And I'm walking out there. Please don't shoot me." He stepped toward the barricade.

Shots rang out at his feet, sending chips of pavement flying. Blake flinched at the gunfire, but did not turn away. No way was he taking those boys back to Gotham to die.

He kept walking.

The convoy rolled through downtown with its deadly cargo. The Bat caught up with it first, swooping down from the wintry grey sky. They reached an intersection and the Bat swung in low, trying to force the truck and its escorts east toward the river. The truck turned quickly to avoid the menacing aircraft, which darted back and forth above it, careful to avoid the tumblers' cannons. Seated in the cockpit, Batman worked the controls. His side still burned where "Miranda" had stabbed him, even as his heart stung at her betrayal. But he could deal with that later. If there *was* a later.

Another intersection was coming up fast. The Bat dived to force the convoy further east. The rear tumbler accelerated to protect the truck, only to be blasted from behind.

Catwoman and her Bat-Pod joined the rolling battle at high speed as she veered past the damaged vehicle, which crashed into the sidewalk, taking out a line of parked cars. Metal crumpled and tore. Burning fuel polluted the air.

Her arrival didn't go unnoticed. Gun turrets swung in her direction, unleashing heavy fire. She swerved to dodge the blasts. The Bat-Pod lacked armored plating, but it was faster and more maneuverable. Catwoman worked that advantage for all it was worth. Weaving, she closed in on the truck, even as Batman harried it from above. The convoy couldn't shake either of them.

They made a good team, he mused, but would that be enough?

Blake walked closer to the barricade. Gunfire tore apart the pavement in front of him, but he still hadn't been hit. He hoped that was a good sign—for the boys' sake.

"Son of a bitch!" the uniformed guard exclaimed. Panic could be heard in his voice. "Blow it! Before he reaches the line—" His partner armed a detonator.

"Get down!" the first cop shouted. "We're blowing the bridge!"

No! Blake shouted inwardly. *Don't do it!*

The ground lurched, and he gaped in disbelief as the bridge blew apart in front of him. A tremendous fireball erupted beyond the barricade, and a roaring drowned out all other sound. He dived for cover as tons of steel and concrete crashed down into the river. Smoke billowed into the sky.

Oh my God, he thought. *They really did it. They blew up the bridge.*

Now there was no way out.

CHAPTER FORTY-FOUR

Lucius fired up the reactor. Alone in the hidden plant beneath the river, he activated the controls and checked to make certain everything was functioning properly, despite Dr. Pavel's tampering.

Without the core, the reactor was useless, of course —all of its sophisticated safeguards and dampening mechanisms had nothing to regulate. But he had to make it ready to receive the core, should Batman recover it in time. With that thought he glanced anxiously at his watch. Every moment counted. They couldn't afford any last-minute glitches or delays.

He hastily scanned the monitors and readouts. At first everything appeared in order, but then something unexpected caught his eye. He stared in shock at the flashing display, not quite believing what he was seeing.

No, he thought with dismay. *Not that*.

* * *

The remaining tumblers stuck close to the truck. Their missile launchers and machine guns fired relentlessly, trying to keep the Bat and the Bat-Pod at bay. Batman frowned at their persistence. Did Talia's men know they were fighting for their own fiery deaths?

Probably, he guessed. Most likely she had surrounded herself with a cadre of true believers— just as her father had done before her. The League of Shadows demanded absolute loyalty.

The Bat unleashed its own armaments. Diving toward the street, it blasted away the pavement directly in front of the convoy. A smoking crater opened up in front of the lead tumbler. The speeding vehicle tried to swerve away from the gaping hole, but it was going too fast. The tumbler toppled over and came to rest with its rear in the air. Its wheels spun uselessly in the smoke.

That's another one down, Batman thought. He briefly entertained the hope that the truck itself would be trapped by the pit, but its driver successfully dodged the obstacle. The truck sped on, leaving its capsized escort behind. Another tumbler moved to take the lead vehicle's place, but Catwoman was on it. Weaving past the scattered debris, she came up behind the tumbler and took it out with her own cannons. The tumbler lived up to its name, rolling sideways across the street until it crashed to a halt. Flames erupted from its undercarriage. Shaken mercenaries crawled out of the wreckage.

Nice work, Batman thought. But there was still one left—and precious little time. A digital chronometer in the Bat's cockpit counted down to Gotham's destruction.

Six minutes.

Staggering to his feet, his ears still ringing from the explosion, Blake gazed in shock through the clearing smoke. The once-mighty Gotham Bridge was shattered. Heaps of rubble piled in the river below. An impassable gap stretched between the island and the mainland. You'd need wings to make it across now—and Gotham was running low on angels.

"You idiots!" he bellowed. "You sons of bitches! You're killing us!"

The trailer swerved sharply, throwing Gordon against the wall. He struggled to keep his balance as the speeding truck buffeted him back and forth. He heard crashes and explosions outside.

What the hell's going on out there?

The temperature inside the trailer was rising by the moment even as the core glowed brighter and brighter. Did fusion reactors produce harmful radiation? Gordon didn't know, and he didn't want to know. At the moment, radiation was the least of his worries. He'd settle for not being incinerated.

Tugging on his collar, his face bathed in sweat, he

averted his eyes from the glowing core and felt like he was trapped inside a microwave oven. But he couldn't let himself think about trying to get away. The jammer was still blinking. For all he knew, it was the only thing stopping Bane from triggering the bomb.

He had to buy Batman time.

The din of battle penetrated the lead-lined walls, as though World War Three was being fought on the streets of Gotham.

That sounds about right, he thought. *Here's hoping the angels are winning.*

The Bat would not die.

Talia cursed beneath her breath as the agile black aircraft strafed the street in front of her. Strapped into the truck's passenger seat, she stared at the battle raging all around her. She had to assume that it was Bruce piloting the Bat, which meant that he had somehow escaped from Bane.

And the woman riding the Bat-Pod appeared to be Selina Kyle, alias "Catwoman." Talia had no idea why the notorious thief had allied herself with Batman, but she regretted not eliminating Kyle earlier.

No matter, she reminded herself. Nothing could prevent Gotham from burning.

The Bat came in for another run. It blasted the road in front of them, forcing the truck to veer right at an intersection. Smoke and flames burst from the flying debris. Against all odds, a random chunk of concrete smashed through the driver's side window, striking the man in the head. He jerked, then slumped forward onto the wheel, blood leaking from a fractured skull.

The truck careened out of control.

Talia shoved the man's body aside and took hold of the wheel. She steered the truck back into the center of the lane. Out of the corner of her eye, she glimpsed the Bat banking off into the sky, no doubt preparing for another assault.

Just as well, she thought. She preferred to be in the driver's seat. *At least for a few more minutes.*

Blake raced back toward bus. Father Reilly had the boys in a huddle outside of it, praying. Soot blackened their faces. He caught snatches of the Lord's Prayer.

"Father!" he called out. "Get the boys on the bus!"

The old priest gave him a puzzled look.

"But there's nowhere to go, son!" Nevertheless, he moved to comply.

A navigation unit was built into the dashboard of the truck. Talia kept one eye on the miniature screen as she sped through the glass-and-steel canyons of downtown. Deserted skyscrapers and office buildings seemed to rush past her on both sides. A concrete divider separated the eastbound expressway from the westbound lanes, which lay one level below. A radio kept her in communication with the last surviving escort.

A glance at the rear-view mirror showed the Bat-Pod trailing her. Irritation flashed across her face. Catwoman wasn't supposed to be a part of this.

The voice of the driver came over the radio.

"*They're trying to force us onto Grand—*"

"Pushing us to the entrance of the reactor," she murmured. Bruce's plan was obvious. "They're going to try to reconnect the core."

"*Can they?*" the driver asked.

Talia smiled.

Alarms blared throughout the reactor plant. Indicator lights flashed red.

Lucius raced toward an emergency ladder, praying that there was still time to escape. He reached the foot of the ladder, only to hear the beginning of a thunderous rumble. The sound grew louder and louder behind him.

He turned, fearing the worst.

Here it comes, he realized. The reactor's last-ditch shutdown procedure, functioning precisely as designed.

Icy water, flooding in from the river above, smashed through the plant, demolishing everything in its path. It poured in from all directions, tearing apart the main reactor unit and destroying any hope of stabilizing the missing core. Lucius winced at the sight, even as a churning wall of white water rushed toward him at heart-stopping speed. Looping his arm around one of the bottom rungs of the ladder, he braced himself for the impact.

I don't understand, he thought, still trying to make sense of it. *Nobody else had the shutdown code except Bruce...and Miranda.*

The flood slammed into him like a battering ram.

CHAPTER FORTY-FIVE

Your ass is mine, Catwoman thought.

Hitting the gas, she closed in on the final tumbler. With time running out, there was no point in conserving her ammo, so she let loose with everything she had.

Cannons blasted the tumbler again and again. It flipped diagonally into the path of the truck, causing the vehicle to lurch onto its side. Both hit the divider and crashed down onto the expressway below. They careened across the pavement before skidding to a stop.

Catwoman accelerated toward the crash site.

Gordon threw open the trailer doors to expose the luminous core. He jumped out of the truck in time to see a masked woman in a tight black suit pull up on what appeared to be Batman's one-of-a-kind motorcycle. Her description matched Selina Kyle.

Catwoman. Blake had nabbed her for abducting the congressman, right before Bane took over Gotham. He wondered whose side she was on.

"Give me a hand!" he shouted. As he did, the Bat touched down on the expressway several yards away, its backdraft stirring up a cloud of dust and litter. The canopy opened and Batman emerged.

He hurried toward them, his dark cloak flapping in the wind. It occurred to Gordon that he had never before seen Batman in the daylight.

First time for everything, I guess, he mused. Then he turned.

The core was throwing off heat like a blast furnace. Gordon started toward it, hoping to haul it out of the trailer, but even the slightest touch showed that it was too hot to handle. He prayed that that it wasn't already too late.

"Let's get a cable on it and drag it out!" he shouted. "Come on, we're almost there—"

Bitter laughter interrupted him.

Startled, he stared as Miranda Tate dragged herself out of the crashed truck. Badly injured, she looked past saving, but her dark eyes gleamed with malice.

"Fox showed me how to operate the reactor core, including the emergency flood—"

* * *

Lucius's left arm felt like it was broken. He cradled it against his chest as he painfully dragged himself up the ladder, trying to keep his head above the rising tide. Choppy waves pounded against him. The frothing water felt cold as ice, and he shivered uncontrollably, every unwanted movement sending another jolt of pain through his fractured limb.

But he kept on climbing, one rung after another. Part of him wondered why he bothered; with the reactor destroyed, the core would inevitably explode. Even if he didn't drown, he was doomed to perish in a nuclear blast. If he was smart, he would just let the freezing water swallow him up.

Some say the world will end in fire, some say in ice, he thought ironically.

Why keep on fighting?

Because I'm not ready to die yet, he realized. *And I've lived too long to give up now.*

So he climbed another rung.

Batman joined Gordon alongside the overturned truck. Talia lay upon the pavement, only half out of the cab. Blood trickled from the corner of her mouth— the same mouth he had kissed in front of the fireplace. Not that long ago. He found it hard to reconcile those tender memories with the vengeful woman who was dying before his eyes.

"There's no way to stop this bomb," she said.

"Prepare yourself." Her eyes met his. "My father's work is done." A smile lifted her lips as her eyes closed. They fluttered briefly, and fell still.

The daughter of Rā's al Ghūl had gone to join her infamous father. A pang of regret stabbed Batman's heart, but only for an instant.

Turning away from her, he located the hoist on the Bat, grabbed the cable, and moved toward the core. He could feel the scorching heat even through his suit, but his gloves protected his hands long enough to attach the line to the core. He tugged on it to make certain it was secure.

"What are you doing?" Gordon asked. He had heard Talia's dying words. He knew the core couldn't be stabilized.

"Two minutes," Batman said. "I can fly it out over the bay."

Catwoman looked over his shoulder. She nodded.

"Rig it to fly over the water, then bail…" she began.

He shook his head.

"No autopilot."

Understanding dawned as he let go of the cable, then turned to face her.

"You could have gone anywhere," she said. "Been anything. But you came back here."

"So did you," he reminded her.

"I guess we're both suckers." She stepped closer and wrapped her arm around his neck. She kissed him, not defiantly like before, not as a challenge, but tenderly and with feeling. He kissed her back, wishing that this moment could be longer, that they had more time.

But time was the one thing they didn't have. He hurried toward the Bat. Gordon kept pace beside him.

"So this is the part where you vanish," Gordon said, "only this time you don't come back." It wasn't a question.

Batman opened the canopy.

"Come on! On the bus!"

Blake hustled the boys through the door. He grabbed one of the smaller kids and shoved him through, then reached for another.

"What are you doing?" Father Reilly asked.

Blake kept it up.

"Protection from the blast."

"It's an *atom bomb*—!"

Blake glared at the priest.

"You think they need to hear that, in their last seconds? You think I'm going to let them die without hope?" *Not a chance*, he thought to himself.

Gordon placed a hand on Batman's arm.

"I never cared who you were—"

"And you were right," Batman said.

"But shouldn't the people know the hero who saved them?" the cop asked.

"A hero can be anyone," Batman replied. "That was always the point." He got into the cockpit, and gripped the controls. "Anyone. A man doing something as simple and reassuring as putting a coat around a little boy's shoulder to let him know the world hadn't ended...."

The canopy closed.

Gordon stepped back as the Bat fired up. A distant memory surfaced from the past.

The boy sat alone at the police station, pale-faced and trembling. A botched hold-up in a filthy alley had just taken his parents from him.

Jim Gordon, an ordinary uniformed cop, knelt to comfort him. He wrapped a rumpled overcoat around the small figure, wishing there was more he could do. The boy looked up at him. Gordon tried his best to be reassuring, even though he knew the boy's life would never be the same...

Gordon stared in wonder at the cockpit, at the Dark Knight fighting one last time to save Gotham.

"Bruce Wayne?"

The downdraft dusted him and drove him back as the Bat rose. The cable—attached to the core—snapped taut, and Gordon dived out of the way as the white-hot mechanism was yanked from the back of the trailer and into the sky. It trailed behind the Bat like a captured sun.

Tilting his head back, Gordon watched anxiously as the Bat ascended with its volatile cargo. Swirling fumes issued from the core. The exotic aircraft struggled with the weight.

Then a towering skyscraper blocked its path. The Bat's engines roared, searching for the power to clear the building. Gordon imagined Batman in the cockpit, fighting the controls, trying to overcome the drag.

It's too heavy, Gordon realized. *He's not going to make it.*

The boys were all loaded into the bus. Frightened faces peered out the grimy windows.

"Heads down!" Blake shouted, leaning in from outside. "Heads down, now!" Father Reilly tried to restrain him.

"Blake, they need to make their peace."

"They're children," Blake snapped. "They have no peace to make—"

A titanic explosion cut off his outburst. It sounded as if it came from downtown. Startled, Blake glanced back at the city. He caught a glimpse of flames and smoke. Turning back toward the bus, he hollered at the kids.

"Get *down*! That's it!"

"No." The smallest boy, whose name Blake couldn't recall, stared out an open window past Blake and Father Reilly.

"That's Batman," he said.

Blake spun around to see the Bat thundering out of the heart of Gotham, coming in their direction, dragging a blazing star behind it. Smoke rose from a busted skyscraper that looked as if a missile had hit it. The cop squinted at the radiant globe hanging from the aircraft. He knew what it had to be.

But where was Batman taking it?

The Bat flew toward the river, growing nearer by the second. Father Reilly crossed himself as the aircraft curved dangerously close to the demolished bridge before heading for the mouth of the river... and the bay.

And the ocean beyond. Moving at uncanny speed.

The Bat and its fiery cargo receded into the distance. Shielding his eyes against the glare, Blake watched as the core appeared to shrink to a tiny point of light—before bursting like an exploding star.

A hellish mushroom cloud blossomed on the horizon. Nuclear thunder could be heard from miles away. For just a second, winter turned into summer. Blake and Father Reilly hurled themselves to the ground moments before the shock wave rushed over Gotham, carrying a ferocious blast of wind, heat, dust, and ash that blew through the entire city, from Blackgate to City Hall. Blake guessed that even the stately walls of Wayne Manor were shaking.

He huddled on the ground, wondering if this was the end.

But then the blast subsided, and he was still there. He lifted his eyes cautiously and saw the city still standing. If anything, it looked as if the blast had scoured away some of the grime that had accumulated over the years. He heard the boys on the bus shouting in excitement.

A grin broke out across his face.

He did it, Blake realized. *He saved us all.*

Army helicopters appeared in the air, coming from the mainland, and boats began to appear on the river, now that the danger had passed. Now that Batman had sacrificed himself. Blake shook his head, took out his badge, and gazed at it thoughtfully.

He threw it into the river.

CHAPTER FORTY-SIX

"'I see a beautiful city and a brilliant people rising from this abyss....'"

The gardens were blooming on the Wayne estate. Gordon read solemnly from his copy of *A Tale of Two Cities*. Lucius Fox, his arm in a sling, stood beside him, along with John Blake, whose expression was grim. A fourth man stood off to one side, lost in his own grief.

"'I see that I hold a sanctuary in their hearts, and in the hearts of the descendants, generations hence. It is a far, far better thing that I do, than I have ever done.'"

Gordon closed the book. He gazed down at a simple grave, its marker bearing the name of Bruce Wayne. His throat tightened as he recited the final words.

"'It is a far, far better rest that I go to than I have ever known.'"

No official cause of death had been released

regarding the last of the Wayne dynasty. The tabloids had indulged in scandalous speculation, but nobody really paid much attention. Too many people had died during Bane's reign of terror for even the death of Bruce Wayne to stand out. Most people simply wanted to move on and put the myriad tragedies behind them.

But for some, this was easier said than done. Gordon looked across the empty grave to the melancholy figure who completed the funeral party. Tears streamed down Alfred's face. He looked older and more frail than Gordon remembered. He could only imagine what the man was feeling, now that he had outlived the entire Wayne family.

Lucius placed a gentle hand on Alfred's shoulder before stepping away to give him some time alone at the grave. Gordon and Blake followed after Fox. Glancing backward in sympathy, Gordon saw the butler cross to the graves that lay next to Bruce's: the resting places of Thomas and Martha Wayne.

"I'm so sorry," Alfred sobbed. "I failed you. You trusted me, and I failed you." His drooping shoulders shook with sorrow.

Gordon and Blake parted company with Fox, and then made their way to the drive in front of the mansion. Gordon turned toward the younger man.

"Can I change your mind about quitting the force?"

"No," Blake answered. "What you said about structures. About shackles. I can't take it. The injustice." He gestured back toward the gardens—and the grave. "I mean, no one's ever going to know who saved an entire city."

"They know," Gordon said. "It was Batman." Plans were already afoot to erect a granite statue of the Dark Knight in a plaza downtown. Gordon had started writing the speech he intended to deliver on the day the statue was unveiled. It was a better and more heartfelt speech than anything he had ever composed for Harvey Dent Day.

At last Gotham knew who its true hero was.

Blake quietly slipped into the office just as the lawyer was getting to the meat of the matter.

"Mr. Wayne's will was not amended to reflect his more modest estate," the lawyer said. "Nevertheless, there are considerable assets to be disposed of."

A small group had gathered in the lawyer's office for the reading of the bequests. The complications regarding Wayne's finances had kept the estate tied up in probate for a time, but everything had finally been sorted out. The ex-cop shifted uncomfortably, feeling out of place.

"The contents of the house are to be sold to settle the estate's accounts," the lawyer declared. "The remainder is left in its entirety to Alfred J. Pennyworth."

Good, Blake thought. He didn't like the idea of the manor's fine furniture and artwork being carted off to market, but he figured the old butler more than deserved whatever was left over. Alfred had given his all to the Wayne family—and then some.

"The house and grounds," the lawyer continued, "are left to the city of Gotham, on condition that they never be demolished, altered, or otherwise interfered with, and that they be used for one purpose and one purpose only: the housing and care of the city's at-risk and orphaned children."

A school bus pulls up in front the mansion, only a few days after the movers delivered the brand-new bunk beds. An elderly man watches as the bus disgorges dozens of wide-eyed children, who gaze in awe at the palatial edifice.

Father Reilly steps from the bus, gathers the children, and shepherds them toward the open front doors, past a freshly-erected sign bearing the new name of the household.

THE
THOMAS AND MARTHA WAYNE
HOME FOR CHILDREN

Alfred suspects his former employers would approve.

The lawyer stood and gathered up his papers. People

began to file out of the office, now that the bulk of the estate had been disposed of. The attorney gestured toward a desk in the corner, where a pretty young woman, who looked fresh out of law school, sat beside a small collection of miscellaneous envelopes, knick-knacks, and minor items of little value.

"My clerk will help anyone with the smaller correspondences and instructions…"

Blake figured that was where he came in. The clerk smiled at him as he approached the desk.

"Blake, John," he volunteered.

She consulted her list.

"Nothing here." Frowning, he started to step away, and then realized what the problem was. He took out his wallet and offered her his driver's license.

"Try my legal name."

She glanced at the ID before checking her list again.

"Yup, here it is." She reached behind the desk and sorted through various items. After a moment, she handed him a bulging sports bag. He hefted it, more confused than ever.

What the hell is this all about?

"You should use your full name," she suggested. "I like that name…*Robin*."

He smiled sheepishly, slightly embarrassed. He had always preferred to go by "John," which had seemed tougher and more suitable for a cop. Then again, he wasn't a cop any more.

He stepped away the desk, wondering what was in

the bag. He was tempted to open it right away, but decided against it. Wayne was gone, but Blake still felt obliged to protect his secrets. He owed the man that much.

The lawyer strolled over to the clerk's desk. Leaning close to her, he lowered his voice. Blake couldn't resist eavesdropping. Detective habits died hard.

"Any word on the missing item?"

The clerk shook her head.

"No, not yet."

"Well, they'd better leave no stone unturned," the lawyer said, scowling. "We can't just put a string of pearls on the manifest as 'lost.'"

Applied Sciences was back in business.

Fox had spent months repairing the damage from Bane's invasion—and beefing up the security—but the underground armory looked as good as new, as did the new and remaining prototypes. Lucius intended to keep a close watch on his inventory, just in case they were ever needed again.

At the moment, a pair of technicians was inspecting the last surviving version of the Bat. The original prototype had been vaporized over the ocean, months ago, but Fox had salvaged a variant model whose components had survived Bane's incursion. The techs were running a systems analysis from the cockpit. Both had passed a rigorous background check before being allowed anywhere near the premises.

"Why worry about the stabilization software?" the senior tech asked impatiently. "This whole autopilot system's obsolete."

"Please," Lucius said. "I just need to know what I could've done to fix it."

The junior technician gave him a puzzled look.

"But, Mr. Fox, it's already been fixed." He called up a diagnostic display on the instrument panel. "Software patch...six months ago."

Six months ago?

"Check the user ident on the patch," Fox suggested.

Who on Earth?

The tech keyed in the request. His eyes widened in surprise.

"Huh? Bruce Wayne."

Bruce?

Lucius stepped away from the aircraft, trying to conceal his reaction. An idea began to form in his mind, as clearly as an engineering diagram. A weight slowly lifted from his shoulders.

Well, as I live and breathe...

CHAPTER FORTY-SEVEN

The woods were miles outside the city, in the middle of nowhere. Blake sat in his car, staring in confusion at the GPS device he held in his hand. The sports bag sat open on the seat beside him. A slip of paper bearing a set of coordinates rested inside, on top of some climbing ropes and other gear.

Puzzled, he double-checked the coordinates. Yep, he was heading in the right direction.

Oh, what the hell, he thought. He'd come this far. So he exited the car, closing the bag and hefting it onto his shoulder.

The GPS guided him toward the waiting trees. Sunlight filtered through the leafy canopy overhead. The forest floor crunched beneath his boots. It looked like he had a hike ahead of him.

Okay, Wayne, he thought. *Let's see what this is all about.*

* * *

It was evening in Florence, Italy. A newspaper under his arm, Alfred strolled down to his favorite café. He sat down at his usual table.

"*Seulement?*" the waiter asked.

"*Oui,*" Alfred answered. "*Fernet-Branca, s'il vous plait.*" He settled in for another quiet evening by the Arno.

The GPS led Blake to a rather impressive waterfall. A wide curtain of water cascaded down a rocky cliff face. He stared up at the falls, feeling the cool spray against his face. Then he checked the coordinates one more time.

There was nowhere to go but up.

Well, he thought, *this explains the climbing gear, at least.*

He opened the bag and uncoiled the ropes.

Commissioner Gordon stepped out onto the roof, making his nightly escape from the hubbub of the department. In the aftermath of the Bane incident, and given his part in saving Gotham, the Harvey Dent scandal had been quickly forgotten. Gordon figured he had the job for life—if he wanted it.

Along with the workload. He carted a stack of

arrest reports under his arm.

Life was getting back to normal, but he wanted to stay on top of things. Bane had taught them all not to become complacent. There was always a storm brewing somewhere, and you never knew when or where the next one might hit. Gordon had no intention of being caught off-guard again.

Especially now that he was on his own.

Alfred sipped the drink, taking his time. Sparkling laughter and conversation drew his attention to a young couple seated one table over. A recurring fantasy tugged painfully at his heart, and he couldn't resist peeking at their faces.

They were strangers, of course.

They always were.

Sure enough, there was a cave behind the falls.

Blake burst through the sheet of falling water and landed awkwardly on a slick limestone shelf. Climbing to his feet, he faced the mouth of the cave, which appeared to extend deep into the earth. Stalactites hung from the ceiling like the jagged fangs of a guardian beast. Apprehension warred with excitement. Wayne had led him here for a reason.

Blake sensed he was on the verge of finding out why. He ventured cautiously into the dark.

* * *

Gordon banged the files against the air duct to straighten them. His gaze drifted across the familiar rooftop, then came to an abrupt stop.

His jaw dropped, and he forgot all about the arrest reports.

The shattered searchlight had been repaired. A brand-new bat-symbol, freshly cast in gleaming steel, was mounted atop an unbroken glass lens.

Stepping over to it—hesitantly, as if afraid it might vanish—he ran his fingers reverently along the outline of the emblem. Then he stared up at the night sky, looking for a sign.

Perhaps he wasn't on his own after all.

Blake left the daylight behind. Descending into stygian blackness, he pulled a flare out of the bag, and then lit it. A bright red flame sparked to life deep inside the cave.

The sudden glare awoke a rustling, chittering mass high above his head. He ducked in alarm as thousands of screeching creatures swooped down from their roosts, flying wildly throughout the cavern. Leathery wings flapped all around him, buffeting him, engulfing him in a flurry of...bats.

* * *

Alfred finished his drink. He folded his paper and took out his wallet. A familiar sense of melancholy came over him as he faced another long night of guilt and regret. Happier people laughed a few tables over. Bracing himself for yet another painful disappointment, he glanced over at an attractive couple—who were not strangers at all.

Bruce smiled at Alfred, looking more relaxed and at peace than the old man would have thought possible.

After a moment, Alfred nodded back at him, knowing that nothing more needed to be said. Bruce turned back to his companion, a lovely young brunette wearing an exquisite pearl necklace. She bore a distinct resemblance to a certain light-fingered maid Alfred had briefly encountered once before.

Selina, I think.

He paid his bill, leaving the waiter a generous tip, and departed with a spring in his step. But he didn't look back.

The bats were everywhere, screeching in the dark. Blake crouched defensively as their wings and bodies swirled around him like a living cyclone. An instinctive sense of panic bubbled up inside him, but he forced it back down.

He knew why Wayne had brought him here.

Bats were more than symbols of fear. In Gotham, they had come to stand for hope and justice and a legend that was bigger than just one man. A hero who could be anyone. He raised his head as the bats welcomed him to their abode.

He rose and was swallowed up by the darkness of their wings.

END

ACKNOWLEDGEMENTS

I've been a Batman fan for as long as I can remember, so I jumped at the chance to novelize the final epic chapter of the Dark Knight trilogy. I'm grateful to all the people who helped make this book possible, including my editor Steve Saffel, my agent Russell Galen, and the enormously helpful people at Warner Bros., including Josh Anderson, Shane Thompson, Izzy Hyams, Jill Benscoter, Erica Rahn, Jordan Goldberg, and Emma Thomas.

The folks at Titan Books also labored heroically to bring this book to press, so thanks also to Nick Landau, Vivian Cheung, Katy Wild, Tim Whale, Cath Trechman, Elizabeth Bennett, Julia Lloyd, and Natalie Laverick.

And, of course, I have to thank Christopher Nolan, Jonathan Nolan, and David Goyer for bringing their saga to such a powerful conclusion—and giving me such a terrific story. I hope I've done justice to it.

Finally, I could not have written this book without the help of my girlfriend, Karen Palinko, who held down the fort at home while I was off doing Bat-business in Burbank!

Greg Cox, Oxford, PA. 2012